P9-BHW-449

The Curious Lobster

Richard W. Hatch

Illustrated by Marion Freeman Wakeman

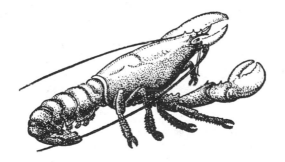

NEW YORK REVIEW BOOKS

New York

THIS IS A NEW YORK REVIEW BOOK
PUBLISHED BY THE NEW YORK REVIEW OF BOOKS
435 Hudson Street, New York, NY 10014
www.nyrb.com

The Curious Lobster text copyright © 1935, 1964 by Richard Warren Hatch
The Curious Lobster's Island text copyright © 1939, 1966 by Richard Warren Hatch
All rights reserved.

Library of Congress Cataloging-in-Publication Data
Names: Hatch, Richard Warren, 1898– author. | Wakeman, Marion
Freeman, illustrator.
Title: The curious lobster / by Richard Warren Hatch ; illustrations by
Marion Freeman Wakeman.
Description: New York : New York Review Books, 2018. | Series: New York
Review Children's Collection | Summary: Curious old Mr. Lobster has
adventures in New England with his friends, good-natured Badger and
grumpy Mr. Bear.
Identifiers: LCCN 2017061213| ISBN 9781681372884 (paperback) |
ISBN 9781681372891 (epub)
Subjects: | CYAC: Adventure and adventurers—Fiction. | Lobsters—Fiction.
| Badgers—Fiction. | Bears—Fiction. | New England—Fiction. | BISAC:
JUVENILE FICTION / Animals / Marine Life. | JUVENILE FICTION /
Humorous Stories. | JUVENILE FICTION / Classics.
Classification: LCC PZ7.H2817 Cur 2018 | DDC [Fic]—dc23
LC record available at https://lccn.loc.gov/2017061213

ISBN 978-1-68137-288-4
Available as an electronic book; ISBN 978-1-68137-289-1

Cover design: Leone Design, Tony Leone and Cara Ciardelli
Cover illustration: Nikki McClure

Printed in the United States of America on acid-free paper.
10 9 8 7 6 5 4 3 2 1

This book is
for Dick and Toph
and for
Charlotte

"IT IS A GOOD THING I CAME ALONG," SAID THE PERMANENT
PARTRIDGE.

Contents

Mr. Lobster Decides to
Travel Up a Certain River

THERE is a certain place known to all the people and the older birds and four-footed creatures as Two Mile. It is a country place, where you can see a good deal of land and woods and sky all at once, which is quite impossible in a city place. Flowing right through the meadows of Two Mile is a certain crooked little river which is called Two Mile River, although it is really much longer than two miles and should be called Ten Mile River at least.

If you go down this crooked river, which is the pleasantest way, or, if you are in a hurry and want to take a short-cut, and go over one of the Two Mile hills, you will come to a place where the little river flows along behind a wide sandy beach. And there you will find meadows wide and free, with no fences at all, where the salt tide comes in each day and there is a warm salty smell in the summer-time. Also you will find the gentle eastern slopes of the hills of that land, and these slopes are grown up with a fine forest, the kind of woods you like to go into looking for flowers hidden under old leaves, and where you can hear whisperings high up in the pine trees even when the wind is not walking along the ground at all.

But the best part of this lovely place is that besides the river and the meadows and the woods there is also the old Ocean, that vast mystery which makes old men rub their eyes and shake their heads and wonder just as much as it makes children. For nobody knows all about the Ocean no matter how old he grows.

At this certain place sometimes the Ocean is like a blue saucer upside down, with ships sailing from the middle right over the edge, and taking with them the fancies of anyone who is watching from the shore. At other times the dark winds ruffle the water, and the Ocean becomes a great disturbance, so that if you happen to be on the beach watching you are glad that you are safe on land where there are houses to go into instead of ships.

Every day the Ocean comes stealing up the river and creeks and over the meadows until they are covered with blue water, and that is what men call the rising of the tide. Then, when all the clams and eels and crabs and small fishes have had their dinner, the Ocean very gently, and so slowly that you can hardly see, steals away again. That is what men call the falling of the tide.

Now it so happens that at the bottom of this Ocean, about two miles from the beach and the hills and the meadows, there lived Mr. Lobster.

Of course, every lobster has a hard shell, eight legs, two great big pincher claws, and a long, wide tail that folds up. So Mr. Lobster had all of these. More than this, Mr. Lobster was the biggest creature of his kind that had ever lived in this Ocean, and his claws were the largest and strongest and his shell the hardest.

On the day when this story starts Mr. Lobster was at home and very pleased with himself. Also, he wanted to enjoy being pleased with himself as long as possible before taking up what he called the cares of life. By these he meant such things as finding food for himself, and keeping a sharp look-out for unpleasant creatures.

Mr. Lobster considered that small fish and clams and such were pleasant creatures. They never harmed him, and they tasted delicious. Such things as whales and sharks, which are exceedingly careless about what they scoop in when they open their huge mouths, he considered unpleasant creatures. Sometimes he had to hurry to escape them.

Mr. Lobster was pleased because he had just moved, and he had found himself a practically perfect house. It was between two big rocks on which grew a delightful

HE HAD FOUND HIMSELF A PRACTICALLY PERFECT HOUSE.

seaweed garden. Nothing could swallow those rocks, he knew; so nothing could bother him when he was at home.

"That," he said to himself, "is what a home is—a place not to be bothered in."

That thought was so pleasing that he uncurled his tail and relaxed.

The second fine thing about his house was that it had both a front door and a back door. If a pleasant creature swam past the front door Mr. Lobster could shoot out frontwards to meet him. If it was advisable to go out the back door he could fold up his tail with a snap and go out backwards even faster. He knew that not every creature could go both backwards and frontwards and be happy no matter which way he was going. That was another pleasing thought.

He reflected that the seaweed garden would attract pleasant creatures. He thought of several that he hoped would come; for instance, a small flounder. With that thought he folded up his tail so as to be ready to leave on short notice.

"You never can tell," he thought, "when some pleasant thing will happen. It is wise to be ready."

You may be sure that Mr. Lobster was far too wise to be pleased with himself without due cause. Besides having a splendid house, he was sixty-eight years old. When he shed his shell the next time, he would be sixty-nine.

"An uncommonly ripe age for a lobster," he told himself. "It is no wonder I know so much."

He was really a charming creature when not too hungry, and he had several friends among the larger fish (that is, not too large) and such creatures as the sea urchins, which are a kind of walking pin-cushion and difficult to digest.

Mr. Lobster owed his long life to a fortunate occurrence. One day a great many years ago, sixty-one to be exact, when he lived on some rocky bottom three miles further out to sea, he went for a walk. Suddenly he saw a large object which looked like a box resting on the bottom. But it was made of slats, so that he could look in and see that there was a large lobster much bigger than himself inside.

"Good morning," said Mr. Lobster. "That seems to be a large house you have, and a very fine one."

"It is not a house," replied the other. "I came in here to get some fish."

Mr. Lobster was hungry. He looked carefully, but he could see no fish.

"I hope it was good," he said, feeling even hungrier.

"It was delicious."

"Since it is gone, why don't you come out?" asked Mr. Lobster.

"I am not quite so stupid as that," came the reply. "I am waiting for more fish."

Mr. Lobster decided to wait too. Evidently this was a pleasant place. But he decided to wait outside. He thought that he might see the fish before it swam into the strange house. Also, he considered it unwise to be inside where the arrival of a fish might cause some argument. That would be decidedly unpleasant, for Mr. Lobster was then only eight inches long, and the other lobster was at least twelve.

"This is a fine day," he said. Since all days at the bottom of the Ocean are fine, he said this merely to be agreeable.

"I've seen better," said the other.

"You have had more experience than I have," said Mr. Lobster.

"Oh, I've seen a good deal. I've traveled. Besides, it is only a matter of patience."

"I beg your pardon," said Mr. Lobster respectfully. "I don't quite understand."

"A matter of patience, I said. If you are patient and sleep when it is bad weather, then you have only good weather. Patience is not doing anything about the things that annoy you. So is sleeping. So they are the same."

Mr. Lobster hoped the conversation would continue until he knew what it meant, but at that moment there was a strange interruption. The house with the big lobster in it suddenly stood up on its end, left the bottom of the Ocean, and sailed upward until it disappeared.

Mr. Lobster waited for it to come back. After a few minutes it came floating down and landed on the bottom again. Mr. Lobster crawled over and looked in. There was some delicious-looking fish hanging in the house, but the other lobster was gone.

Mr. Lobster drew his tail up very tight. That is the first

thing a lobster does when he feels cautious. "That lobster," he said to himself, "was very wise, and so he must have been very old. If he was very old, then the time may have come for him to be gone, for he certainly is gone now. And now I know enough not to go into one of those houses for fish unless I want to be gone. Surely, I am not old enough or wise enough yet to be gone."

So he did not go after the fish in the house, and all his life he had never gone into those houses, which he saw quite frequently on the bottom of the Ocean. That was how he had lived to be sixty-eight years old and was not gone yet.

Even when he became sixty-eight he did not consider himself ready to be gone. "It would be absurd," he said, "for me to be gone, for I enjoy living here on the bottom of the Ocean. Besides, there are several things I don't know yet."

When Mr. Lobster didn't know a thing, it was serious, for all his life he had been curious, and as soon as he heard about a thing he wanted to know all about it. One of the things he was the most curious about was the land. In fact, that was one of the reasons for moving to his new home, which was much nearer shore than his former home. He hoped to be able to investigate the land, a very mysterious place to him.

He lived happily in his house between the big rocks and made several friends in the neighborhood, among them a skate, two old flounders who looked very tough and moved away from him whenever he came too close, and a large sculpin. The sculpin was mostly large fins and tail and horns, none of which was good to eat. So he had no need to be suspicious, like the flounders, and used to talk for hours on end with Mr. Lobster.

Each day the sculpin disappeared for a long time. At first Mr. Lobster thought he had gone for good, as he knew that many fish went hurriedly upwards just like the lobster in the house many years ago. And they never came back unless they were very small, obviously being not wise enough or old enough to go and be gone. But the sculpin always came back from wherever it was he went.

One day Mr. Lobster decided to satisfy his curiosity about the sculpin. "Because," he said to himself with a great deal of wisdom, "satisfying your curiosity is what brings knowledge. Besides, it is a very pleasant thing to do." So he asked the sculpin a question:

"Would you mind telling me where you go each day? You are always gone so long that I am sure you must know some delightful place."

"Sir," said the sculpin, "I proceed up the river."

The sculpin was so very ugly that he had to be dignified in order to win the respect of other fishes. He was so ugly that he should have carried a handkerchief and used it all the time—but of course he had no pocket for a handkerchief. He always took a formal tone, even when talking to Mr. Lobster, for he believed that such a tone preserved his dignity.

"Do you go up the river and down it each day?" asked Mr. Lobster.

"Exactly."

"May I ask whether the purpose of your travel is pleasure?"

The sculpin ruffled a large fin, and his horns stood right up straight with anger.

"Only children and others who are irresponsible travel purely for pleasure. The aim of travel should be to procure food and knowledge. It is desirable to combine those pursuits."

"I beg your pardon. I quite agree with you," said Mr. Lobster politely.

"I procure my food in the river," said the sculpin in a little more friendly tone.

Mr. Lobster listened with respect to the sculpin, but he sometimes thought things about the sculpin which were not exactly complimentary. Right now he thought that the sculpin moved so slowly, being so dignified, that it did not seem possible that he could go up the river and down in a single day. Mr. Lobster hesitated about asking another question. It seemed that dignified people were the very worst about questions, and yet they were always the ones who knew so much you just had to ask them.

Finally he said: "I should think that going up the river and down it every day would be a lot of work."

"One goes up the river when the tide goes in, and one comes down the river when the tide goes out," said the sculpin in a very superior way. "It is not an arduous procedure."

"Oh, how very convenient!" exclaimed Mr. Lobster.

"That is the reason there are tides," said the sculpin.

"It is?"

"Exactly."

At that moment a shadow passed over the bottom of the Ocean.

"I should be pleased to continue this discourse," said the sculpin very amiably, but still in a dignified manner, "as I delight in instructing those who are ignorant. But I perceive that there is a shark hereabouts. In any case, it is four o'clock, and the tide starts to go in today at seventeen minutes past four. We are one hour later than Boston."

The shadow returned just then, and it was a very large shadow.

The sculpin immediately squddled himself into the sand until he was completely out of sight. Mr. Lobster snapped his tail twice very quickly, and went into his house backwards at high speed.

After the shadow had gone and Mr. Lobster had waited several minutes to be sure, he went out very cautiously, with his tail all curled up ready to snap at a moment's notice. But the sculpin had gone.

"He has started for the river," thought Mr. Lobster. "It is a pity we are always an hour later than Boston, but I suppose nothing can be done about it. However, I have certainly increased my knowledge today, thanks to the sculpin. And I have a curiosity that fairly aches, now that he has told me about the river. I think that tomorrow I shall go up the river and increase my knowledge even more. Unquestionably, the river goes near the land. I am glad the tide goes in and out for the purpose of helping fishes to travel, and I shall go with it."

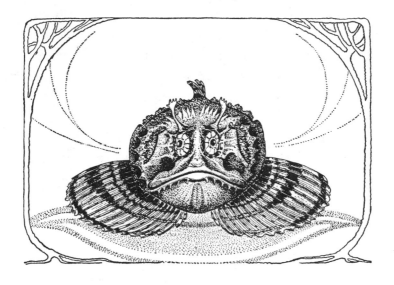

Mr. Lobster Discovers the
Land and Also Mr. Badger

THE NEXT day Mr. Lobster left his house just before seventeen minutes past four. As he was leaving he looked back, thinking that it really took a good deal of courage to leave such a safe place just to travel up a certain river. There were times when he preferred not to go too many tail-snaps away from home, and often, just when he was starting out on an investigation, the whole business would seem very unwise. Right now, when the time had come for him to start on his latest trip, going up the river seemed a risky undertaking.

"You must have courage to satisfy your curiosity," he said to himself, "and also to get knowledge."

So he kept going until he found the sculpin, who was resting in a lovely cool spot under some sea-trees, which are of course taller than seaweeds, and more suitable for fish of dignity like the sculpin.

"Good afternoon," said Mr. Lobster. "I am ready."

"Ready?" The sculpin blinked a large eye. That is, he rolled it unpleasantly, which is the same as blinking for a sculpin. "Ready for what?"

"If you will tell me the way, I should like to go up the river with the tide. I have no knowledge of traveling with the tide, and I want to try it. Also, I am sure the river must go to the land, and I want to see the land."

"If you take my advice, though you look a great deal too old to take anybody's advice, I must say, you will keep strictly away from the land." The sculpin said this in a very decided tone.

"Why?" asked Mr. Lobster.

"The land, as you would know if you had had experience, is a dry area. It would be exceedingly unfortunate for you if you should be left there."

"Thank you," said Mr. Lobster. "But I have no intention of remaining on land to be dried up."

"Very few people dry up intentionally," said the sculpin in his coldest tone. "However, permit me to say that there are such things as accidents." The sculpin raised up his horns and then scratched himself with one fin and looked as dignified as possible immediately after the scratching was finished. He knew that it really was not dignified to itch, of course. "Anyway," he said, "if you knew anything about the tides, you would know that the tide goes in about an hour later each day. It is arranged that way so that we do not have to hurry. We are on time even if we are late. But you are early."

"I am very careful," said Mr. Lobster. "So I go slowly."

"Then go slowly in the direction of the north," said the sculpin. "When you come to a place where there is mud on the sand, you will be where the river comes out into the Ocean. You will feel the tide when it goes in. At present, I am going to take a short nap, and you have disturbed me."

"That is too bad," said Mr. Lobster.

"And don't go near the land. Remember that under your shell you are at heart a fish!" And with these wise words the sculpin fell asleep.

Mr. Lobster traveled very carefully until he came to the place where there was mud on the sand, mud that was brought out by the river when it rained far up in the country. Once he saw a shadow and had to squddle in the sand and try to look like nothing worth eating, but the shadow was made only by a big boat going over his head; so nothing unpleasant happened. Still, it made Mr. Lobster tremble a little, and the joints in his tail felt shaky.

Once he had to hurry for two or three minutes in order to catch up with a pleasant creature, a small sand-dab which tasted delicious.

He had to wait for a short time for the tide to start flowing in, but soon he felt the gentle movement of the water, and he began to swim along with it. It was easy, much easier, in fact, than any other traveling he had ever done; and he enjoyed it very much. He began to think with pleasure of what he was going to see when he got up the river and right near the land.

A great many fish were going with the tide, mostly sculpins and flounders. But there were also some perch, and Mr. Lobster saw one cod-fish with long chin-whiskers, and two very large skates. They were strangers to him; so he did not stop to speak with them. He was too busy wondering what was going to happen to him to stop to make new acquaintances.

When he was finally in the river the tide grew stronger and stronger, and he traveled at a fine rate of speed.

He said to himself: "I guess this is some speed for a lobster. At least four miles an hour. Probably it is a record achievement." Of course, this pleased him, but he reminded himself: "I must not be reckless."

So he slowed up and swam in under the bank of the river where the tide was not so strong. He knew that he was very near dry land, and he wondered how he could see the land without too much danger. Perhaps he could even explore the land. It was a perilous thought, and he recalled the sculpin's warning.

"All my life," he said to himself, "I have been curious. That is why I know so much now. And I have wanted to see the land, and I must do it."

So he went along slowly, looking for a place where he could crawl up the bank of the river, put his eyes out of water, and look around. And suddenly, as he was looking at the bottom of the river, he saw a pleasing thing. It was a large clam without any shell, all ready to be eaten and lying still on the river bottom.

"Now I understand why the sculpin comes up this river," he said to himself. "Here clams grow without shells, and everybody knows that a clam-shell is just a nuisance."

But before he could swim over and take the clam a large flounder same scuttling past him, raising a great deal of sand like a cloud of dust, and greedily gobbled up the clam. Immediately the flounder went rapidly upwards and disappeared with a splash. And in a minute down came another clam without any shell and rested on the bottom right where the first one had been.

Mr. Lobster was wise enough to know that such clams must be different from the ones he had eaten. At the present moment he had no desire to go upwards for good. But he still wanted to see the land; so he took the clam very carefully in one claw, not trying to eat it, but just holding it to see what would happen.

And what happened was surprising, indeed. The clam gave a jump, which Mr. Lobster knew was very uncommon behavior for a clam, and Mr. Lobster found himself going up just as the flounder had gone, and going so fast that his feelers were bent backwards, and he almost lost his breath.

He almost forgot what to do next, thinking that his last hour had come. But when he jumped right out of water and suddenly saw the land right in front of him, he opened his claws in amazement, dropping the clam; and he fell back on top of the water with a tremendous splash which shook every joint in his shell.

There he lay, floating on the surface of the river, looking all around, trying to gather his wits together, and at the same time holding his tail all ready to give a good snap which would send him safely down to the bottom again if there was danger.

"Well!" exclaimed a hearty voice. "Well, indeed! I have never seen anything like you in this river before. For goodness' sake, what are you?"

Mr. Lobster jumped at that voice, and very nearly snapped his tail and disappeared right then and there. But he was too curious really to do that. He had to look around first. And when he looked around, there, sitting on the bank of the river, was such a creature as he had never seen in his life before, evidently a land creature. And right beside the creature lay the greedy flounder that had just gone upward so fast. Mr. Lobster also saw the land and the sky, but for the moment all his attention was on the creature who had spoken.

Mr. Lobster decided to answer.

"I am Mr. Lobster," he replied courteously.

"You don't say!" exclaimed the creature. "I have always wanted to see a lobster, and what a joke on me nearly to catch one."

"Did you say joke?" It didn't sound like a joke to Mr. Lobster to be caught.

"Of course. Anything that doesn't work must be considered a joke. Then there are no hard feelings."

"I see," said Mr. Lobster, although he was not so sure that he did see.

"You know," the creature was saying, "you must be the largest lobster in the world."

"Probably I am," replied Mr. Lobster with all modesty. "I am sixty-eight years old. That is rather unusual, you know."

"I am sorry, but I didn't know," said the creature.

"What I should like to know," said Mr. Lobster, "is who are you? Are you a land creature?"

"I am different things."

"I beg your pardon!" Mr. Lobster exclaimed. "Did you say—"

"Oh, yes, I am several different things. Thank goodness I don't have to be the same thing all the time as most creatures do. It all depends on where I am. In some places I am a bandicoot, in others a rock wallaby. At my very fiercest I am a brock. Here I am a badger."

As he said it, the creature smiled very pleasantly. He was not such a very big creature, and not such a very small creature; and he had grayish fur and a short tail and looked very strong. And his eyes were exceedingly bright and mischievous.

"What do you look like when you are a bandicoot?" asked Mr. Lobster.

"Why, I look just the same. Only I am a bandicoot instead of a badger."

"Oh." Mr. Lobster was disappointed. He was going to ask the badger to change into a bandicoot.

"You may call me Mr. Badger today," said the creature. "And by the way, I very nearly caught you. I did catch a fine flounder, although he is flat just like all the rest of them."

"But all flounders are flat," said Mr. Lobster.

"I know it. I know it. But I would like to catch one that isn't, just the same. That would be accomplishing something."

"Did you place the clams without shells on the bottom of the river?" asked Mr. Lobster. At the same time he gave a very gentle tail-snap and went backwards a bit. He wasn't sure what Mr. Badger would do next.

"Yes," said Mr. Badger. "I placed the clams there. I am fishing for my dinner today. It is a good joke on the fish, isn't it? But don't be afraid, I beg of you. I can see that you are a very rare creature. And I am the only badger this side of the Mississippi River, which makes me exceedingly rare in these parts. That's why I stay here. I wouldn't live where I was common. You know, speaking of us two rare creatures, birds of a feather should flock together."

"Birds?" asked Mr. Lobster, who was having a hard time understanding Mr. Badger.

"Yes, of course."

"I don't see any birds," said Mr. Lobster.

"Look over by the cliff. Do you see those white things

in the air?" Mr. Badger pointed a paw with long claws in it.

"Yes, I see them," Mr. Lobster answered.

"Well, those are birds, and they are flying."

"Oh," said Mr. Lobster. "I understand that. I have heard something about birds. But I can't see that it makes any difference whether they flock together or not. I really don't."

Mr. Badger was laughing. "Please excuse me," he said. "I am never serious. What I meant was that you and I are both very rare, and that therefore we should be good friends. Of course, we haven't really got any feathers, I am glad to say. Fur is bad enough this summer weather."

"Oh, no," agreed Mr. Lobster.

"Though I shouldn't mind flying," Mr. Badger added. "It might be cooling."

"It is very comfortable in the water," said Mr. Lobster.

"Oh, no, thank you. I could never stand it there. It's over my head, you see."

Mr. Badger chuckled pleasantly over his own joke. Mr. Lobster wanted to be polite, but he didn't see anything funny about it. So he didn't even smile, but he did snap his tail gently and come in near shore.

"What I should like to know," said Mr. Badger almost seriously, "is why, when you have the whole ocean to live in, you come up this little river. Certainly you are not so foolish as these flounders."

"Hardly," answered Mr. Lobster with some pride. "I travel for pleasure, it being my special pleasure to satisfy my curiosity. In other words, I travel to gain knowledge. I like to think that is one of the great aims of my life."

"Really! Well, I travel only for pleasure, too. That's why I never go anywhere at all."

"You don't say!" gasped Mr. Lobster. "How can that be?"

"I hate traveling," said Mr. Badger.

Mr. Lobster thought this over for a few minutes, but he couldn't see how Mr. Badger traveled only for pleasure and yet hated to travel. He felt confused. He took in a great gulp of clear salt water to refresh his brain, and moved his claws and his tail to see if everything was all right. The wisest thing to do, it seemed to Mr. Lobster, was to change the subject.

"I came in here," he said to Mr. Badger, "because I am curious to know about the land. I have always lived at the bottom of the Ocean."

"What! At the bottom of the Ocean for sixty-eight years! Why, you ought to come ashore this very minute!" exclaimed Mr. Badger. "Imagine staying at the bottom of the Ocean sixty-eight years. It's a wonder you are not so rusty you won't work." Mr. Badger chuckled.

"I am not sure about that," said Mr. Lobster, who again did not quite understand what Mr. Badger was laughing at. "At any rate, you see I hesitate about coming ashore. I might dry up, and that would be the end of me—though I do want to see the land."

"You could try it a little at a time," said Mr. Badger. "A

few minutes today, a few more minutes tomorrow. That is how animals learn to go in the water. You can do anything if you only practice, anything but flying and living without anything to eat."

"Oh, could I?"

"Certainly. Why, I once saw a mouse swim a hundred feet with very little practice."

Again Mr. Lobster did not understand.

"What is a mouse?" he asked.

"Let me see." Mr. Badger thought very hard. "A mouse is a very hard thing to explain," he said. "In fact, there is no explanation. A mouse is simply a small squeak with a long tail."

"Oh." Mr. Lobster didn't know any more than he had before. He knew what a long tail was, but he had never seen a squeak.

"The squeak," went on Mr. Badger, "is his sound. But a mouse is insignificant, anyway. And not at all rare, like us. I have eaten quite a few, and I know. But do come ashore. You can go back into the water the instant you want to."

Mr. Lobster swam over to the bank and looked up. His tail joints were shaky with nervousness and excitement. He knew that now he was beginning a real adventure. But the bank was just too high.

"I can't climb it," he said.

Mr. Badger looked over.

"I have only a short tail, I am glad to say. Not one of those common ones which drag on the ground if you are not careful," he said. "But I am sure it is long enough for this. I will back up and hang my tail over the edge. You take hold, my dear Mr. Lobster, and I will pull you up."

Mr. Badger backed over to the very edge of the bank. Mr. Lobster reached up both of his big claws, which were very strong, because he was sixty-eight years old, and grabbed Mr. Badger's tail. He held on for dear life.

"Ow!" Mr. Badger screamed and gave a tremendous jump, and Mr. Lobster went flying through the air so fast that he let go of Mr. Badger's tail and landed all in a heap on the grassy meadow. The shock frightened him and made him feel dizzy. At first he didn't know where he was, and he snapped his tail furiously in order to go somewhere at high speed. But of course he went no-where, because he wasn't in the water, and his tail was just snapping in the air.

Mr. Badger was running around in a circle trying to catch up with his tail to see if it was all there. Suddenly he stopped running and sat down and began to laugh.

"That was an awfully good joke on me," he said. "You took hold of my tail so hard that I thought it was bitten in two. I did say something about having a short tail, but mine is short enough already, thank you. I really am very sorry I jumped so and sent you flying through the air. I usually jump when I am surprised. I hope you are not hurt."

By this time Mr. Lobster had gotten his breath, but his thoughts were still badly shaken. He thought that if see-ing the land was like this, perhaps he had made a mistake

"OW!" MR. BADGER SCREAMED AND GAVE A TREMENDOUS JUMP.

in leaving his nice safe house between the two big rocks at the bottom of the Ocean.

"I think I am all right now," he said, "although it hardly seems possible."

Mr. Badger laughed.

"You look splendid," he said. "You are probably the first lobster in the world to fly, also. That ought to make you feel better than ever."

That thought did cheer Mr. Lobster, and he began to look around. It was a beautiful summer day, with a high blue sky and a bright sun that made all the meadows warm.

"Now you can see the land," said Mr. Badger, "which I am sure you will find superior to the bottom of the Ocean. Come with me."

Mr. Lobster was still not sure of all his joints, but he crawled along beside Mr. Badger. Very slowly they started across the meadow, and Mr. Lobster saw tall grass, some bright blue flowers of the blue-grass, and, farther away, some trees. He even heard birds. Those were red-winged blackbirds, who live in the meadows and scold everybody else who comes near their homes.

Mr. Lobster became so interested in all the new things that he was seeing that he overlooked one very important thing. That was the sunshine. He had never been out in the sunshine, and he didn't know that it would dry him up in no time if he wasn't careful. So he kept walking along with Mr. Badger, turning his eyes this way and that, and trying to see everything in the new land-world, and not paying any heed at all to the fact that the sun was shining and he was going farther and farther away from the river.

And then, suddenly, like a pain in the stomach after eating green apples, the sort of pain you hope is just a mistake and will not return again, Mr. Lobster had a most unpleasant sensation. He was getting dry.

He stopped crawling to make sure that he was right. The feeling came again, as pains are so likely to when you stop and wait for them, and then he was sure.

"I must go back!" he exclaimed. "I am beginning to get dry!"

"We shall turn around," said Mr. Badger calmly.

They started back toward the river. Mr. Lobster tried to hurry, but his legs would not hurry on grass. He snapped his tail, and then remembered that it was no use unless he was in the water. And he was getting drier and drier.

He felt sure now that he was going to perish, for he couldn't see the river anywhere.

"I have felt very dry twice already," he said to Mr. Badger. "If I feel dry for the third time, I am done for. And now it is coming on! I can never get back! It's too far!"

"You must hurry!" cried Mr. Badger.

"I can't hurry any faster. What shall I do?" Poor Mr. Lobster began to moan, and as soon as he began to moan he began to go even more slowly, because the more sorry you are for yourself the more slowly you go, always. "This is no way to get knowledge," he moaned. "My

knowledge won't do me any good. There's no use in satisfying your curiosity if it leaves you dead when you've
satisfied it. The sculpin was right. I am perishing!"

He was really in a desperate plight.

"I tell you what!" exclaimed Mr. Badger. "I will show
you that I am your friend, and will risk my tail again.
Hang on, and I will drag you to the river. But please
spare me as much pain as possible."

Mr. Lobster grabbed Mr. Badger's tail with both claws.
He honestly tried not to pinch too hard, but he was so
frightened that he held on like death. Poor Mr. Badger let
out a scream, and jumped. That made Mr. Lobster all the
more frightened, and he held on all the harder.

"Ow! Ow! Ow! Ow!" screamed Mr. Badger, crying
"Ow!" at every leap, and leaping farther every time.

Mr. Lobster was half on the grass and half in the air,
and more frightened than ever.

Fortunately, the louder Mr. Badger yelled, the faster he
ran. So the two of them went across the meadow at such
a great rate of speed that they reached the bank of the
river in no time at all. There Mr. Lobster had the good
sense to let go of Mr. Badger's tail and drop off the bank
with a splash into the river.

In a few moments Mr. Lobster was quite himself again,
for the salt water very quickly restored him. He went
down to the bottom of the river and then came up to the
surface.

"Thank you very much," he said to Mr. Badger. "You
frightened me nearly to death, but you saved my life."

"Don't mention it," said Mr. Badger. "You are entirely welcome, but I must say I hope I never have to save your life again in that manner. Once more, and I shall have no tail at all."

"I have had an adventure," said Mr. Lobster, "and I have learned a great deal."

"I trust that we have both learned not to practice too much the first time," said Mr. Badger. "Also, it might be wise the next time to look behind us as well as in front of us when we go walking. Then you will know how far away you are from the river."

"How true," said Mr. Lobster. "Well, I must return home now, and I hope that the next time I come up the river I shall meet you again."

"Do come again!" exclaimed Mr. Badger. "I've had more excitement this afternoon than I've had before for a long time. And I love excitement. Good-by!"

Mr. Lobster slowly sank in the waters of the river and, delighted to find that the tide was now going out, went easily along down the river and back to the Ocean.

He had a good deal to think about. In the first place, he had started to satisfy his curiosity about the land; but he had not entirely satisfied it because he had been rudely interrupted by that dry feeling. And in the second place, he had had a narrower escape from death, and a more exciting experience, than ever before in all his travels. And lastly, what pleased him very much, for he was a friendly creature at heart, he had found a new and strange friend, Mr. Badger.

Just before he got home, whom should he meet but the sculpin.

"I see that you have returned safely," remarked the sculpin. He looked a bit disappointed. He did not like to have people succeed when they didn't take his advice.

"Oh, yes, indeed," answered Mr. Lobster.

"Then you have not been on land, we can be sure of that," said the sculpin confidently. He would have said more, but Mr. Lobster was already moving along. He felt good and cross at Mr. Lobster, but he didn't have to scowl because a sculpin always scowls.

"Oh, yes, I have," said Mr. Lobster very casually. "And I have had a delightful time."

And with those words, he tail-snapped contentedly home.

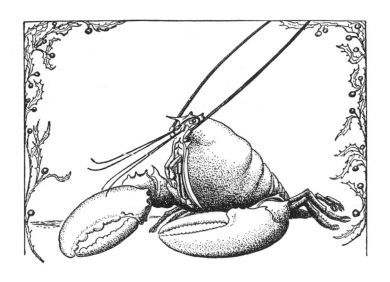

Mr. Lobster Satisfies
a Little of His Curiosity

SECRETLY, WHEN Mr. Lobster was safe in his own house, and no one else could see him, he trembled quite a little in all his joints as he thought about his narrow escape. He had nearly gone too far on land and dried up there. In fact, he had gone too far. As long as there was nobody around to hear him, he admitted it. If it had not been for Mr. Badger, he would have been gone—just as the ugly old sculpin had warned him he might.

Mr. Lobster decided that he would not tell the sculpin about that experience. It seemed unnecessary. The sculpin certainly knew a great deal, but there had to be some things that Mr. Lobster knew that the sculpin didn't, so that Mr. Lobster could meet the sculpin and talk to him and feel superior.

When he woke up bright and early the next morning Mr. Lobster thought at once of going in with the tide. Again he thought of the dangers of the land and of his narrow escape, and so he hesitated. But then he began to feel curious. He said to himself:

"You will never satisfy your curiosity if you let a little fright keep you at home. It is always the things away from home that you have to find out about. Home is where you come to think over things you've found out."

Then he answered himself back: "But suppose you get too far on land and start to dry up. Maybe Mr. Badger won't drag you to safety. And besides, think how much you know already."

So he spoke up to himself very sharply, saying, "It is unworthy to be satisfied with what you know." And he added in a low whisper to himself, so that he could hardly hear: "Besides, you know you are just as curious as you can be about the land, and you will never be happy until you explore it some more."

So he went out of his house, wondering if it was too late to catch the 6:17 tide. He was determined not to run for it.

On the way he met the sculpin.

"You don't seem to be in any great hurry," said the sculpin unpleasantly. "Surely, if you had such a delightful time yesterday, you are going ashore again today."

"I have been planning my excursion," answered Mr. Lobster, which, he felt, was very near the truth. "I am leaving now. What a pity it is you cannot go ashore."

"I wouldn't think of it," said the sculpin. "Fortunately, age has brought me good sense. But are you really going?"

"Yes, indeed," said Mr. Lobster, now very pleased with himself, because he knew he had made the sculpin furious with envy.

"Probably for the last time," said the sculpin in a gloomy tone. "There comes a day when the wanderer does not return."

Mr. Lobster gave three tremendous tail-snaps and shot away. It was so depressing, anyway, just to look at the sculpin without having to listen to such dire thoughts. He wondered if the sculpin always had such unhappy ideas. Perhaps that explained why the sculpin was so ugly.

"Just for that, I shall think joyous things all day," he told himself. "I never want to look like a sculpin."

He had his first joyous thought just after he reached the river. There he saw that a great many small fish were going in with the tide, and he thought how joyous it would be to catch them and eat them.

"It will be a little late for breakfast, and a little early for lunch," he explained to himself. "So I shall be eating between meals. Everybody knows that is joyous. In fact, I am sure that one of the best things about meals is to eat between them."

And that was just what he did on his way up the river.

A GREAT MANY SMALL FISH WERE GOING IN WITH THE TIDE.

He kept a sharp look-out for clams without shells. When he found several all together he swam to the surface of the water, but there was a boat. So down he went and continued going along the bottom.

He noticed that the water in the river was dirtier than before, for there was brown in the green today; so he knew that it had been raining. Although he had never seen any rain, it had been explained to him years ago by a large eel.

"I shall find out about rain," he thought. "One can never know too much. Evidently rain happens on land."

Just as he was thinking this, and being very curious about rain, which was a second joyous thought, he came to another clam without a shell. He swam right up to the surface of the river and looked around, and there was Mr. Badger sitting on the bank.

"Well, good morning," said Mr. Badger. "I say good morning, though it is really a very bad morning for fishing, because one must be polite. Couldn't you bring a fish or two with you when you come in from the Ocean? Though of course, I am delighted to see you even if you bring nothing but yourself. Friends are people who don't have to bring anything when they come to see you, aren't they?"

"But I have brought six small flounders," replied Mr. Lobster joyously. "Only they are under my shell, so to speak."

Mr. Badger laughed.

"That is a fine joke," he said, "but the next time please

bring them in a paper bag so that I can count them. Will you come ashore? Let me give you my tail."

Mr. Lobster went ashore, being very careful this time not to hold too tightly to Mr. Badger's tail. He sniffed the air and was delighted to find that it was quite cool, for this was one of those summer days when the sun was resting, and the sky was down low over all the earth. Also, he saw with pleasure that there were pools of water on the meadow, which made the place seem very safe.

"I'll never dry up today," he said, "and I shall take time to look around and see everything. You know, Mr. Badger—"

"Oh, pardon me for interrupting," said Mr. Badger with a twinkle in his eye. "But today I am pretending that this part of the meadow is Australia. That makes me in Australia also, fortunately; so I am no longer a badger. I am a wallaby. Just for today, I assure you, but I beg of you to take it very seriously. You see, if you don't pretend seriously, there is no use pretending at all, and there is really nothing like pretending. You know, it is a great relief to me not to be a badger some days. But do continue. I am afraid I interrupted you."

"I was going to say, Mr. Wallaby—"

"Oh, thank you, thank you, Mr. Lobster."

"I was going to say that I must be careful not to walk too far, although I see that this meadow—"

"Oh, pardon me again," put in Mr. Badger. "This is Australia."

"I don't understand at all," said Mr. Lobster. "But let

me see—this Australia has so much water on it that I am sure I am in no danger of drying up. These little pools are a very good idea."

"Very good! Very good!" exclaimed Mr. Badger. "It has been raining today."

"I was thinking of going for a short walk," said Mr. Lobster.

"Very well," said Mr. Badger. "I know it will make me hungry and I shall want to catch more fish than ever, but I will go with you. Just in case, you know."

They walked slowly across the meadow. Mr. Lobster, who was looking as hard as he could, finally pointed a claw toward a hill at the edge of the meadow.

"There," he remarked, "at the very edge of the meadow—"

"Pardon me."

"There at the edge of the Australia," began Mr. Lobster again, "is a creature standing perfectly still with his tail in the air. You can see it move, Mr. Badger."

"I beg your pardon. Were you speaking to me?"

"I mean Mr. Wallaby."

"Oh, yes, I hear perfectly now. Do go on."

"You can also see its scales," said Mr. Lobster. "It is an enormous creature, but I am very curious, and as soon as I can walk that far I shall go over there."

"That is a tree," explained Mr. Badger.

"Is it dangerous?"

"Oh, no, not unless it falls, and it only falls when there is a storm, and all sensible creatures stay at home during storms. So falling trees fall only on foolish and stupid creatures. So falling trees are good things. There, do you see?"

"I think so. I mean, I hope so," said Mr. Lobster. "And I think we had better turn around now."

"Very well. Besides, trees are not creatures, you know. They are only things. They were made for unimportant creatures like birds and squirrels to live in. Trees are not important." Mr. Badger seemed very positive.

"Still, I want to see one close to. I am curious," said Mr. Lobster.

"Some day you must come and see me. That is, when you have learned to stay ashore long enough," said Mr. Badger pleasantly. "At present I am living in the woods. Somebody planted a tremendous number of trees in the woods. They are all over the place there. I suppose it was because there are so many birds in the woods. Of course, trees do give shade, but wouldn't one know enough to stay home when it is too hot?"

That thought made Mr. Lobster feel a trifle too warm himself. In fact, he felt a trifle dry. He knew that he could stay on the meadow (which Mr. Badger said was now an Australia) for some time yet before he would be in any real danger, but he wanted to satisfy his curiosity about the rain. So he said to Mr. Badger, "Please excuse me for a moment, as I am going to try the rain." And he crawled over and plumped himself into the biggest pool and took a good deep breath.

Immediately he gave a terrible tail-snap which made

him come out of the pool backwards and land on the meadow right near Mr. Badger.

Then he tumbled over and sneezed four times. And each sneeze was so hard that it shook him down to the very last joint in his tail.

Mr. Badger tried to be polite, but he did love to laugh, and the sight of Mr. Lobster sneezing was so funny that this time he just laughed right out loud.

"I am furious!" exclaimed Mr. Lobster. "I might have been drowned! Why didn't you tell me that was not water I was jumping into?"

"But, my dear Mr. Lobster, that is water," cried Mr. Badger.

Mr. Lobster curled up his tail very tightly, which he did only when he was cautious or angry or when he was about to go somewhere at full speed. This time he was angry.

"I am sixty-eight years old," he said, "and I guess I know what water is, having lived in it all my life. There is no salt in that pool. Therefore it is not water."

Mr. Badger laughed so hard that Mr. Lobster tried to curl his tail even tighter. In fact, he was just about ready to crawl to the edge of the bank and fall in the river and go home.

But Mr. Badger finally stopped laughing.

"You really must pardon me," he said. "But that is really about the best joke of all. You see, water has no salt in it unless you put it in. Somebody has put salt in the Ocean. Probably the same person who planted all the trees in the woods. I never dreamed that you did not understand that."

Mr. Lobster let his tail uncurl a little.

"I forgive you," he said. "I must say that it is a good thing somebody put salt in the Ocean. Otherwise I should live somewhere else."

"Of course! Of course!"

"But I do think," went on Mr. Lobster seriously, "that it would be a good thing if the rain were salted as well."

"Oh, no doubt." Mr. Badger nodded his head.

They were quite near the bank of the river by this time; so Mr. Lobster hurried over and fell in. Then he had a good swim, several long breaths, and got good and cool and wet.

Mr. Badger hung his tail over the bank.

"Won't you come ashore again?" he invited.

"Well, just for a few minutes," answered Mr. Lobster. "You notice that I did better today than I did yesterday."

"I should say you did."

When Mr. Lobster was ashore again, Mr. Badger said:

"I don't know whether it is a pity or a good thing that I cannot see my tail. But I know that if this goes on long I shall lose all the hair out of it." He was craning his neck, trying in vain to see his tail. "However, I do admire your courage, Mr. Lobster. I admire it because I have courage myself. That is how I know it is a good quality. If I find that you have the same opinions I have, I shall know you are perfect. But tell me, did you ever wonder why I come here fishing?"

"Why, no," answered Mr. Lobster. "To tell the truth, it seems to me a very natural thing. Of course, everybody likes fish."

"Oh, not at all!" exclaimed Mr. Badger. "Would you like to hear my story?"

Mr. Lobster wondered if the story would be so long that he would feel dry, but he was near the river, and he was curious. So he begged Mr. Badger to tell it.

"Well," began Mr. Badger. "It is this way. Not all creatures like fish, strange as it may seem to you. Now I found out from an owl in the woods—"

"Excuse me, did you say an owl?"

"Yes. An owl is a very old bird who is so wise that he never goes out except at night, because he knows so much he cannot associate with other birds and has to go out when he will be sure not to meet them. And night is the only time. You can easily see how that would be."

"Oh, of course," agreed Mr. Lobster. "Do go on."

"Well, the owl informed me that all badgers and wallabies and bandicoots and brocks, which I am, you remember, lived in burrows, that is, nice warm holes in the ground, and ate only meat. He said that they were never allowed to do anything else. Of course that made me furious. I had a fine burrow with a bed of dry leaves and hay; but of course I moved out at once, and since then I have lived under an old stump in the woods. It is a very unpleasant place. There is a good deal of noise from other creatures passing by, and it leaks when it rains. But of course I shall stay, since the owl said that I couldn't."

Mr. Badger drew a long breath of satisfaction. Then he continued:

"And then, when I realized that badgers were allowed to eat only meat I immediately decided to live on fish. It has been hard at times, for I hate fish, but I am glad to say I have succeeded. You see, I am independent, just as you are curious."

"Is that being independent?" asked Mr. Lobster in some surprise.

"It is. The owl said I was contrary, but that is what other people always say when you are independent."

"I see."

"I lead a hard life in some ways," Mr. Badger went on, "as you can easily understand. But I do not complain. Of course, one never complains about the troubles he makes for himself, such as eating fish and living in a miserable hole under a stump where the rain leaks in. Oh, no, I never complain, but right now I would like to eat seven pounds of meat and go to sleep in my own burrow."

"I wonder if I am independent," said Mr. Lobster.

"Of course you are. You live in the Ocean, and you want to be on land. When you are in one place and insist on being in another, that is a sure sign of independence —especially if you go there, as you do."

"That pleases me," said Mr. Lobster. "All in all, this has been a joyous day; I have learned so much. And you have no idea how much I have enjoyed your story. But now I must go home."

With that he said "Good-by," waved his right claw at Mr. Badger, and fell in the river.

On his way home he thought: "What a wonderful day! I have learned about a tree and an owl. I have satisfied more of my curiosity about the land. I have shown the sculpin that I am independent, for I have gone ashore again and am returning safely. Another thing—I have discovered that rain is not good at all, since it is nothing but water with the salt left out. Just wait until I see the sculpin!"

There Is
Trouble Brewing

As LUCK would have it, before Mr. Lobster reached home he saw the sculpin in the distance. At first he thought that he would swim right over and tell the sculpin what a joyous day he had had. But then he remembered just in time that he was independent. If the sculpin wanted to hear the news he would have to come to Mr. Lobster. So Mr. Lobster went quite near the sculpin but pretended that he didn't see him at all. Instead of looking the sculpin's way, he gave some especially tremendous snaps of his tail and went past the sculpin at a very good rate of speed, sending up a great cloud of sand as he went along. That night he had an enjoyable rest. Mr. Lobster found that he slept best after a happy day, which was one of the reasons he liked happy days.

In the morning, when he looked out from his house, he saw the sculpin approaching. The sculpin was being very slow and dignified, and was going along as though he were just out for any old kind of a swim, but it was plainly to be seen that he was really coming to Mr. Lobster's house.

"So," thought Mr. Lobster.

The sculpin swam up to a place just in front of Mr. Lobster's house and then, it appeared, accidentally discovered that he was there.

"Good morning," said Mr. Lobster.

"Why, good morning," said the sculpin. "This is indeed a very agreeable surprise—to go out for a short swim and meet you."

"You will usually meet me if you come to my house when I am home," remarked Mr. Lobster.

"Since I am so fortunate as to encounter you this morning," said the sculpin in a grand manner, spreading his largest fin, "I believe I shall pay a little call."

"That is very nice of you, I am sure," said Mr. Lobster.

The sculpin cleared his throat and then coughed. You could tell that he did by the bubbles, and by the fact that his fins trembled and his eyes rolled.

"You know," he said, "of course, I have been practically everywhere on the bottom of the Ocean and up the river. There is very little left for me to discover." He was

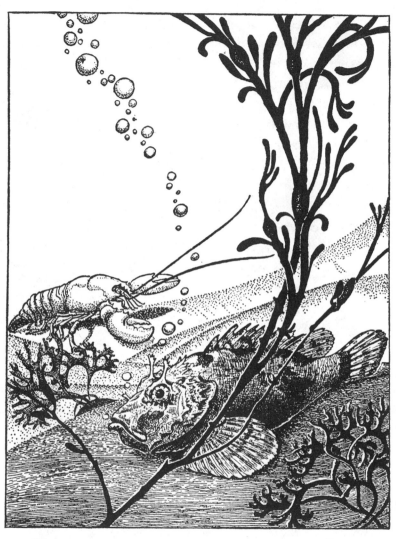

"THERE IS VERY LITTLE LEFT FOR ME TO DISCOVER," SAID
THE SCULPIN.

trying very hard to be charming without losing any of his importance. "But I must confess that I have never been on land."

"Going on land is difficult for some people," observed Mr. Lobster, coughing modestly. "It takes a great deal of practice, naturally. There are a great many little things, such as getting dry, for instance, which one has to keep in mind. You may remember that you said yourself that the land is a dry area. Still, I find that one who is skillful and courageous can acquire a great deal of knowledge by going ashore. And then, too, I have a good friend who lives ashore all the time."

The sculpin sighed and waved his fins. He was not an ill-natured fish at heart, but if there was one thing he could not stand it was anybody who knew more than he did. Being wise and dignified, the more he couldn't stand a person the sweeter he was in conversation with that person.

"You are a very wise—I should say, a very brilliant lobster," he said now in his most gracious tone.

Mr. Lobster realized at once that the sculpin was no fool after all.

"I should be pleased," the sculpin went on, "if you would tell me about the land. Unfortunately, one can't have both wisdom and youth, and I have reached an age when I no longer care for adventure, or I should certainly go ashore myself."

"Of course," agreed Mr. Lobster. "And I shall be delighted to tell you about it."

He thought he saw a look of slight pain come into the sculpin's face as he settled down to listen, but the sculpin was so ugly it was hard to tell when he was pained and when happy. So Mr. Lobster started to tell about the land.

This was the beginning of what appeared to be a friendship between Mr. Lobster and the sculpin. And it seemed to be a fine friendship, because each one realized the merits of the other without forgetting for a moment that his own merits were also very great. Some days the sculpin came to call. On other days Mr. Lobster stopped to talk on his way home from the river after a particularly nice walk which he knew the sculpin would love to have taken himself.

Mr. Lobster explained the land almost faster than he learned about it. He explained trees and birds and rain.

The sculpin explained more fully than before about the tides, how they worked, and why it was that, besides being an hour later each day, some days the tide went in the river in the morning and other days it went in in the afternoon.

"You observe," he said, "that it would be inconvenient for us fish to go up the river always in the morning or always in the afternoon. And it would be very monotonous. So the tides are arranged at different times of day."

Mr. Lobster was glad to know that. It was a relief to know that he would never have to go up the river by night. He did not like the dark. As he explained to himself: "Home is the best place to be after dark. In fact, that is one of the reasons for having a home, and I am wise enough to know it."

Some days after the beginning of this friendship between the sculpin and Mr. Lobster, there came about a change in Mr. Lobster's habits. He learned that instead of going up the river, he could swim straight to shore and walk right out on the beach. That is, if the waves were not too big.

As Mr. Lobster observed to himself after he tried this the first time, "Either the beach is just the bottom of the Ocean where it is out of water, or the bottom of the Ocean is the beach where it is under water. It is a very happy arrangement and was probably done by somebody on purpose."

It was Mr. Badger who had first suggested that Mr. Lobster come walking ashore on the beach.

Mr. Badger said: "I suggest that now that you can walk so far and so well on the meadow you ought to walk on the beach. There you can practice for miles. Besides, I find it necessary now to fish from the beach. The owl has told me that badgers are never found on beaches; so of course I am going to see about that. I must preserve my independence. And besides again, if I keep hoisting you over the bank of the river I shall wear all the fur off my tail where you grab it. That will either make my tail look like a muskrat's tail, which is a miserable object indeed, or it will make rings around my tail and I shall look like a raccoon. And a raccoon is an inferior creature. It can't dig burrows but has to climb trees, which is extremely silly."

"I should say it was," agreed Mr. Lobster, who knew that he could never climb a tree. "Who would want to climb trees?"

"No one in his right mind, of course," said Mr. Badger. "Trees are for poor things like birds, who have nowhere else to go. Besides, you are supposed only to fly into trees. And besides again, the tops of trees are a long way from the ground."

Mr. Lobster shuddered at the thought of being in a tree and not having wings. He wondered, though, what it would be like to fly. In fact, now that he came to think about it, he began to feel curious about it, and he wished that he could fly just once.

But he said nothing. He did not care to diminish Mr. Badger's respect for him, and he suspected that Mr. Badger had no use for creatures that flew.

Mr. Lobster said to himself: "I find that it is necessary to have some secrets even from my friends. I shall say nothing to Mr. Badger about flying until I have fully accomplished it. It is wiser to tell modestly about what you have done than to brag about what you are going to do."

Almost every day he walked on the beach, and almost every day Mr. Badger fished from the beach, throwing his line out into the Ocean beyond the waves, and sometimes catching some very fine fish.

"I have discovered," he told Mr. Lobster one day, "that the biggest fish live in the biggest places. Now either somebody made the place big because the fish were so big, or the fish are big because somebody made the place so big. I wish I knew which. But even if I don't it is a delightful thought to meditate upon, because it is a riddle without any answer."

"I realize that it is a deep subject," said Mr. Lobster, "but I do not know what a riddle is. I have never seen one."

"You don't see them. You hear them," explained Mr. Badger. "A riddle is just a question with an answer that makes you angry if you don't know it, and makes the person who asks it angry if you do know it."

"I see."

"You mean, you hear." Mr. Badger chuckled. "Riddles are usually very silly. This one is a delightful one because there is no answer. So nobody will be angry."

Mr. Lobster enjoyed walking on the beach, even though he never met anything pleasant to eat there. He could look away into the blue distance and see the woods, which he was curious to see close at hand. And he walked farther and farther every day, getting stronger and stronger, and able to stay out of water longer and longer. He was just waiting for the time when he could walk so far and stay out so long that he could go anywhere.

Mr. Badger warned him not to go too far alone.

"Don't fear," said Mr. Lobster, who was becoming very confident. "I always keep a weather eye out."

"Good heavens, how do you do that?" exclaimed Mr. Badger. "You don't mean to tell me that you have more eyes than I can see, and that you keep one out?"

Mr. Lobster was delighted to find out that he knew

something Mr. Badger didn't. It seemed to him that he was always asking Mr. Badger questions.

"That is a sea-faring expression," he said. "It means that I am always on the watch lest some unpleasant event catch me unawares. Like drying up, or a shark."

The reason that Mr. Lobster had to walk back and forth on the beach all alone was that Mr. Badger would not go with him.

"Walking is supposed to take you somewhere," Mr. Badger explained carefully. "But walking to and fro only brings you right back where you started. That isn't really walking. It's only exercise. And I hate exercise; it has no excitement in it. So you will please excuse me from walking with you here."

One day when the tide was going in during the afternoon there began a most unpleasant adventure for Mr. Lobster.

Mr. Lobster was late. He met four small flounders and one very small sand-dab on his way to the beach. So he stopped to catch them, which was pleasant; but he was late getting ashore. And when he walked down the beach to the place where Mr. Badger was fishing he saw at once that something was wrong. Mr. Badger, usually the happiest person in the world, and full of jokes, looked unhappy.

Mr. Lobster thought that he would cheer up Mr. Badger.

"What a beautiful day," he said. "Are you a badger today or something else?"

"It is a terrible day," said Mr. Badger in a gloomy voice.

"A terrible day. The most terrible day I have ever seen. And what I am today is a miserable creature."

"Why, what is the matter?"

"It is a long story," Mr. Badger sighed. "And I may not live long enough to tell it before a disaster befalls me, but I shall try."

"You must!" cried Mr. Lobster. He was instantly sympathetic and terribly curious. "You must tell me, and maybe I can help you and restore your happiness."

Mr. Badger sighed again more deeply than before.

"No, I am afraid I am beyond your help, though you are very kind indeed. I am afraid the time has come for me to suffer, and I hate suffering. It's all the owl's fault."

"But the owl isn't here," put in Mr. Lobster.

"I will tell you," said Mr. Badger. "You remember, I told you that the owl said no badger ate fish or was found on the beach. And how I immediately began to eat fish and finally even came to this beach, even though I hate fish, and I would much rather be in my own burrow. Well, last night I decided that I would go back to eating meat and living in my own warm burrow instead of under a leaky old stump in the woods. I have really been quite homesick."

"I remember," said Mr. Lobster. "I did not understand very well, except that you were being independent."

"Exactly." Mr. Badger sighed deeply. "Now last night, when I decided to go back to my old way of life, I thought I had better see the owl and ask him if there was anything else a badger didn't ever do. Because I knew that if there wasn't then I could go home in peace. You have no idea how I have longed for the comforts of my home."

"Oh, I have! I have!" exclaimed Mr. Lobster. "Home is always the place where you are the most comfortable."

"How true that is." Mr. Badger groaned. "Well, the owl said, after a great deal of thought and keeping me waiting, that there was one other thing a badger never could do. He could never eat vegetables. So I decided that I would eat a vegetable immediately and then go home. And, as it seemed foolish to bother the owl with any more questions, I decided that once I had eaten a vegetable I would never ask him another thing. Then I stole the vegetable."

"You stole it!"

"I stole it." Mr. Badger's tone was serious. "It is very difficult to find vegetables at night. They are inferior, and do not make noises or move about like a proper diet. So I went to the house of Mr. Bear, the finest house in our woods, and there was Mr. Bear asleep by the stove. And I went in very quietly and stole all his corn. Corn is a vegetable. It didn't taste a bit good, but I ate it all. Of course, you have to eat whatever you steal. And Mr. Bear woke up and saw me, and I had to run for my life. I can tell you, I was frightened almost to death. And all the owl's fault, you see."

"Of course," agreed Mr. Lobster. "Although I don't see why you had to steal the corn."

"We won't discuss that now," said Mr. Badger. "To discuss why you do foolish things after you do them is useless. What I am about to tell you is that Mr. Bear didn't catch me, but today, while I was fishing here, he did catch me."

"Well, you are still alive," said Mr. Lobster.

"For the present, yes. But only for the present, I am afraid. You see, when I begged his pardon for stealing his corn, and explained that it was all the owl's fault, and that the owl had made me miserable for weeks by telling me things I couldn't do, so that I had to do them, Mr. Bear said: 'Very well, you must catch me six large fish for my supper, to take the place of the corn you stole. And if you don't—' I shudder to think what he meant. And I have caught only five fish. I have given those to him, but he says I must catch another. And there isn't another. So I am lost."

Mr. Lobster thought seriously.

"I have it," he said. "I shall go out into the Ocean and swim around and see where there is a large fish near shore. Then I shall come back and tell you where to throw your line."

With these words Mr. Lobster crawled down to the water and began swimming. He swam all along the bottom of the Ocean just beyond the breakers and looked as hard as he could. But he didn't see a single large fish. He caught a small fish and thought of taking that to Mr. Badger, but then he knew it would not be big enough. So he simply ate it.

Finally he returned to the beach and went up to Mr. Badger.

"I am very sorry," he said. "I did not see a single large fish."

"I knew it," said Mr. Badger. "I knew it. This is probably the end of our friendship. Doubtless I shall be fried."

"Fried?" asked Mr. Lobster. "What do you mean?"

"That means being burned with fire, which is the hottest heat there is and extremely dangerous. Mr. Bear boasts that he is the most civilized creature in the woods, and so, to prove it, he fries much of his food. He will probably fry me with the five fish I have succeeded in catching him."

"I suppose," said Mr. Lobster thoughtfully, "that frying dries one up."

"Frying does," said Mr. Badger sadly. "Also, frying is permanent."

Mr. Lobster could feel himself getting dry at the very thought of such a thing. But at the same time he was thinking a heroic thought.

"Pardon me for a few minutes," he said. "I feel a bit nervous." And he hastily crawled back into the Ocean and got himself good and wet, so that all the hinges of his tail and all his other hinges felt fine.

Then he crawled back to Mr. Badger.

"Where is Mr. Bear?" he asked.

"He is behind that huge boulder over there." Mr. Badger pointed a sad and drooping paw toward a great boulder at the edge of the beach.

"Very well," said Mr. Lobster. "Mr. Bear is not my enemy, for I have not stolen from him. So I shall go over and engage him in conversation. I can tell him a great many things. While I am talking to him, and he is carefully listening, you can run away and he won't see you go."

"How brave you are!" exclaimed Mr. Badger. For the moment Mr. Badger seemed almost happy. "But you are nervous, Mr. Lobster. I can see your joints shaking."

"Being brave is the most nervous thing there is," replied Mr. Lobster. "Nevertheless, I shall go."

"No." Mr. Badger's tone was sad again. "Mr. Bear is not to be trifled with. I shall not let you risk your life for me. I can't allow it."

"Nonsense!" exclaimed Mr. Lobster. "As if Mr. Bear could hurt me. I have one of the hardest shells you have ever seen. Besides, I am your friend. And a friend has the right to do anything for you that he sees fit."

And with these words, and before Mr. Badger could say another thing, and trembling in every joint of his shell and every hinge in his tail, Mr. Lobster started on his way to Mr. Bear.

Mr. Lobster Has
a Desperate Time

MR. BEAR, who happened to be the largest bear living
in the woods of that certain place, was sitting behind the
big boulder, looking at his five fish which Mr. Badger had
caught for him. Also, he was enjoying the warm afternoon sun. It was a great pleasure to sit in the sun while
someone else did all the work of catching his dinner. So
Mr. Bear was in a happy frame of mind.

"Good day," said Mr. Lobster by way of greeting as he
came around the boulder.

"Humph!" said Mr. Bear, and he gave a low growl. And
immediately he looked very cross, for, being a bear, no

matter how contented and pleased he was, he always was also cross as a bear when small creatures spoke to him.

Mr. Bear got up, and Mr. Lobster suddenly realized what a tremendous creature a bear was, and he began to tremble in all the joints in his shell in spite of himself.

"And what in the world are you?" asked Mr. Bear in his gruffest voice, just as though he had a very bad throat indeed and was very hoarse.

Mr. Lobster wished instantly that he could be back at the bottom of the Ocean. He didn't feel half so brave as he had when he told Mr. Badger he would come and speak to Mr. Bear. But he managed to speak, and he folded up his tail tightly so that Mr. Bear would not see it trembling.

"I am a lobster," he said. "I have a home at the bottom of the Ocean. At present I am walking on this pleasant beach." He did not think it was a pleasant beach at all just at that moment.

"Ah, then you are a fish!"

"I am a lobster," replied Mr. Lobster, "and very superior to fish."

"Well, what are you doing here? If you live at the bottom of the Ocean, I say you are a fish, and a fish belongs either in the Ocean or in the frying-pan." Mr. Bear was being as cross as he could, considering that a few moments before he had been exceedingly contented. "If you are superior, I suppose that means you are superior to fish when fried?"

"Oh, no, not at all! Not in that way! Please do not misunderstand me!" begged Mr. Lobster. "I was going to say, what a pleasure to meet you, and what a delightful day it is, isn't it?"

"Things are going very well, I suppose," said Mr. Bear, "but that's no sign that they'll continue to go well. I do not take too much stock in today. What I am interested in is always tomorrow."

"I never thought of that," said Mr. Lobster, hoping that now the subject was changed from such things as frying fish.

"No, you wouldn't," remarked Mr. Bear, a little less gruffly, and a little more as though he were satisfied with the way things were going even if it was not tomorrow. "Of course, you are not civilized. No civilized creature would live in water or at the bottom of an Ocean. And only civilized creatures have the intelligence to think about tomorrow. You have no worries."

"I suppose you are highly civilized." As Mr. Lobster made this flattering remark, he edged away. He wanted to be as far as possible from Mr. Bear, and he wanted to look around and see if Mr. Badger had escaped yet.

"I am. I have a house with windows, and I fry much of my food," said Mr. Bear. "Especially fish. All fish were made to fry." And he looked unpleasantly at Mr. Lobster.

Mr. Lobster realized that the subject had changed to frying again. He was very much frightened. So he looked quickly around, stretching his eyes as far as he could. Mr. Badger had disappeared.

"I am very sorry, but I believe I must be going," he said to Mr. Bear, trying to seem quite at ease, but speaking over his shell because he was already started. And he began to hurry toward the water without waiting to hear what Mr. Bear said.

"Possibly I am being discourteous," he said to himself, "but this is a difficult situation, and I hope I may be excused."

He crawled as fast as he could.

"There's one thing about it," he told himself as he drew near the Ocean, "I know now that I am not at all curious about bears. I've learned all I want to know about them."

He was almost to the water. He thought that he was safe. But then there came a frightful roar, and before he could go any faster or even think another thought Mr. Bear came rushing along behind him and grabbed him by the tail.

"I've got you!" growled Mr. Bear, and it was no slight growl but a great big double-barreled one that terrified Mr. Lobster.

"Pardon me," said Mr. Lobster. "I should love to stay and talk with you, but at present I must go into the water. I am getting dry."

"Oh, no, you don't! I know now what you did. You came over and talked to me so that the miserable corn-thief, Mr. Badger, could run away. I saw you talking with him." Mr. Bear was not just cross now. He was furious.

"Please let me go!" begged Mr. Lobster. "I have done you no wrong!"

"Oh, haven't you, though!" exclaimed Mr. Bear, growling at the same time he talked. "You let that Mr. Badger get away when I had only five fish. It was a plot!"

"But I don't even know what a plot is," protested Mr. Lobster.

"A plot is a mean trick to cheat people out of their dinner," growled Mr. Bear. "Now you know. And now you shall be the sixth fish for my dinner."

And with that he picked Mr. Lobster up and carried him off. Then he gathered the five fish Mr. Badger had caught, and started for his home in the woods.

"I shall have six fish for dinner after all," he said.

Poor Mr. Lobster was so frightened now that he could scarcely speak. Mr. Bear was so big and strong that Mr. Lobster was helpless. He couldn't even reach around and bite with his big pincher claws. When he did manage to speak, it was only in a whisper:

"What are you going to do with me?"

"Cook you for my dinner."

"But I am sixty-eight years old. And I have such a hard shell you can never fry me," said Mr. Lobster.

"Maybe that's so."

"Oh, it is!" exclaimed Mr. Lobster. "And if you let me go I will catch you a fish."

"If I let you go, you will hide in the Ocean," answered Mr. Bear cruelly. "Besides, I won't fry you. I'll boil you."

Mr. Lobster shuddered. He began to feel dryer than he had ever felt before. He saw the beach and the beautiful Ocean disappearing in the distance. Now Mr. Bear was carrying him right into the woods he had wanted to visit, but he forgot all about that. He was too unhappy even to look around.

"I WON'T FRY YOU. I'LL BOIL YOU," SAID MR. BEAR.

"I hope," he said to himself, "that the sculpin never hears about this. He said that the wanderer sometimes does not return. I never knew that getting knowledge would lead to this. This is a frightful thing. It must be all the owl's fault, as Mr. Badger said."

Then he saw Mr. Bear's house. It was made of stones, and there was a window right beside the door. And there was a chimney with smoke coming out of it. Mr. Lobster felt so badly that he would have closed his eyes if he could, but of course no lobster can close his eyes; so he had to look right at Mr. Bear's house.

"You observe the window," said Mr. Bear. "A sure sign of being civilized. Presently you will observe the fact that I cook my food. I believe you will make an excellent dinner."

Mr. Lobster was too unhappy to reply. He knew that Mr. Bear had no mercy.

Mr. Bear put the five fish on his table. He put Mr. Lobster in a corner, where Mr. Lobster lay, not daring to move. Then Mr. Bear stirred up his fire until he had a good blaze. Although he never admitted this to the creatures he met, the reason he was so civilized was that he had once spent several years with a circus; so of course he knew all about civilization.

Finally he filled a big kettle half full of water, put in a good measure of salt, and put the kettle on the stove. Then he dumped Mr. Lobster into the kettle.

At first Mr. Lobster felt much better. The salt water refreshed him at once, and it was so pleasant to feel wet and salty again, that he thought that maybe there was still a chance for him to escape.

But then the water began to get hot. Mr. Lobster had never been in hot water before, but he knew instantly that it would be the end of him if he stayed in it now. He put his head and eyes out to cool them, but he knew that that would never save him.

"This time I am lost," he thought.

And then suddenly there was a shout from the woods.

"Ha, ha! There's Mr. Bear, who is so stupid he can't even catch his own fish!"

It was Mr. Badger, and he stood right outside Mr. Bear's door, shouting over and over, making insulting faces, and doing everything he could think of to make Mr. Bear angry.

But Mr. Bear did not move. He was watching the big kettle that held Mr. Lobster.

And Mr. Lobster felt hotter and hotter. He could feel his shell, which was a lovely dark green color when he was in good health, turning red. He knew that when it was red all over he would be dead.

"What a terrible way to be gone!" he thought. "O that Mr. Badger could save me!"

"You can't catch me!" shouted Mr. Badger to Mr. Bear. "You are too clumsy! You have no brains! And how easy it was to play a trick on you! Ha! Ha! Ha!"

Mr. Bear was furious, and each moment he was getting more furious. He growled terribly.

"I won't chase you now!" he cried out to Mr. Badger.

"I'll get you some other time, you insulting, inferior, corn-stealing creature! I am going to stay right here until your friend Mr. Lobster is cooked to a turn."

Mr. Lobster groaned. Mr. Badger was brave indeed, but it was no use. It had been all a mistake ever to leave such a place as the bottom of the Ocean.

And just as he was thinking the most unhappy thoughts a huge stone came crashing through Mr. Bear's one window, of which he was so proud, breaking the glass all to bits.

And then another stone came crashing into the house and broke all the dishes on Mr. Bear's table.

"Hooray!" cried Mr. Badger. "Isn't that fun! Did you hear that noise?"

Mr. Bear could stand it no longer. He gave a roar and rushed out of his house to catch Mr. Badger.

Mr. Lobster was left all alone. He jumped as hard as he could and as high as he could, but he couldn't jump out of the kettle. He was getting hotter and hotter and redder and redder. And this was his last attempt to escape.

"My last minutes have come," he said to himself.

At that moment, and just in the very nick of time, Mr. Badger came running right into Mr. Bear's house, with Mr. Bear right at his tail. There were terrible sounds of panting and growling.

Mr. Badger reached up a paw and knocked the big kettle smash onto the floor, and Mr. Lobster and all the water were spilled out. Then Mr. Badger ran under the table. When Mr. Bear tried to get under after him he was too big, and he tipped the table over. There was a fearful crash and clatter, and everything went this way and that in small pieces, showering Mr. Lobster and covering the floor.

At that moment Mr. Badger stopped to laugh and then ran outdoors again. Mr. Bear gave the loudest roar he had ever made and ran out after Mr. Badger.

Mr. Lobster was so bewildered and hot and red that he hardly knew what to do next. But he gathered his wits together and realized that he was all alone, and that if ever he was to escape now was the time, before Mr. Bear came back and caught him again.

Very feebly he crawled out of Mr. Bear's house and started through the woods. He did not know which way to go. He dared not look this way or that. He was still so hot that he felt very uncomfortable. And he was getting dryer every second. So he just crawled along slowly, dragging his tail behind him, and feeling very lame in all his joints.

Just when he thought he could not crawl another inch, the little path he was on crossed a brook. And just then Mr. Lobster thought he heard the sound of Mr. Badger laughing somewhere in the woods.

He knew he could not wait for Mr. Badger.

So he crawled into the brook and began to swim down it, not going very fast, but helped along by the flowing water. The water was fresh, of course, and Mr. Lobster coughed and sneezed. If he had had to stay long in such water he might have been ill. But fortunately the little

THERE WAS A FEARFUL CRASH AND CLATTER.

brook flowed into a creek, and the creek flowed into the river, and Mr. Lobster found himself once again in salt water.

Then he knew that he was safe, and he began to swim down the river at a pretty fair rate of speed, although he was still far from well.

He did not want to see the sculpin; so when he reached the Ocean he went home as fast as he could—which wasn't half so fast as it ought to have been, and not a tenth as fast as he wanted it to be. And, as bad luck would have it, the sculpin saw him and came swimming right over into his path.

"You are very late, Mr. Lobster, and I have been worried about you," said the sculpin. He was looking Mr. Lobster over with a sympathetic eye, but with one of those looks of a wise person who is missing nothing. "You don't look at all well, my dear Mr. Lobster. What can be the matter with your shell?"

"I am tired," said Mr. Lobster. "I really can't stop to talk just now. I made a long and important trip on land today. In fact, it has been a busy day for me."

"Indeed!" The sculpin looked as important and wise as he could, at the same time being envious and suspicious. "If you are so exhausted," he said, "I suppose you will hardly care to go ashore again."

Now Mr. Lobster knew then and there that he never wanted to go ashore again as long as he lived, but he also knew that he could never let the sculpin know that. The sculpin would think he was afraid and would probably say, "I told you so."

So he had to say to the sculpin just what he didn't want to say:

"Of course I shall go ashore again. I would not miss it for anything."

And then, a little sadly, and very tired, he crawled home. And as he curled up his tail and prepared for a long rest, he said to himself:

"Home is certainly the place where you are the most thankful to be."

Mr. Lobster and Mr. Badger
Meet Mr. Bear Again

MR. LOBSTER rested for a long time, and when he woke up he felt much better than he had when he returned home from nearly being boiled. He remembered right away, however, that he had told the sculpin he was certainly going ashore again, and he realized that had been a rash thing to say. Right now he did not want to go ashore again.

And then he noticed that there were still some red places on his beautiful dark green shell, and he realized with sorrow that they would probably stay there until he shed his shell the next spring.

"I am not so very happy," he said to himself. "I must

therefore think a pleasant thought as soon as possible. Let me see. . . . Ah, when I shed this shell I shall be sixty-nine years old and my new shell will be number seventy. How fortunate I am to be able to shed my shell and get a new one every year. That's more than the sculpin can do, and it is a pleasant thought."

So, since it was a pleasant thought, and a superior one as well, he started the day by feeling better right then.

But he did not go out of his house at all, except to catch two small flounders who came to play in his seaweed garden.

In the afternoon he saw the sculpin come swimming up, and he immediately pretended to be sleeping. So the sculpin, being dignified, and therefore always polite, did not disturb him.

The next morning when he looked out, there was the sculpin again, moving his big fins slowly and staying right in one place.

"He is watching for me, and I have no desire to see him," said Mr. Lobster to himself. "But if he does not go away I shall get hungry and have to go out. In fact, I am hungry now, come to think of it."

He waited for quite a while, getting more and more hungry, until he felt actually hollow in a certain place under his shell. He looked at his shell to see if the red places were gone. No, they were still there. He knew the sculpin would say something unpleasant, but there was no waiting any longer. So he crawled out, looking just as pleased with himself as he could, which is the way to deal with stern and dignified people, but really not feeling at all pleased about those red spots.

"Well, well," said the sculpin, "at last you have come out. I was really worried—deeply perturbed, I might say. I was afraid that something had happened to you and that you were not well. You know, you did look so poorly when you returned the other day."

"Oh, not at all. Not at all," said Mr. Lobster. "I am in fine condition. A person has to rest once in a while, you know. And I have been very busy these past weeks. It requires some effort to go ashore each day."

"No doubt," said the sculpin, without trying to look pleasant, which is the least he might have done. "But what has happened to your shell? I thought it looked strange the other day, and now I see that it is getting red! You really don't look healthy."

"That?" asked Mr. Lobster as though he were very much surprised at the sculpin's question. "You mean that trifle of red? Don't think of it. This shell is getting old, you know. I shall discard it in the spring." He said this lightly, but he felt annoyed. The sculpin's bright eyes saw too much sometimes.

Mr. Lobster decided to crawl right past the sculpin lest there should be any more annoying conversation to remind him of the unhappy meeting with Mr. Bear. So he started to go on without saying another word.

"Of course," said the sculpin, swimming up very near, "now that you have had a rest, you are going ashore again at once."

Now that was just what Mr. Lobster had been afraid the sculpin would say, and it was just the question he did not want to answer. It was strange how people of the dignity and wisdom of the sculpin always made the most unwelcome remarks when you did something which caused trouble just because you hadn't followed their advice.

"At present," Mr. Lobster answered sharply, "I am going to get my dinner."

And with that, he tail-snapped away.

He did not go ashore that day. The next morning when he came out of his house to see if there were any pleasant creatures in his garden, who should come along but the sculpin.

"I wondered if you were going ashore today," said the sculpin. "Because if you are, I'll just go along a way with you."

There was a suspicious look in the sculpin's eyes.

"Not today," said Mr. Lobster, and he started to move away.

"I see," said the sculpin. "I see."

Mr. Lobster did not wait to hear the sculpin say "I see" again. He gave two of his hardest tail-snaps.

But every day the sculpin came to ask him whether he was going ashore. Mr. Lobster didn't know what to do. He wanted to go ashore just to show the sculpin that he wasn't afraid, but he didn't want to go because he thought of Mr. Bear, who might very well be on the beach. In a way, he wanted to see Mr. Badger, because they were friends; but in another way he didn't want to see Mr. Badger for fear there might be more trouble.

After a few days Mr. Lobster was surprised to find that his curiosity was returning. He wondered what Mr. Badger was doing, and whether he could ever go into the woods in a pleasant manner, not being carried by Mr. Bear, and whether he could still get along all right out of water—and lots of other things.

"I suppose," he said to himself, "that I shall be curious as long as I live, and I might as well face that fact. I wonder if anything cures curiosity. I really do want to go ashore again. And yet I am really afraid to meet Mr. Bear."

He thought and thought and thought, and his curiosity got stronger and stronger. And then his wisdom came to the rescue. If he wanted to go ashore but was afraid to meet Mr. Bear, why not go to the river bank again, where Mr. Bear did not come? It was a wonderful thought.

This time when he met the sculpin he was glad to see him. "You are the gladdest to meet people," he said to himself, "when you have nothing to hide from them." And he spoke up quickly when the sculpin asked him if he was going ashore.

"Yes, I am," he said. "It has been very nice staying here at home for a while. All travelers appreciate home, but of course I couldn't live such a dull life all the time. It must be miserable not to be able to go ashore, and I don't see how you stand it."

The poor sculpin couldn't say a word.

Mr. Lobster went in with the tide that day, but he did

not hurry. In the first place, he stopped to catch several pleasant creatures on the way. In the second place, now that he was really on his way ashore again, he remembered the red places on his shell, and Mr. Bear; and he wondered just how wise it was to go ashore.

"After all," he said to himself, "you should always think before you go into danger. It just does no good to think afterwards. Still, I am curious to know how Mr. Badger is, and whether the land is still pleasant."

So he kept swimming until he came to the place where he used to meet Mr. Badger. Then he came up to the top of the water and looked around.

At once he saw Mr. Badger and at once Mr. Badger chuckled joyfully.

"Ha, ha! I knew you would come!" cried Mr. Badger. "I felt it in my bones you were safe. Come right ashore."

Mr. Lobster went up the bank in the old way, hanging on to Mr. Badger's tail.

"I am very sorry to have to use your tail again," he said.

"Don't mention it! Don't mention it! You can pull all the hairs out of my tail if you want to on such a glad occasion as this. When old friends meet again for a reunion after great danger, such trifles as hairs don't matter." Mr. Badger seemed very happy. "Besides, you saved my life."

"Oh, no," protested Mr. Lobster, "you saved my life by knocking that kettle on the floor."

"But you saved my life first by talking to Mr. Bear; so you really saved your own life."

"But you saved my life yourself after I saved your life," insisted Mr. Lobster.

"But I had such a good time," said Mr. Badger. "I enjoyed teasing Mr. Bear. I always love a good joke, and it is such fun breaking things in a good cause. I did love to hear Mr. Bear's window and dishes breaking. And you must admit that I couldn't have saved your life if you hadn't saved my life first."

"Perhaps that's true," admitted Mr. Lobster. "It is a little confusing. I guess we're even."

"We are both heroes!" exclaimed Mr. Badger. "That's what we are, and that is the important thing. It is delightful, isn't it? And such a joke on Mr. Bear, who didn't get either one of us! But you know, I did a very fine deed after you escaped."

"Please tell me about it!" Mr. Lobster was curious at once.

"Well, it is all very well to have an enemy if he is a small enemy," said Mr. Badger, his eyes twinkling. "It can be quite interesting. But when your enemy is as big as Mr. Bear it becomes a serious matter. So after you escaped and Mr. Bear went home, I went and gathered a great lot of fine corn and carried it to his door. I worked all night to get it there."

"You did it at night—in the dark?"

"Oh, yes. You understand, it is the custom of badgers to go out only at night. We fear nothing. That is how I met the owl, and it was the owl who told me that badgers never went out in the daytime. Ever since then I have been out every day. You know, I told you the owl started all my troubles." Mr. Badger sighed, but it was not an unhappy sigh, for he really loved trouble—so long as it was not as big as a bear. "Yes, I think it was very fine of me to return Mr. Bear's corn."

"Where did you get it?" asked Mr. Lobster.

"I stole it," said Mr. Badger.

"Then you will have to return that also sometime, won't you?" asked Mr. Lobster.

"Let us not go into that now," said Mr. Badger. "The point is, I did a fine thing."

"Well, anyway, you are very brave," said Mr. Lobster.

"How brave we both are!" exclaimed Mr. Badger. "And what a happy occasion this is, to be together again. Two heroes—one a land hero, and the other a sea hero. And how lucky we are that our escapes were so narrow!"

"Pardon me," put in Mr. Lobster. "Did you say 'lucky'?"

"Of course. There is nothing in the world so delightful as to talk about the narrow escapes you have had. They are a great pleasure after they are all over."

"I never thought of that," said Mr. Lobster. "I see what you mean, though I myself am simply very glad my escape is over."

They sat together on the bank of the river for a few minutes, very pleased with themselves. Mr. Lobster was especially delighted to realize that he was a hero who had had a narrow escape. And then suddenly he had an interesting thought which showed how wise he was.

"You know," he said, "I have thought of another good

thing. Each one of us has somebody else who knows he is a hero, and that is what really counts. I know you are a hero, and you know I am a hero. I suppose it is no fun at all being brave and a hero if no one knows but yourself."

"Why, of course. What a brilliant thinker you are, Mr. Lobster!" Mr. Badger was happier than ever.

"And you also, Mr. Badger."

"Oh, I beg your pardon, but not today," put in Mr. Badger quickly.

"Not today?"

"Exactly. I mean I am not a badger today, though of course I am a hero. Once a hero, always a hero, is my motto."

"Then you are a wallaby."

"Oh, no, I was a wallaby before. Today I am a bandicoot. I must tell you why. You see, I knew that if the owl told me another thing I couldn't do, I just wouldn't be able to stand it. You see, now that I am eating meat again and living in my own house, I am quite happy. Well, the owl always calls me Mr. Badger; so now, whenever I go through the woods, I am a bandicoot. Naturally, when the owl calls out, 'Good evening, Mr. Badger,' I know he isn't speaking to me because I am a bandicoot. And so I don't have to answer. It is perfectly fair not to answer if people don't know your name. As long as I don't answer, the owl can't tell me anything more I can't do, because he can't be talking to me." Mr. Badger paused after that long explanation, looking quite pleased. "It is quite simple, you see," he added.

"Perhaps it is," said Mr. Lobster, "but I think it is very confusing. In many ways you baffle me. How am I going to keep you straight?"

Mr. Badger laughed out loud.

"It delights me to baffle people," he said. "And think what a joke it is on the owl!"

Mr. Lobster did think of that, and he wondered what Mr. Badger would be tomorrow.

"Well, Mr. Bandicoot," he began.

"Yes, yes, do go on," said Mr. Badger, very much pleased.

But just then came an interruption—a horrible interruption. It was a cough, a very deep cough that ended in a low growl. And it came from behind Mr. Lobster and Mr. Badger, because they were sitting on the bank of the river looking over the water.

Mr. Lobster trembled in every joint. He knew that he had heard that growl before.

Mr. Badger instantly stopped being happy.

Then they looked around.

There stood Mr. Bear, looking as big as a hill.

Mr. Lobster and Mr. Badger both started to move at the same time.

"I beg your pardon," said Mr. Bear, in such a deep voice that Mr. Lobster's tail curled and Mr. Badger's hair stood up straight all down his back. "I didn't mean to cough, and so the cough made me a little cross, and I growled. I tried to be very quiet."

JUST THEN CAME A HORRIBLE INTERRUPTION.

For a moment the two heroes were silent.

Then Mr. Badger said, "I hate to swim, but I believe I will cross the river."

And Mr. Lobster said, "I am feeling very dry. I really must be getting home."

"Oh, no, please don't do that!" exclaimed Mr. Bear. "I realized after I found the corn at my door that you were both so clever and so brave we all should be friends. Besides, you are both such good fishermen, and I love fish. I thought we could be friends and fish together."

"But we can't all be fish," said Mr. Badger.

"I mean we ought to go fishing together."

Mr. Lobster had been moving slowly backwards so that he could drop off the river bank into the water.

"Please don't go, I beg of you," said Mr. Bear. "It will make me very cross. I mean what I say about being friends. A bear is always cross but never deceitful. You know, you can trust cross people because they mean what they say, but you have to be careful of people who smile all the time."

Mr. Lobster was so near the edge of the bank that he thought he could safely talk to Mr. Bear.

"Are you cross now?" he asked.

"I am furious," said Mr. Bear calmly. "So you can believe every word I say."

Mr. Badger's back hair was lying down again.

"I feel better," he said. "I am very independent; so it does my heart good to see people furious. But why are you furious now?"

"I have fished for hours on the beach and haven't caught a thing."

"I see," said Mr. Badger thoughtfully.

"I am the largest creature in these parts, and I am the most civilized," said Mr. Bear. "I had a window in my house until you broke it, and I fry much of my food. Now will you be friends? You know I am speaking the truth."

"I know the window part is true," said Mr. Badger, a rascally look gleaming in his bright eyes.

"I know a few things too," said Mr. Lobster.

"Of course, you must realize that we are both heroes," said Mr. Badger, still looking rascally.

Mr. Bear growled terribly.

"You both make me furious!" he exclaimed.

"Ah," said Mr. Badger. "Then that settles it. We must be friends, because nobody but a friend can have the privilege of making one furious without suffering for it; and Mr. Lobster and I hate to suffer."

"I should say so," agreed Mr. Lobster, thinking of the red places on his shell, and the great heat that had caused them.

"Very well," said Mr. Bear crossly. And he came and sat on the bank, unwound the fishing line which he had in his paw, and began to fish.

Mr. Lobster and Mr. Badger were not fishing, but they watched, and all three of them talked pleasantly, although Mr. Bear did not get any bites and so was very cross.

Mr. Lobster went into the river to get wet and to look around for fish. But there were no fish to be seen.

"Just my luck," growled Mr. Bear. "It is always my luck to get places just too late. I shall probably be especially hungry today, too. I shall go home and eat blueberries for supper. I am very fond of blueberries, but you can't fry them, and so whenever I eat them, no matter how good they taste, I feel uncivilized." He began to wind up his line, growling softly to himself.

"I think," said Mr. Badger, "that we had better plan some way of getting fish for Mr. Bear. Let us all meet here tomorrow and plan a fishing expedition."

"We probably won't get any, but I will come," said Mr. Bear.

"And so will I," agreed Mr. Lobster.

So Mr. Badger and Mr. Bear started home together.

"Good-by, Mr. Bear," called Mr. Lobster, and then, "Good-by, Mr. Bandicoot.'"

"Thank you! Thank you!" called Mr. Badger.

"Now what did he mean by that?" asked Mr. Bear. "Was he calling names?"

Mr. Lobster did not wait to hear what Mr. Badger said, for he was sure it would be confusing. He just slipped off the bank, fell with a splash into the water, and started for home.

When he met the sculpin, just as he was getting near home, he said, "You know, there is nothing like going ashore. Such interesting and wise creatures there—and absolutely nothing to be afraid of."

And he continued on his way, very happy indeed.

Three Friends Go Fishing
and Something Happens

EARLY THE next morning Mr. Lobster was up and prowling around looking at his seaweed garden and being pleased with his home. He spent a good deal of time rubbing his shell very hard back and forth along the big rock that was the wall of his house. This made his shell shine beautifully, but it did not rub out the red patches, as he hoped it would.

Still, Mr. Lobster was happy. Now he could go ashore and he and Mr. Badger could be heroes without having a single enemy, for Mr. Bear was their friend.

"And that," said Mr. Lobster to himself, "is the pleasantest kind of hero to be. It is all very well to have adventures and narrow escapes, but I prefer a friendly life."

He was so curious to find out about Mr. Badger's fishing expedition that he could hardly wait for the tide to go in. When it did start to flow in, Mr. Lobster chased only two small flounders, he was so busy swimming. Besides, the bottom of the Ocean was dark today, and it was hard to see.

When he had swum up the river to the right place, there were Mr. Badger and Mr. Bear waiting for him.

"Good day!" called Mr. Badger. "Of course it is a pretty gray day, and it looks like rain, but that makes it a good day for fishing; so it's a good day for us."

Mr. Lobster saw that it was a very darksome day, and he heard the waves on the beach making a rather stormy sound, and he saw that the sea gulls were flying around restlessly and screaming to each other. When he looked up he saw that the sky was restless and moving too. Evidently nothing was quite contented this day. But of course Mr. Lobster didn't care, because he knew that whenever there was a storm all he had to do was go down to the bottom of the Ocean, where it was always calm. It was only near shore, where the water was shallow, that the great storms disturbed the fish and tore up the seaweed and scattered the clams.

Mr. Lobster did notice a rather unpleasant thing. Mr. Bear looked especially cross, even for a bear.

"Good morning," he replied to Mr. Badger. And then

to Mr. Bear, very politely, "And good morning, Mr. Bear. I hope you are feeling well and happy."

Mr. Bear growled.

"I am perfectly well," he said. "In fact, I am too well. My health is so good that my appetite is tremendous, and we've been waiting for you and fishing two solid hours and haven't caught a thing. It is high time you came, and I am furious. If we don't catch any fish today I shall have to go on eating berries, which are perfectly delicious, it is true, but which will soon make me completely uncivilized. I tell you, I've got to have something to fry!" He growled again, and began pulling in his line to see if there was any bait on the hook.

The bait was gone.

"There, look at that!" he exclaimed in disgust. "The bait is gone, but I've caught no fish. I never have anything but bad luck. You don't wonder I'm cross, do you?"

"I think," observed Mr. Lobster, "that it wasn't bad luck but crabs that took your bait. I saw a great many crabs as I came along."

"They're the same thing," growled Mr. Bear. "No fish is bad luck, and if crabs mean no fish then they're bad luck. And I'm disgusted."

"Don't mind him," said Mr. Badger to Mr. Lobster. "Come ashore. I've already learned that as long as Mr. Bear growls and complains he's all right. It was my idea to start our fishing expedition here, and he has been growling ever since we got here."

"A very poor idea it was," said Mr. Bear crossly.

"Oh, I have other ideas," said Mr. Badger cheerfully. Nothing could put Mr. Badger down.

Mr. Lobster went ashore by way of Mr. Badger's tail.

Mr. Bear was winding up his fishing line, growling softly to himself, just as though a kettle were boiling inside of him.

"What I would like to know," he said when he had his line wound up, "is what is your next idea?"

Mr. Lobster was stretching himself and letting his tail out to its full length. It was so nice to be ashore again, and to feel safe at the same time. He looked off towards the hills and the woods and wished that Mr. Badger's next idea would take them all there.

Mr. Badger began to speak.

"I had three ideas," he said. "I must admit that one of them is no good, since there are no fish here. So I will now tell you the second."

"What is it?" asked Mr. Bear.

"We shall go now and fish from the beach, and Mr. Lobster can tell us where the big fish are."

"That is not very remarkable for an idea," said Mr. Bear.

"But the third idea is remarkable," said Mr. Badger. "It is stupendous!"

"What does that mean?" asked Mr. Lobster.

"Well, stupendous is three times as remarkable as remarkable." Mr. Badger chuckled.

"Oh." Mr. Lobster thought for a time. He knew that he could not conceal his curiosity. So he had to say, "Then tell us what the third stupendous idea is."

"Oh, no!" protested Mr. Badger. "That would spoil the fun. There must always be a surprise ahead. Life is very dull if you are sure of what is going to happen next."

"It is dull if you don't have anything to eat," growled Mr. Bear.

"Let us go right away and try the second idea," said Mr. Lobster. "Then we can learn the third." And he said softly to himself under one corner of his shell, "I must learn Mr. Badger's third idea."

So Mr. Badger and Mr. Bear walked along the river to go over the bridge to the beach, and Mr. Lobster said that it would take him so long to walk he guessed he would swim across the river and meet them on the other side.

Mr. Badger looked quite small and unimportant beside Mr. Bear, but as Mr. Lobster watched them walking away he realized that Mr. Badger was a hero, and so size didn't matter.

"It goes to show that you can never tell a hero by his size," he said to himself. "I will remember that bit of wisdom. It seems to me that I get wiser every time I come ashore, and goodness knows I satisfy a great deal of my curiosity, too. Traveling is evidently a very good thing—so long as you have a good home and know enough to return to it."

When the three friends were together on the beach Mr. Bear baited his hook and threw his line so that he could fish way out beyond the waves. Then Mr. Badger did the same.

"Now we shall see," said Mr. Badger.

"I hope we shall see some fish," growled Mr. Bear. "Do you realize that you have done nothing but make me cross ever since we met?"

"Let us not speak of the unhappy past," said Mr. Lobster. He was thinking of the disgraceful red spots on his shell. "I will go right out and see if I can find you some fish."

And he crawled into the waves, sank to the bottom, and then began tail-snapping along to see what he could see. Back and forth he went, and back and forth. He saw Mr. Badger's bait and Mr. Bear's bait. He saw crabs and clams and dabs and small flounders, but he didn't see a single big fish.

"Well," he said to himself, "probably I am very mean, but I am really glad. If there are no fish here I shall certainly learn Mr. Badger's third idea, which is stupendous."

So he went ashore and crawled out trying to look sorry, but really not feeling sorry at all.

"I must tell you," he said to Mr. Badger and Mr. Bear, "that I did not see a single big fish. I think we had better try the third idea."

"I think," said Mr. Bear with a low and disgusted growl, "that I might just as well go and pick blueberries. At least, a blueberry does not run and hide as soon as you come after it."

"But you haven't heard the best idea of all," protested Mr. Badger. "Listen to me. Over in the river near here is a good-sized boat. It belongs to a sailor who lives in an old sea shanty on the beach. We can take the boat, and

Mr. Bear can row because he is the biggest and strongest, and we can go way out on the Ocean where we know the big fish live. We can catch a boat full."

Mr. Lobster was delighted at this idea. He had been under the Ocean all his life, but he had never been on top of it in a boat. It *was* stupendous! But then he thought of something else.

"We would be stealing the boat," he said.

"Oh, no," said Mr. Badger quickly. "When you steal things you don't bring them back. We shall borrow the boat and bring it back, and we shall leave enough fine fish in it to pay for using it."

"It sounds shady to me," said Mr. Bear.

"But think what an adventure it will be!" exclaimed Mr. Badger. "And you just can't help it if an adventure is just a little shady."

"Humph!" Mr. Bear gave a small growl. "It may be an adventure for you, but as I am to do the rowing it sounds like work to me. And I hate work."

"We must be cautious," put in Mr. Lobster at this point.

"If you are cautious you never have any adventures," said Mr. Badger. "I am surprised at you two. A hero being cautious! A great strong bear being unwilling to row for his good friends!"

There was nothing to do but give in to Mr. Badger. So the three left the beach and returned to the river, Mr. Badger leading the way and smiling to himself at his success.

Just as he had said, there was a fine boat, a fisherman's dory with two oars in it, tied to a stake in the meadow. Mr. Lobster got in first and sat in the bow, or rather he folded up his tail and lay on the bow seat. Mr. Bear took the middle seat, which bent dangerously under his great weight. Mr. Badger untied the boat and then jumped in the stern. When he jumped in he gave a push. They were out in the river.

"The adventure has begun!" he cried.

"But it is not finished yet," added Mr. Bear.

"Row! Row!" called out Mr. Badger.

Mr. Bear took up the oars, put them in the right places between the tholepins, and gave a mighty pull. As Mr. Bear was facing the bow of the boat just as the others were, the boat went suddenly backwards and bumped into the bank, almost knocking Mr. Lobster off his seat.

"Something is wrong!" cried Mr. Lobster in alarm. "We are going backwards!"

"A very poor beginning for an adventure," said Mr. Bear.

"Wait a minute. Let us think," urged Mr. Badger. "Let's all turn around and face the other way. Then we'll be going frontwards."

So they all turned around, and Mr. Bear, being altogether too big for the boat, nearly tipped them all over.

"Now row again!" cried Mr. Badger.

Mr. Bear was terribly strong, and he gave a tremendous pull on the oars. This time the boat shot away from the bank and down the river. The boat was going frontwards beautifully, but Mr. Badger, Mr. Bear, and Mr. Lobster were still going backwards.

"This is a fine boat!" exclaimed Mr. Bear, giving a particularly unpleasant growl. "No matter which way we sit, we go backwards. I don't like it. I like to see where I am going, and I'm not in the habit of going backwards to get to a place."

Mr. Badger was thinking again. He had never been in a boat before in his life. That was why he had suggested the trip. And now he was a little surprised, himself.

"I tell you what," he said. "Mr. Lobster and I will turn around so that we can see where we are going. But you will have to go backwards, because evidently that is the way oars work."

"I knew it," said Mr. Bear. "In every adventure someone gets the worst of it. I have to do all the work, and I am the one who has to go backwards. That's life for you."

"I think it's fun," answered Mr. Badger. "I think life is fun, and I love life—especially here where the owl can't come. And think of the pleasure you are giving Mr. Lobster and me." Mr. Badger was smiling happily.

So Mr. Bear rowed and rowed, though almost every time he pulled the oars he gave a growl of disgust because he had to go backwards.

They went down the river and out of the mouth and out on the Ocean. They went farther and farther from shore, and every time Mr. Bear slowed up the least little bit Mr. Badger called out to him to keep going.

Mr. Lobster did not like the growling of Mr. Bear, but

he was enjoying the ride very much. For the first time in his life he was going up and down on the surface of the great Ocean, where he could look away for miles and miles and see nothing but water, which was all perfectly safe for him. And it was such a dark day that he wasn't getting dry or hot at all. He was very happy.

"Wait till I see the sculpin," he thought.

"What an adventure! What heroes!" Mr. Badger cried out. He was joyous, because, being mischievous, he loved to see Mr. Bear working so hard, and he loved to hear Mr. Bear growl. Mr. Badger thought that was a good joke.

"Aren't we nearly there?" asked Mr. Bear for the thirty-third time. "You may not realize it, but I have to row back after the fishing is done."

"What do you think?" asked Mr. Badger of Mr. Lobster. "You know all about this Ocean."

"I think there must be fish here," replied Mr. Lobster.

So Mr. Bear stopped rowing, and he and Mr. Badger began to fish. Mr. Lobster just watched.

At once they began catching large fish. Mr. Badger and Mr. Bear were soon working furiously, for the Ocean was very deep and it was a long pull to get a big fish all the way from the bottom clear up to the boat. Sometimes the fish got away while being pulled up, and then Mr. Bear growled and Mr. Badger laughed at him.

Mr. Badger caught fish so big that it was all he could do to haul them up and get them into the boat. All the time he was laughing and chuckling, and every now and then he would say to Mr. Bear:

"Now what do you think of my ideas?"

Mr. Bear seemed to be too busy fishing to answer. In fact, it seemed that he did not even hear what Mr. Badger said.

Mr. Lobster was so busy watching the two fishermen that he was thinking of nothing else.

And so it was that the fine fishing went on and on, and the boat was beginning to get filled with fish. And not one of the three friends was thinking at all about that important matter—the weather.

Suddenly Mr. Lobster thought he heard an unusually bad growl from Mr. Bear, and he thought Mr. Bear must have lost a very big fish.

"I wish," he said to Mr. Bear politely, "that you wouldn't growl quite so loud."

"I didn't growl," said Mr. Bear. "For once in my life I am too happy to growl—though I know it won't last."

"Well, I didn't growl," said Mr. Badger.

And just then came another ominous sound.

Then they all looked up. There was no mistaking that sound this time.

"That was thunder!" exclaimed Mr. Badger.

A great black cloud was coming up the sky, a cloud darker than any other part of the gray and hurrying clouds that had been in the sky all day. The Ocean looked black and strangely still. Another peal of thunder rolled across the great spaces of heaven and sea, sounding much nearer this time. And then there was a puff of wind, and a sound in the far distance, and a few drops of rain.

"A storm!" cried Mr. Lobster.

"This will be a real adventure after all," said Mr. Badger.

"I knew it!" said Mr. Bear. "I knew that something unpleasant would turn up! You call this an adventure, do you?"

Just then there was a bright flash of lightning and a crash of thunder, and the wind and rain came in a great rush together. It was almost as dark as night. The Ocean began to show white and angry, and the boat rocked and tossed so violently that Mr. Lobster had hard work to keep on his seat, and Mr. Badger and Mr. Bear held tightly to the sides.

Mr. Bear managed to pick up the oars and get them in place.

"Row for dear life!" cried Mr. Badger.

"Where is the land?" asked Mr. Bear.

Everyone looked, but the land was nowhere to be seen.

"I know where it is without seeing it," said Mr. Lobster. "I will show you how to go."

Mr. Bear gave such a terrible pull on the oars that the boat jumped ahead. Then he gave another terrible pull. Crack! The oar in his right paw broke in two, and half of it floated away.

A great wave slapped the side of the boat, dumping a lot of water over the side so that it ran over the bottom and over the fish. The rain was pouring down.

"Now we'll sink!" cried Mr. Badger. "This is turning out very badly!"

"ROW FOR DEAR LIFE!" CRIED MR. BADGER.

"I told you so!" growled Mr. Bear.

Mr. Bear stood up to paddle with the one oar he had left, and he was strong and so frightened that he paddled too hard. Snap! And the other oar broke in two.

They were helpless. The wind was raging, and the waves were getting higher and higher. More and more water was dashed into the boat. It was a wild storm, and the thunder and lightning were enough to frighten even old sailors.

"We're done for!" exclaimed Mr. Bear. "This boat will sink soon, and I could never swim from here to shore even if I could see the shore."

"Neither can I!" cried Mr. Badger. "This is the worst adventure I have ever had."

"I hope this will teach you a lesson about adventures!" growled Mr. Bear. "I'll never believe in your ideas again."

"It was a good idea!" shouted Mr. Badger. "It is the storm that is somebody else's idea—not mine. And think of the fish we caught!"

"Think of getting drowned way out here!" Mr. Bear shouted back.

"If you would stand up, you would be as big as a sail, and maybe the wind would blow us ashore!" shouted Mr. Badger.

Mr. Bear tried to stand up, but the wind was blowing so hard and the boat was rocking so much that he immediately slipped and fell down with a crash. The boat very nearly tipped over then, and Mr. Bear nearly went overboard.

"That was another of your ideas!" he growled at Mr. Badger. "I am going to stay right here in the bottom of the boat. Also, I am going to close my eyes. I don't want to see what certainly is going to happen."

And he lay as still as he could, but he growled every time the least thing happened, and as something was always happening he was growling all the time.

Mr. Badger looked out at the wild Ocean, and then he spoke to Mr. Lobster.

"I've had a good many bad times in my life," he said. "I suppose it is very fitting that the worst time should be the last, but I hate to think of it. This was such a stupendous idea, too. I suppose, Mr. Lobster, that you can just climb overboard and sink, and you will be perfectly safe. But I have to die like a hero."

Mr. Lobster was holding on for dear life. It is true that he was not worried about himself, because if the boat sank he would sink too, and then he simply would be at home. Home was always a comforting thought to him, but now he was thinking as hard as he could about other things, because he wanted to save his two friends.

"It is true that I am quite safe," he said to Mr. Badger.

"Well, I'll say good-by now," shouted Mr. Badger. "Here we go, I guess!"

A mountainous great wave dashed against the boat, covering Mr. Bear and the fish, who were now all thrown together in the bottom of the boat, with water.

Mr. Bear closed his eyes even tighter than before and growled harder than ever.

But still the boat did not sink.

"Maybe we did steal the boat," said Mr. Badger. "I've nearly always been punished when I've done anything shady, and this must have been shadier than I thought."

After this no one said anything for some time. The danger was now so great that gloom and unhappiness had descended on them all.

And then Mr. Lobster, who was still thinking with all his might, and looking everywhere, saw the rope that was fastened to the bow of the boat. And he had a stupendous thought.

"I will pull you ashore!" he shouted.

He seized the rope in his big claws and climbed overboard, letting himself go splash in the stormy sea. The water of the Ocean was nice and salt after the rain which had been falling on Mr. Lobster, and he felt strong.

He began to swim. It was fortunate that he was the oldest and biggest lobster in that Ocean. Certainly no other lobster would have been strong enough to swim and pull that boat with all the fish and Mr. Bear and Mr. Badger in it.

But Mr. Lobster could pull it, and he did. Very slowly they went, to be sure, and the storm howled louder and louder, and the Ocean grew rougher and rougher, but the boat was moving toward the shore.

Mr. Badger was trying to throw water out of the boat, using both of his front paws like a scoop.

"Hurry!" he cried to Mr. Lobster. "I can't throw it out as fast as it comes in. We'll sink before we get to shore."

Mr. Bear just lay still with his eyes shut. He was half covered with water now, and his growls were low and sad.

On and on they went. It seemed hours to Mr. Badger and more hours to Mr. Lobster, who was working as he had never worked before in all his life.

"Hurry!" Mr. Badger kept crying.

Mr. Lobster was in the rolling waves of the mouth of the river. He gave every bit of his strength to his task. The waves caught the boat, and it almost tipped over. Mr. Badger had to stop throwing water and just hold on. Mr. Bear gave the worst growl of the day.

And then, as sudden as darkness when a light goes out, there were no more waves. They were in the river itself. The rain was falling and the wind blowing and the thunder rolling far over the great Ocean. The boat was more than half full of water and just barely floating. But they were safe!

At the sudden stillness Mr. Bear sat up, but he still kept his eyes closed.

"It is so quiet we must be dead," he said.

Mr. Badger laughed.

"We are saved!" he cried. "Mr. Lobster, the hero, has saved us!"

And then Mr. Bear dared to open his eyes and look around.

"I want to go ashore right away," he said. "I won't believe I am safe until I am at home and smell my fish frying."

Mr. Lobster pulled the boat over to the bank where they had found it.

"I am sorry to have to say this," said Mr. Badger, who was quite restored now that he was safe, "but of course we have to leave some fish for the use of the boat, and I am afraid that as you broke both the oars you will have to leave all your share of the fish to pay for them." Mr. Badger's eyes twinkled. Once he was feeling well, it did not take him long to think up a joke.

Mr. Bear saw the twinkle.

"You are not sorry at all!" he growled.

"Well, you have to admit that's a joke on you," said Mr. Badger. "And after all, you thought you were dead, and here you are alive."

"What's the use of being alive if I've got no supper?" asked Mr. Bear unhappily. "Do you mean to say I must leave all my fish?"

"Yes, I think that would be just right to pay for the oars. It will be a lesson to us not to borrow things and break them."

"How about your fish?" asked Mr. Bear.

"I shall take my fish, thank you," said Mr. Badger. "I must be rewarded, for it was my idea to go out on the Ocean and catch them."

Mr. Bear growled in such rage that it looked as though the three fishermen were going to part anything but friends. Mr. Lobster trembled so that his shell rattled. Mr. Badger was just enjoying himself.

"I think I shall be going home," said Mr. Lobster.

"So shall I," said Mr. Badger. "Sometime I shall be able to thank you fully for saving my life a second time. It was a beautifully narrow escape, and as soon as I am dry and at home it will give me a great deal of pleasure."

Mr. Badger started to walk away.

"You haven't taken your fish," called Mr. Bear.

"Oh, I have changed my mind," answered Mr. Badger. "I don't really care for fish. Wouldn't you like a few, my dear Mr. Bear?"

So Mr. Bear got his fish after all, and they all went home happy, although Mr. Bear, as he went, was growling softly over the trick Mr. Badger had played on him.

The Three Friends
Almost Have a Picnic

OF COURSE, Mr. Lobster went ashore again the very next day. He knew that Mr. Badger and Mr. Bear would be grateful to him for saving their lives; so of course he was eager to see them.

"There is nothing so pleasant," he said to himself, "as going to meet two friends for whom you have done a great favor. And I do like pleasant meetings. They add pleasure to life."

It was a beautiful summery day, the kind of day that often comes after a storm to make up for all the trouble the storm has caused. The sky had been washed clean.

The clouds were snowy white. Even the old Ocean seemed in a very contented state, for its waves were small and gentle and made very little noise upon the beach.

When Mr. Lobster reached the river bank, Mr. Badger and Mr. Bear were waiting for him.

"Hail to the hero!" cried Mr. Badger. "How are things going under the Ocean today? Take hold of my tail and come ashore."

When Mr. Badger had pulled him ashore, Mr. Lobster answered his question.

"Things are very quiet under the Ocean," he said.

"Well, they are quiet here too," said Mr. Badger. "Very quiet after such an exciting day as yesterday. Mr. Bear and I have just been talking with pleasure about the narrowness of our escape. I shall get pleasure from remembering it as long as I live."

"Pardon me," put in Mr. Bear gruffly, "but Mr. Badger has been doing all the talking, as usual. I am sure I get no pleasure at all from narrow escapes. But I do want to thank you, Mr. Lobster, from the bottom of my heart for saving my life."

"Oh, it was nothing," said Mr. Lobster, trying to be modest, though he was glowing with pleasure under his shell.

"There now!" Mr. Badger broke right out laughing. "You see, Mr. Bear, he says your life was nothing."

"What! Why, it has always meant a great deal to me," said Mr. Bear, beginning to look cross.

"Please!" exclaimed Mr. Lobster. "You must not take

Mr. Badger seriously. Why, he does not take himself seriously, and some days he isn't even a badger. I meant that
what I did was nothing."

"Just what I said!" exclaimed Mr. Badger. "He said
that saving your life was nothing. Think of it! It was an
act of no importance."

"You know very well I meant nothing at all like that!"
protested Mr. Lobster.

Mr. Badger chuckled.

"I'll tell you something," he said. "When people thank
you for a gift or a great favor you must never say it is
nothing. That makes the gift or favor seem very mean.
You should say very kindly: 'You are very welcome,' or 'I
am very glad I could be of service.' You don't get any
credit in this world if you are always belittling yourself.
Now I, for instance, know I am a hero and admit it
freely."

"You certainly do," said Mr. Bear. He growled softly.
He was not really cross, because now he saw that Mr.
Badger had been having one of his jokes.

Everybody was happy and contented, it seemed.

"As I was going to say," Mr. Badger remarked finally,
"it is very quiet here. That is wrong. I believe that something should always be happening. That is my motto. And
if it isn't happening, then I believe in making it happen."

"What would you suggest happening?" asked Mr. Bear
suspiciously. "Something a little different from going out
on the raging Ocean and nearly getting drowned, if you
please."

"I have an idea," said Mr. Badger.

"I was afraid of that," said Mr. Bear. "I think I shall go home. Your last idea was enough for me."

But Mr. Lobster, of course, was curious.

"Tell us what it is!" he begged.

"I will," said Mr. Badger happily. He loved to be the center of attention, just as all jokers do. "I propose that in honor of Mr. Lobster's saving Mr. Bear's life, which was nothing, and mine, which was the life of a hero and worth a great deal, we all have a picnic."

"A picnic!" growled Mr. Bear. "Well, that might be a pleasure after all. Surely there is no risk in that."

"Oh, you never can tell what will happen on a picnic," said Mr. Badger. "That's just why I want to have one."

"Please excuse me for being so ignorant," murmured Mr. Lobster. "But you land creatures do such strange things. My curiosity is aroused at once. I don't even know what a picnic is."

"Oh, it is quite simple," said Mr. Badger. "A picnic means not eating your food at home, but wrapping it up and taking it away and eating it somewhere you would never think of eating it naturally. It takes twice as much work as a regular meal, you have to carry it so far; but it is twice as much fun eating it, because you don't have to have any manners to speak of."

"I don't see how anything that is twice as much work can be twice as much fun," said Mr. Bear. "That is beyond me. It sounds unreasonable."

"A picnic is always unreasonable," agreed Mr. Badger.

"Everything is that's done just for fun. And you wait and see if you don't have a good time."

"I would like to try a picnic," said Mr. Lobster.

"Good!" said Mr. Badger. "Now my idea is that this will be a surprise picnic. Each one of us must bring lunch for someone else. I shall bring Mr. Lobster's lunch. Mr. Bear will bring my lunch, and Mr. Lobster will bring Mr. Bear's lunch. And we mustn't tell what we're going to bring."

"That will be fun!" exclaimed Mr. Lobster. He was already curious about what Mr. Badger would bring him.

"Where shall we have the picnic?" asked Mr. Bear.

"Well, the important thing about a picnic is that a place to eat the lunch you have brought is never really suitable unless it is hard work getting the lunch there. The hardest place I can think of is the very end of the beach, by the cliff. It is also lonely, and there is no shelter if storms come up, which is one of the important chances you must take on a picnic."

"It will take me all the morning to bring lunch there," said Mr. Bear. "And I shall have a terrible appetite."

"It will take me hours and hours," added Mr. Lobster.

"Fine!" exclaimed Mr. Badger. "Then it is just the place."

"If you don't mind," said Mr. Bear now, "I think I'll be going home before you have another idea. I can see that this is going to require thought."

"We must all meet at the picnic tomorrow," said Mr. Badger.

So the three friends parted, and Mr. Lobster went slowly down the river and home again.

As soon as he was home he began to think about what he would take to the picnic for Mr. Bear. The most delicate pleasant creature he could think of catching was a small sand-dab or a flounder. Possibly a perch would be all right. So he sat where he could look out of his house and watch the beautiful seaweed garden.

Not a single pleasant creature came into the garden all the afternoon. One old gray cod came along who was so big Mr. Lobster knew he could never catch him. A little later there was an enormous skate who looked most unpleasant. There were also two or three crabs, very young crabs, who came and played in the garden, chasing each other backwards, but they were distant relatives of Mr. Lobster.

Finally Mr. Lobster went out for a short crawl, just to look around and see what he could catch. He realized that it would be disgraceful if he did not catch something for Mr. Bear's picnic lunch.

"Why, if I don't get Mr. Bear's lunch I can't go," he thought. "And I have to go because the picnic is in my honor."

He had been out about a half-hour when he met the sculpin.

They exchanged greetings in a dignified manner, as usual.

"You know," said Mr. Lobster, "I am going to have lunch ashore tomorrow with some friends, and I must take lunch for one of my friends when I go, but I don't know just what to take."

"I wish that you wouldn't say that I know when I don't know," said the sculpin sternly. He was envious because he could not go ashore himself, and therefore more dignified than ever. "I did not know. Of course, if you must persist in your reckless wanderings, and must go ashore where you do not belong, it is obvious that the greatest of all delicacies is clams without their shells."

"Of course!" exclaimed Mr. Lobster. "To think that I was so stupid as to forget clams!"

"I should say there were other things more stupid," said the sculpin severely. "Such as going ashore, for example."

Mr. Lobster did not want to wait to hear any more advice from the sculpin.

"Please excuse me," he said, and he tail-snapped away very rapidly.

As the beautiful green daylight was fading before the night, Mr. Lobster went straight home.

Now Mr. Lobster considered clams without their shells the finest luncheon—or dinner, for that matter— that could be had. In fact, they were so good, they were good even for breakfast. The reason he did not have clams often was that it was very hard to get them. In the first place, the clams were shy, always hiding in the sand with only a small hole to show where they were buried. And then—and this made it even harder—it was a great deal of work to open a clam's shell and get him out. And no one likes to eat clam-shells.

"I suppose," Mr. Lobster said to himself as he thought about the clams, "there must be a reason why things which are good to eat inside are not good to eat outside. But it seems very unfortunate at times, especially when the outside is as hard as a clam-shell."

He thought that he might gather a great many clams and take them to Mr. Bear in their shells.

"No," he decided, "that would be discourteous. A wise person is never discourteous, especially to anyone as big as a bear."

So very early the next morning he went out and started gathering clams. He had to hunt hard to find them, and each one he dug up he had to take home and take out of its shell. And each one looked so delicious when it was out of the shell that it was all Mr. Lobster could do not to eat them as fast as he caught them and got them ready.

But he did not eat a single one, and he grew hungrier and hungrier because he didn't have time to stop for any breakfast.

After he had gathered and opened clams for hours, he looked around until he found an empty turtle-shell almost as big as he was. He dragged it home and put all the clams in it.

"Certainly," he said, "no one has ever seen any lunch as delicious as this. I bet there are a hundred clams without their shells here. How lucky Mr. Bear is! I wish I were bringing my own lunch!"

When he began to drag the turtle-shell full of clams from his home all the way to the beach, he found that was the worst and hardest work of all. Mr. Badger had certainly told the truth. He dragged it with his tail when he went frontwards. Then he took hold with his claws and went backwards. Both ways the dragging was very difficult.

"Surely I shall get some great happiness as a result of all this work," he thought.

Anyway, although he was tired and hungry, he dragged the turtle-shell all the way to shore and then up the beach to the lonely place at the foot of the great cliff. Then he covered it with a flat stone and was all ready before the others came.

Mr. Badger came first. He was pushing a package wrapped in leaves, a very dirty and bedraggled package which kept coming unwrapped and rolling in the sand. Mr. Badger kept stopping to wrap it up again.

"I have had a terrible time," he said. "I have had to push this heavy package all the way. But it is delicious, I am sure of that. Wait until you see it."

Just then the package came unwrapped again, and a large object, already dirty and covered with sand, rolled out and became even more dirty and covered with sand.

"Don't look!" cried Mr. Badger, and he hastened to wrap it up.

But Mr. Lobster was so curious that he had already looked before Mr. Badger spoke. However, as he couldn't see anything but sand, his looking did not matter, and he was just as curious as ever and even more hungry.

Mr. Lobster looked down the beach.

A strange creature without any head was coming toward them.

"We are going to have another narrow escape, I am afraid," said Mr. Lobster.

"No," said Mr. Badger. "That must be Mr. Bear. For no one would come to such a desolate place as this unless he was coming to picnic."

Sure enough, it was Mr. Bear. He was coming backwards, dragging a tremendous parcel with his teeth. And now they could hear him growling as he came, and coughing from the sand in his mouth.

"He is the funniest thing I have ever seen!" exclaimed Mr. Badger joyfully. "Mr. Bear will be furious. I knew a picnic would be lots of fun, and this one is starting out beautifully!"

Mr. Bear kept coming backwards, his growls sounding louder and louder. Finally he almost backed into Mr. Badger.

"Greetings!" said Mr. Badger. "Isn't this going to be fun?"

Mr. Bear looked up.

"Well, I certainly hope so," he said. "It hasn't been anything but work so far. I have been walking backwards for hours. I kept running into things, and I am bruised all over."

"Cheer up!" said Mr. Badger happily. "Now we can eat our picnic."

Mr. Badger at once took charge of things. First they all sat in a kind of circle, although it was hard to make a circle out of three people, and so it was really a triangle.

Then Mr. Lobster put the turtle-shell with the stone on it in front of Mr. Bear.

Next Mr. Bear put his big package, which was almost as long as Mr. Badger, in front of Mr. Badger. The package was wrapped in newspaper, that being one of the signs that Mr. Bear was civilized.

Lastly, Mr. Badger put his battered package in front of Mr. Lobster.

"Now," said Mr. Badger, "we can open our surprise packages and eat."

Mr. Bear was the biggest and so, of course, the hungriest. He removed the stone from the turtle-shell and looked at the big pile of clams without their shells.

"What is this?" he asked rather impolitely.

"Clams! The most delicious thing I know of," answered Mr. Lobster proudly. Mr. Lobster's mouth watered at the sight of them.

"Oh," said Mr. Bear, and there was a note of sad disappointment in his voice.

In the meantime Mr. Badger had unwrapped his tremendous surprise package, and there was the biggest fish he had ever seen. And it was beautifully fried to a turn.

"A fish!" he cried, almost in horror.

"Exactly," said Mr. Bear. "That is the finest fish I have ever fried," and he looked at the fish with the most hungry look a bear could ever have.

Mr. Lobster had no difficulty in opening his surprise package because it was all in pieces anyway. There was a large piece of something all covered with sand.

"Would you mind," he said, looking at Mr. Badger, "telling me what is under the sand?"

"Meat!" said Mr. Badger. "Yes, the most delicious piece of meat I ever stole. I got it this morning." And he looked at it with such longing that the tears came into his eyes.

"I see," said Mr. Lobster.

Then they all sat very still, not saying a word. And nobody started eating.

Mr. Bear hated clams, especially clams which were not fried.

Mr. Badger hated the very thought of fish after all he had eaten because the owl told him he mustn't. And he hated fried things especially.

Mr. Lobster never ate meat.

And so there was a rather unhappy situation.

"Well," said Mr. Lobster sadly, looking at Mr. Bear's delicious clams.

"Well," said Mr. Bear, looking at Mr. Badger's delicious fried fish.

It seemed as though nobody happened to be hungry now. The picnic suddenly had turned out to be a sad failure.

Mr. Badger brightened up.

"I have an idea!" he exclaimed. "It is polite to share one's food, and we must be polite in some ways even on a picnic. So let us play a game. We must all get up and walk around and then sit down in somebody else's place."

"Ah!" said Mr. Bear. This time he did not growl. He was looking at the fried fish.

"I think that would be a good thing to do," said Mr. Lobster. He was looking at the clams.

"First, I had better do something," said Mr. Badger. He was looking at Mr. Lobster's meat. And he took the sandy object to the water, washed it carefully, and put it on a stone in front of Mr. Lobster.

Mr. Lobster thought the meat looked worse than ever.

"Now!" cried Mr. Badger. "And no fair crowding or pushing. One, two, three!"

There was no crowding at all. In no time Mr. Badger jumped right over to Mr. Lobster's place where the meat was. Mr. Bear moved quickly over to Mr. Badger's place where the fried fish was. So there was nobody at Mr. Bear's place, and Mr. Lobster crawled over there as fast as he could crawl.

"There," said Mr. Badger. "This way we can share our picnic politely. And then if we want to move again, we can."

"Do we have to move even if we don't want to?" asked Mr. Bear.

"Of course this is Mr. Lobster's picnic," answered Mr. Badger, "and it is up to him."

"I say we don't have to move," said Mr. Lobster.

So at last everybody was happy. They were just about

AT LAST EVERYBODY WAS HAPPY.

to take the first mouthful when Mr. Badger called out sharply.

"Wait! Don't eat yet!" he cried. "I have just remembered something very important. I saw the owl last night, and I forgot to be a bandicoot and answered him when he spoke to me. And then he was so friendly I told him about our picnic. He said that no picnic was any good without pickles. You see, 'picnic' is short for 'pickle-nic.' We must have pickles."

Then Mr. Bear really growled.

"Do you mean to say that we can't eat until we have pickles?" he demanded.

"Absolutely," said Mr. Badger.

"But I thought you never did what the owl said," put in Mr. Lobster. "At least, you always do what he says you can't do."

"Very true," agreed Mr. Badger. "But you must remember that I am independent. The owl thinks that I will disobey him this time, and so I will fool him. I will obey him. You see, being independent, I simply cannot do what he expects me to do."

"I think this is an outrage!" growled Mr. Bear.

"In a way," said Mr. Badger, "everything that has happened to me because of the owl has been an outrage. But we must not let the owl get the best of us. We must take a little time now before we eat, and all go and hunt to see if we can find or catch a pickle."

"Can't we eat our picnic first and have the pickle for dessert?" asked Mr. Bear.

"No, that would be against the rules of a picnic," said Mr. Badger firmly. "You can't even start a picnic unless you are sure you have pickles."

It was a great blow to all of them, for they were all hungry, and they had just been made happy at the thought of eating the delicious things they had brought. And now there was no knowing when they would eat. But as both Mr. Lobster and Mr. Badger were heroes they had to be fair and obey the rules. And Mr. Bear, much as he disliked the idea, felt that he must do what his friends did.

So the three friends started down the beach, each one searching carefully as he walked. Soon the delicious picnic was far behind. When they finally went over a big sand dune, it was out of sight.

How a Picnic Disappeared
and What Happened Next

MR. LOBSTER thought it was very hard on him, after all his work gathering clams, to have to crawl miles in search of pickles. The worst of it was, he was curious about pickles at the same time, but he hated to show his ignorance. It seemed to him he was always asking questions.

Finally, after it seemed to him the three picnickers had walked for much too long a time, he decided that he would have to ask the question.

"Would you mind telling me," he said to Mr. Badger, "what a pickle looks like? I don't like to appear so ignorant about these land matters, but I must confess I don't know."

"Me too!" exclaimed Mr. Bear. "I had a dreadful appetite an hour ago from dragging my package to the picnic, and now I am half starved. And I haven't the faintest idea what a pickle is. Does it swim or fly or walk?"

For almost a minute Mr. Badger was so upset by laughing that he couldn't answer.

Then he said, "What a joke!" And he almost got started laughing wildly again, but Mr. Bear gave a long growl. "Why didn't you tell me? Well, well!"

Mr. Bear growled again.

"Well, well, indeed," he said gruffly. "What is a pickle?"

"You must excuse my laughing," said Mr. Badger. "But you see, I don't know what a pickle is myself. I have never seen one. I had never even heard of one until the owl made his unfortunate remark. That is why it is such a wonderful joke—it is on all of us!"

"Is that a joke?" asked Mr. Lobster.

"I must say, it makes me miserable," growled Mr. Bear.

"Of course," agreed Mr. Badger. "But when anything very unfortunate occurs which makes you miserable, if you laugh at it, it becomes a joke."

"I am afraid," said Mr. Bear sternly, "I am too hungry to laugh. Perhaps you can think of something else for us to do instead. I want to go back to our picnic."

"So do I," said Mr. Lobster. "I want to eat Mr. Bear's delicious clams."

"Don't be alarmed, my good friends," said Mr. Badger.

"This is very simple, for already I know what we can do. When we find anything at all interesting, we can take a vote to decide whether it is a pickle. If we all vote that it is a pickle, then it is a pickle, and we can all return and eat our picnic."

"Which is the main thing," said Mr. Bear. "This looking for pickles has already gone too far."

"Do we have to eat the pickles?" asked Mr. Lobster. "I am very hungry, but I am not sure about eating pickles."

"I vote that we don't have to eat any pickles," said Mr. Bear positively.

"No, we don't have to," agreed Mr. Badger. "All the owl said was that we couldn't have a picnic without pickles. He didn't say a thing about eating them. Probably they are not good to eat, anyway."

So it was decided that they did not have to eat the pickles after they were caught, which made it very much easier, as now it didn't matter what a pickle was like as long as it was not too big to carry back to the picnic.

Immediately the three friends started to search again, and they looked very carefully. Almost at once Mr. Bear found a piece of wood and wanted to vote that it was a pickle, but Mr. Badger said "No," because everyone knew what a piece of wood was and it was never a pickle.

Then Mr. Lobster, who of course was down the lowest and could easily see low things, saw two round things lying on the sand under an old plank from a boat.

"Look!" he cried, and he moved the plank so the others could see.

The two round things were orange colored, almost as big as baseballs, and had crinkly skins.

"I vote that these are pickles!" cried Mr. Bear at once.

"So do I!" exclaimed Mr. Lobster.

Mr. Badger hesitated a moment just to make the others nervous, but when Mr. Bear started to give a low and unpleasant growl, he said:

"So do I."

"Thank goodness!" exclaimed Mr. Bear. "Now we can eat."

"We must take these to our picnic," said Mr. Badger.

Mr. Bear objected to that, but finally he picked up one of the round things in his teeth and began to carry it. Mr. Badger took the other one. Then the three friends started to walk back to their picnic, Mr. Bear and Mr. Badger having to go rather slow on account of Mr. Lobster, who could crawl only so fast, and who was really tired now.

It seemed to Mr. Lobster that it took forever to get back to the desolate place where they had left their delicious picnic. His mouth fairly watered at the thought of the delicious clams he was going to eat any minute. He was glad now that he gathered so many for Mr. Bear.

"It all goes to show," he said to himself, "that generosity always pays in the end."

Finally they came to a place which seemed to be the exact place where they had met for their picnic. Mr. Bear dropped his pickle.

"There," he said. "That's done." And he looked around.

Then Mr. Badger and Mr. Lobster looked around.

There was no picnic to be seen.

"Maybe we have come too far," suggested Mr. Badger.

"Look!" exclaimed Mr. Bear. "There is the paper I wrapped my beautiful fried fish in!"

"And here is my turtle-shell!" cried Mr. Lobster. "And it is empty!"

There was no picnic. That was the awful truth. They had come back to the right place, but their picnic was gone. And they were all tired and hungry, and there was nothing to look at but the wrappings of their picnic, which are a sure sign that a picnic is all over.

For a moment no one could speak.

Then Mr. Bear let out a horrible growl, the worst Mr. Lobster or Mr. Badger had ever heard.

"And we were so near perfect happiness!" wailed Mr. Badger.

"There is no such thing as perfect happiness," growled Mr. Bear.

"Oh, yes, there is," Mr. Badger protested, "even if we are not having it today. Perfect happiness occurs when you are not afraid of anything and have all you want to eat."

"Well, we're not perfectly happy now," grumbled Mr. Bear. He paused for two short growls. "At least, I'm not. And I think that this picnic is the worst idea you have ever had. Someone has stolen my fish. It was the biggest, most beautiful fish I have ever fried. If there is anything I am perfectly, it is furious."

"I spent all the morning gathering clams," said Mr. Lobster mournfully, "and didn't eat a one. And now I am sure I am getting dry. If you will excuse me, I shall go into the Ocean for a little while."

"Do," said Mr. Badger kindly. "But be sure and come back as soon as you can. We must have a meeting and plan to catch the thief who stole our picnic. I never realized until now how serious stealing is."

Mr. Bear growled some more at that. He remembered that Mr. Badger had stolen from him in the old days when they were unfriends.

Mr. Lobster crawled wearily and sadly down to the edge of the water, crawled through a wave, and had a good swim. He stayed a little longer than was necessary, for he saw a perch and a small flounder, and he pursued them. When he returned to the shore he was feeling a little better.

When he reached his friends he found Mr. Badger quite excited.

"Do you see those?" he asked Mr. Lobster, pointing to a great many tracks in the sand.

"Yes, I do," said Mr. Lobster

"Well, what do you think they are?"

"I think they are the tracks of a sea gull."

"Ah." Mr. Badger was pleased. "Just what I thought. A sea gull was the thief."

"Excuse my interrupting," said Mr. Bear so crossly that they knew he didn't care whether he was excused or not, "but I happen to be hungry. I can't see any use in talking. Let us admit that picnics are very bad ideas, and then never have another one."

"We can't have another one," said Mr. Lobster wisely, "until we have had this one."

"Exactly," agreed Mr. Badger. "So we must have this one so that the one we never have would be another."

Nobody else understood this. Mr. Lobster said nothing. Being wise, he considered silence important at times. Mr. Bear simply growled. He always growled when he did not know what to do or say.

"And," Mr. Badger was saying importantly, "even if this picnic has turned out rather badly, it just goes to show that you never can tell about life—it's so uncertain. And uncertainty is the next best thing to adventure."

"It is the next worst thing, you mean," said Mr. Bear. "And besides, I don't care for uncertainty about my food. That's going too far."

"Please let me finish," said Mr. Badger. "Now we can have an adventure. We must set a trap to catch the thief who stole our picnic. Catching him will be as much fun as eating."

"Nonsense!" exclaimed Mr. Bear. "How can anything be as much fun as eating?"

"And what shall we do with the thief when we catch him?" asked Mr. Lobster.

Mr. Badger smiled happily.

"That's just the fun of it," he said. "I don't know what we'll do with him. When we catch him we shall have a new problem."

"Your ideas always end in problems!" protested Mr. Bear. "First, it was fishing in a boat, which caused the awful problem of how to row without oars. Then it was a picnic, and the problem of how to carry a fried fish several miles. Then it was pickles, and the problem of finding something not one of us had ever seen. And now we have the fine problem of building a trap to catch a thief. And when we catch the thief we shall have the problem of what to do about it. Is your life always a problem?"

"Of course." Mr. Badger grinned. "Life is one problem after another. That's what makes it fun. There is always something to solve. Think how miserable we should be if everything were solved."

"That is ridiculous!" said Mr. Bear. "I would be anything but miserable if the problem of my lunch and dinner were solved right now. In fact, I wish someone would solve it, for I know very well that I can solve it only by hard work." He stopped to growl a good deal. "I think I'll go home," he added.

But Mr. Bear didn't go home. He was really too good a friend to do that, even if he did growl a great deal.

Mr. Lobster noticed that. He said to himself: "I've learned one thing from knowing Mr. Bear. Growling does not change the situation at all. After you have finished growling, you are right where you started."

Instead of going home the three friends worked most of the afternoon making a trap out of wood and pieces of things they found on the beach. When it was done, after a great deal of work, and a great deal of complaining by Mr. Bear and chuckling by Mr. Badger, the trap was arranged so that if the sea gull walked under it to touch the pickles, which Mr. Badger placed there to attract the thief, a big box with a piece of fish-net for a bottom would fall and imprison the sea gull securely.

Mr. Badger and Mr. Bear had done most of the work, for Mr. Bear could pull things and Mr. Badger was very clever with his paws. Mr. Lobster was too clumsy on land to be of much use, but now he was a great help.

"The thief may not like pickles," said Mr. Badger, "but he certainly likes fish. So Mr. Lobster must go and catch us some kind of fish to put under our trap."

Mr. Lobster was glad to be of some service. He hated to miss anything. So he hurried out into the water and caught a fairly large flounder. He wanted to eat it, for he was still hungry, but instead he carried it to Mr. Badger, and Mr. Badger placed it beside the pickles.

"Now we can all go home," said Mr. Badger. "And tomorrow morning we shall return here and see what sea gull stole our picnic."

"Which won't do a bit of good," growled Mr. Bear.

"But what shall we do to punish the thief?" asked Mr. Lobster, who was very curious and hated to wait until the next day to find out.

Mr. Badger smiled one of his happiest smiles. "We mustn't decide that now," he said. "Life would be uninteresting if we knew exactly what we were going to do tomorrow."

So Mr. Lobster had to go home without satisfying his curiosity.

Mr. Bear started off muttering, "I hope we never have any more picnics."

And Mr. Badger went off quite happy in spite of everything, because it had been an interesting day even if his picnic had been spoiled, and tomorrow promised to be even more interesting.

Mr. Lobster was so curious about the punishment of the thief, and whether they would succeed in catching him in the trap, that he almost forgot to have dinner before he went to bed. And after he had crawled into his fine house he was so curious he could hardly get to sleep.

"Curiosity," he told himself, "can be very trying at times, but I suppose there is no easy way to gather wisdom."

In the morning, when Mr. Lobster started for shore, he was eager indeed, and he traveled at a good rate of speed. When he came out on the sandy beach he saw that the morning was bright with sunshine, and the sky was as blue as a fairy's eyes. All the world seemed to be made to be enjoyed, and he felt that he was surely going to enjoy it.

He had gotten up so early, because of his curiosity, that he reached the trap before Mr. Badger and Mr. Bear.

The trap was sprung—and in it, safe and sound but unable to escape, was the largest sea gull Mr. Lobster had ever seen.

"So," said Mr. Lobster, "you were the thief that stole our picnic." He spoke sternly, for he believed that was the proper manner in which to address all criminals.

"Look here!" cried the sea gull, who was very much excited, and who had been beating his wings until he had broken several feathers, "do let me out of here, will you please?"

"Let you out, did you say?" Mr. Lobster was shocked by the request. The idea of a thief asking to be released from a trap.

"Of course," said the sea gull. "Everyone knows you, Mr. Lobster. You are the first lobster ever to be smart enough to come ashore, and you are the wisest lobster in all the Ocean. All of us gulls know about you, for we have watched you. We consider you a brilliant specimen. You are so wise and so famous that you can afford to be generous. Do let me out."

For a moment Mr. Lobster did feel generous. The gull seemed to be speaking true and kind words. Furthermore, the gull seemed a courteous sort of bird, and it seemed impossible that he was a thief.

"It hardly seems possible," said Mr. Lobster, looking at the sea gull closely, "that you could have done such a thing."

"Surely, Mr. Lobster, a creature as wise as you are wouldn't think such a ridiculous thing as that!" The sea gull spoke in the most flattering manner. "You will let me out, won't you?"

"I must think first," answered Mr. Lobster. "It is true that I am very wise. I am sixty-eight years old, you know. But a wise person does not act without thinking about it first. Thinking afterwards is always too late."

There is no knowing what Mr. Lobster would have thought if the clever sea gull could have talked a little longer. But just then a tremendous and furious noise came rushing over the beach, a noise of growling and roaring and panting; and there was Mr. Bear, coming as fast as he could, the sand flying in every direction. Mr. Badger was close behind him.

"Ah!" exclaimed Mr. Bear. "The thief himself! We have caught him!"

Mr. Badger came up puffing.

"There!" he said. "Don't ever say that I don't have good ideas. Isn't this interesting? Isn't this as good as an adventure?"

"Pardon me," put in Mr. Lobster. "I am not sure we haven't made a serious mistake. This sea gull seems to be a very courteous bird."

"A thief always tries to seem honest after he has done his stealing," said Mr. Badger. "I wouldn't trust him."

"Do you speak from experience?" asked Mr. Bear.

Mr. Badger did not answer. In fact, he seemed a trifle deaf for the moment. Instead, he looked the sea gull right in the eyes.

"Did you steal our picnic?" he asked.

"It was all a mistake," whined the sea gull.

"Ah," growled Mr. Bear. "You will find that it was a very serious mistake, indeed. You just wait."

Everyone knew that the sea gull was guilty now, for he just hung his head and said nothing.

Mr. Badger tried to look serious, although he was

pleased with himself for catching the sea gull, and, if the truth were told, he had done a good bit of stealing himself.

"You understand," he said to the miserable bird, "that stealing to get a bite of dinner is one thing, and stealing a whole picnic is another. Stealing a picnic is a hideous crime."

"I realize that now," said the sea gull, and his head went even lower.

"Too late," growled Mr. Bear.

"I should say," offered Mr. Lobster, who was feeling extremely wise, "that the pleasure in stealing totally disappears when you are caught. I am convinced that it must be wrong, therefore; for whatever is without pleasure is wrong."

"That is not new," said Mr. Badger with a chuckle. "Everyone knows that it is wrong to be caught for stealing."

"You know very well that I didn't mean that," said Mr. Lobster sharply.

"Let us not waste time in silly arguments," said Mr. Bear gruffly. "Let us decide the punishment."

So the three friends made a circle around the unhappy sea gull, who now stood with his head almost on the sand, and his bright eyes shut tight, and looking so ashamed of himself that it was hard not to pity him. In fact, Mr. Lobster, who had a soft heart under his hard shell, as so many persons do, did pity him.

"I say," began Mr. Bear, "that since this bird stole our picnic and ate it, he should be eaten also."

"It does seem fair," said Mr. Badger.

"I suppose I shall have to vote for that if my two friends do," said Mr. Lobster.

"Oh, please don't eat me!" cried the sea gull.

"Well, of course, I shan't," said Mr. Bear. "You are all covered with feathers, and I should hate to eat feathers."

"I should not think of it," said Mr. Badger.

"I never eat birds," said Mr. Lobster.

"There is a problem already," said Mr. Bear. "How can we punish him if no one will do it?"

"I suppose," said Mr. Badger, "that we had better decide that eating is not the punishment. Then it will be no problem."

And the three friends decided that at once.

Then there was a long silence, while the matter of punishment was still unsolved.

"I guess we shall have to keep the sea gull in prison," said Mr. Badger finally.

"A very good idea," growled Mr. Bear. "That will teach him a lesson."

"I agree," said Mr. Lobster, who thought this was much kinder than eating the sea gull. "But who will feed him? We can't let him starve to death here."

"Another problem," said Mr. Bear in great disgust. "If we have to get his food and bring it to him we shall be just punishing ourselves, for we shall have to do all the work. Eating him would be a punishment for us, and feeding him would be a punishment for us. It seems to me that this business of giving punishments is pretty poor."

By now the sea gull's head had come up a little, and he was looking more hopeful.

"Also," said Mr. Lobster, who was really wise this time, "it is evident that such punishments would do no good, for how could the sea gull profit by being eaten, and learn to be a better bird? And could he learn to be a better bird if he was kept all the time in this prison?"

What Mr. Lobster said was so true that everyone was silent.

But the sea gull had one eye open now.

"This is going to turn out just like all of Mr. Badger's ideas," said Mr. Bear.

"Wait!" exclaimed Mr. Lobster. "I seem to be able to think very clearly today. I am sure it is because I got up so early this morning. I say that if the sea gull will promise solemnly to gather us another fine picnic, with fish for Mr. Bear, and meat for Mr. Badger, and clams without their shells for me, we let him go free."

"Wonderful!" cried Mr. Badger. "That is the best suggestion of all! We can have the fun of eating our picnic after all, and the sea gull will certainly learn a lesson."

"You are very astute," remarked Mr. Bear in the pleasantest tone he had used for some minutes.

"Astute?" asked Mr. Lobster. "Do tell me what that means?"

"It means being wise at the right moment," explained Mr. Badger. "And that is very much wiser than just wise, and very much more important."

Mr. Lobster felt happy, indeed. This was certainly a beautiful day.

The sea gull, who had been listening carefully, now put his head all the way up and opened his other eye.

"I will promise," he said. "If you will let me go, I will have a fine picnic for you here tomorrow, even if I have to work every minute to do it."

"Are the three judges willing?" asked Mr. Badger seriously.

"I am," said Mr. Lobster, "for I thought of it."

"I am," said Mr. Bear. "I suppose I shall have to be, for it is a wise thing to do. But I know very well that the sea gull can never catch a fish as big as the one I had, and even if he could catch it he couldn't fry it. Still, it is a pleasure to be uncivilized at times, and picking blueberries will be a good hard job for the sea gull; so I say that he has to pick two quarts of blueberries, and I'll have those instead of the fish. No, I'll make it three quarts."

"Oh, I will do that," said the sea gull.

"Well, I am willing," said Mr. Badger.

Mr. Badger then lifted up the trap, and the sea gull flew away.

"I think," remarked Mr. Badger in a satisfied tone, after the gull was far away, "that everything has worked out very well. We should be pleased with ourselves."

"I'll wait until tomorrow before I am pleased," said

THE SEA GULL FLEW AWAY.

Mr. Bear. "Being pleased in advance often ends in disaster."

"What shall we do now?" asked Mr. Lobster.

"Go and catch our dinner," said Mr. Bear, "and hope we don't have to catch it tomorrow, too."

The three friends then parted for the day. It was such a beautiful day that Mr. Lobster was tempted to stay ashore. But he didn't. He went home under the Ocean where the sunlight was a lovely green, and he caught small pleasant creatures, opened two clams, and then met the sculpin and talked with him for hours.

When the three friends met the next day they were all delighted to find that the sea gull, who must have been honest at heart, as all birds are, except possibly the black crow, had brought everything he had promised.

"I have been very busy," he said. "I could carry only seven blueberries in my bill at a time, and I have had to make over 900 trips between here and the place where they grow. And I had to drop each clam upon the rocks to break the shell and then bring it here. But I have everything, and I want to know if I may go now."

The three friends agreed that the sea gull had carried out his promise, and he flew away, probably a very much better bird.

Mr. Badger got the two round things which had been voted pickles, and put them down near the picnic. Then they all sat down and had a joyous time, for Mr. Bear had blueberries, Mr. Badger had a fine piece of meat, and Mr. Lobster had a great heap of clams without their shells.

When it was all over there was nothing left but the pickles.

"My meat was perfect," said Mr. Badger. "Our picnic turned out very well after all."

"My clams were delicious," said Mr. Lobster, "and I think your ideas are wonderful."

"Well," said Mr. Bear, "my blueberries were fresh and nice, but I do love fried fish." And he gave a growl, but it was a low growl and a soft growl, for he was really very happy.

Mr. Lobster Takes a
Very Dangerous Trip

EVER SINCE Mr. Lobster had first come ashore he had been curious about the woods, where Mr. Badger and Mr. Bear lived, and where there must be a very different kind of world from any that Mr. Lobster had ever seen. The only time he had ever been in the woods was the time Mr. Bear carried him home to cook him, and that had been such an unpleasant event, and Mr. Lobster had been so frightened and miserable, that he had forgotten all about looking closely at the woods.

"I guess," said Mr. Lobster to himself, "that was the one time in my life when I forgot to be curious. But you can't expect a person to be curious just before he is going to be cooked, because at such a time further knowledge seems to have little value."

So he thought a good deal about the woods in the days that followed the picnic, and he mentioned to Mr. Badger that he might walk to the woods some day.

One day Mr. Badger brought the news that he had moved into a new burrow, the finest burrow anywhere in the woods.

"It would be a great honor to me," he said, "if you would come to the woods and visit my new home. Also, it would cause some excitement among the creatures who live in the woods, for they have never seen a lobster. Also, again, we might make a call on Mr. Bear."

"Oh, no, thank you," said Mr. Lobster quickly. "You are very kind to invite me to your home, but I really couldn't bear to go to Mr. Bear's house again. My memory of the first visit is too unhappy."

"Very well, but I do hope you will come. Of course, it will be a risky trip for you, but you are a hero, and all heroes are unafraid of danger. Besides, if you should start to get dry, Mr. Bear or I could easily pull you back to the beach."

"I would rather not think of getting dry," said Mr. Lobster, "though I know it is wise to think of everything first."

"Well," said Mr. Badger, "remember that you just walk straight for the woods. Go up the long hill and go straight to that tallest tree, where the permanent partridge lives, and ask him the way."

"Is he friendly?" asked Mr. Lobster.

"Oh, yes, indeed."

"Well, what is he?"

"He is a bird," replied Mr. Badger. "He is the fastest and most cunning bird in our woods. We call him the permanent partridge because he has escaped all foxes and hunters and other vermin for so many years that he just seems to be permanent."

"I am very stupid about your land creatures, I realize," said Mr. Lobster. "You see, I didn't know there were any permanent creatures, as I don't know of any where I live. With us, permanent is practically forever. But what a wonderful thing it would be to be permanent! Think how wise one could become!"

"And old, too," added Mr. Badger. "And probably you would have rheumatism if you were permanent."

"I don't see any necessity for such a thing," Mr. Lobster objected. And then he added: "Whatever it is."

"Do you mean to tell me you don't know what rheumatism is?" Mr. Badger was amazed.

"I have never heard of it."

"Why," said Mr. Badger, "it is the very handiest of all ailments, because whenever you have a pain without any reason for it, or don't feel like doing something you should, you say you have rheumatism."

"I see," said Mr. Lobster. "I should explain that we sea-creatures don't have such things. We are all either alive or gone. You should try living in salt water."

"Oh, but you are most unfortunate," exclaimed Mr.

Badger, who pretended to be serious now but could not conceal the rascally twinkle in his beady eyes. "You can never know how good you feel until you have had rheumatism."

"I feel well now," said Mr. Lobster.

"But just how well? Just tell me that."

"Why, very well," said Mr. Lobster.

"And just how well is that?" insisted Mr. Badger.

"Why, it's very well, of course."

"Exactly. You see, you don't really know how well you are, because you don't know how well very well is. Take my advice, and have rheumatism. Or at least think about having it. You know it is my motto that a little excitement and a little misery are necessary once in a while to make us appreciate peace and happiness. A little rheumatism, just a slight twinge every now and then, say on a very damp morning, will make you appreciate how well you are when you don't have it."

Mr. Badger was smiling now. He loved foolish arguments, and he knew how serious Mr. Lobster was about such things.

"Perhaps I should think that over," said Mr. Lobster, "but I don't think I shall believe a word of it. Those who cannot appreciate their good fortune and never count their own blessings are fools. As I am sure you are no fool, I know you are joking."

The conversation ended here because it was time for Mr. Lobster to go home, and they parted in very good humor, for Mr. Badger had had his joke and Mr. Lobster had shown his wisdom; so they were both satisfied and happy.

Of course, Mr. Badger's invitation made Mr. Lobster all the more curious about the woods. And finally, when he went ashore one day and Mr. Badger was not there, he realized that he could not stand being curious about the woods any longer but must go and visit Mr. Badger.

It was a coolish sort of day, for now the long summer was passing, and there were days of clouds and gray skies as the season drew to its end. Mr. Lobster thought that his shell would not get dry for a long time in such weather.

"This is the day I am going," he said to himself. "I know that it is a very dangerous trip, but, as Mr. Badger said, I am a hero. Besides, you never get anywhere by just sitting down and wishing."

And with these words of wisdom, and trying to forget about the danger of such a long trip, he started in a straight line for the tallest tree that he could see above the woods in the distance.

Now Mr. Lobster had never before walked nearly so far on land, and he did not realize when he started that it was almost a mile to the woods. It was much farther than he supposed, the way it is so often when people start boldly to go somewhere they have never been. Also, it was rather late in the day when he started, for he had been delayed on his way by stopping to open three large clams, which had tasted very good.

On and on he went, keeping his eyes on the tallest tree where lived the permanent partridge. There was a good deal of up-hill going, which was hard for him, and which might have turned some travelers back. But not Mr. Lobster.

"In life," Mr. Lobster said to himself as he struggled up a hill, "you must never stop for the up-hills. There has to be a down-hill for every up-hill, but you never can have the down-hill until you have conquered the up-hill. I shall have the down-hill when I go home."

So he climbed up and up the hill, and, although he didn't turn around to see, which would have been a wise thing to do, he was getting high above his home in the blue Ocean, and quite a distance away.

When he reached the woods he found that he could no longer look up and tell the top of the tallest tree from the tops of other trees, for the sky was gray, and all the tops of the trees were so far above him that it was impossible to tell which was which from his position. He did not want to go outside the woods again to look; so he decided to keep walking anyway.

He was delighted with the woods, and he kept looking every way to see the flowers and bushes and small trees.

"If we only had something like this at the bottom of the Ocean," he thought. "I wonder why somebody didn't plant woods there."

As soon as Mr. Lobster satisfied his curiosity about one thing he was curious about another.

He crawled through the woods in a very happy frame of mind, and in a rather forgetful one. For suddenly he realized that it was getting dark, and he had not found the permanent partridge, and he had not come to Mr. Badger's home.

"I must now go home myself," he thought.

So he turned right around to look for the way back to the beach, but all that he could see was trees, and the great sky dark with the oncoming night.

"Perhaps it is this way," he said to himself, and off he went.

"No, it must be this way," he said then, and he went in another direction.

But none of the directions seemed to be right, because he could not see the edge of the woods, and he could not see the Ocean.

Then Mr. Lobster knew that he was lost. He was a sea creature lost on land! And he was alone. All the birds seemed to have gone to bed, and he didn't see a single creature moving about; so there was no one from whom he could ask the way to go. If only Mr. Badger had been there to remind him that he was a hero things might have been better, but there was no Mr. Badger, and Mr. Lobster forgot all about being a hero. He was just plain afraid, terribly afraid.

"I shall certainly dry up without a chance to save myself," he thought. "When Mr. Badger finds me there won't be anything left but my shell. I shall be gone. That will make Mr. Badger miserable, and it will be the end of our friendship."

Sadness overpowered Mr. Lobster, and he was unable to move for some time. He had been in some pretty tight places in his long life, but never had been in a tight place so far from home and, worst of all, on land. This seemed to be the most unhappy moment of his entire existence.

The sun went down red in the far west, and the glow of it came in through the trees so that every great trunk stood out black and straight. From the distance a small creature who had been waiting for the dusk sent out a little peep to try the air and see if it was time for him to come out. The gray gloom in the woods darkened, changing from the dim light of evening to the silent dark of the night.

Fortunately the night was cool with the blessing of falling dew, and Mr. Lobster realized that possibly he would not get dry after all so long as the night lingered and the woods were damp. But he did not like the dark, and he did not like the thought of having to stay where he was until morning.

Just then there was a whush, like silence rushing by, and something scratched along his shell.

Mr. Lobster thought that he was being attacked, and he raised up one big claw and snapped, and he just missed catching something big and blurry in the darkness.

"Who are you?" he asked. He was frightened, but he tried to make his voice sound bold and angry.

"Someone you can't catch!" answered a proud voice.

"Who are you?" demanded Mr. Lobster again.

"So you are the friend of that contrary Mr. Badger," came the answer. "He never would take my advice, and evidently you don't take advice either, or you wouldn't be here."

"Ah, I know," guessed Mr. Lobster. "You are the owl."

"A much wiser bird than you will ever be," said the unpleasant voice.

"I am thankful to say I shall never have to be a bird," answered Mr. Lobster angrily.

"If you were, you could see your way home now." The owl was chuckling in a most disagreeable manner.

Mr. Lobster realized that he had made a mistake in speaking crossly, and now he tried being polite.

"Perhaps," he said, "since you are the wisest bird in these woods you would show me the way home. I fear I am lost."

Again the owl chuckled disagreeably.

"Perhaps," he said, "since you are the wisest lobster in the Ocean you will show yourself the way home. It is a foolish person, indeed, who doesn't know the way to his own home. What is home for, anyway, if it is not to go to when you have been away long enough?"

Mr. Lobster groaned. The mention of home made him more unhappy than ever.

"How true," he murmured.

"Everything I say is true," said the owl. "And now I shall say 'Good night,' and resume my hunting."

"Wait a minute, I beg of you!" exclaimed Mr. Lobster.

But there was just another whush in the darkness, and the owl was gone.

"I hope," said Mr. Lobster to himself, "that I never let

my wisdom make me so disagreeable as that. Really wise persons are glad to share their knowledge and help others. Wisdom is never selfish. I dare say the owl is not so wise as he thinks he is."

He knew there was no use trying to go home now. He knew also that he did not like the idea of staying where he was and having things whushing over him in the black dark.

So he crawled around from tree to tree and from stump to stump, looking for shelter, and all the time wishing all the harder that he was back in his own home under the ocean waves.

"Oh, the perils of curiosity," he said to himself. "But anyway, if I ever do get home again, I shall know what the woods are." And he tried to get comfort from that thought.

Finally, seeing a hole under an old stump, he backed in very carefully.

Almost before he was safely inside he heard a terrified squeaking in the farthest corner of the hole.

"Who is there?" he demanded.

"Just a mouse, sir," came the answer in a very squeaky and frightened little voice.

"Ah," said Mr. Lobster, remembering what Mr. Badger had said. "Then besides your squeak you have a long tail."

"Yes, sir."

"And you are a very insignificant creature."

"Oh, yes, indeed, sir."

"Well, may I ask you why you are making all that noise?" asked Mr. Lobster.

"I was saying my prayers, sir." The little small voice from the corner was still trembling and frightened.

"Why were you saying your prayers?" asked Mr. Lobster, who, of course, was curious.

"You see, sir," answered the mouse, "no one ever comes into a mouse's home except to eat him. So I knew, sir, that you would eat me immediately. And I didn't dare run out because if I do the owl will eat me. So there was nothing left for me to do but say my prayers. It is miserable to be a mouse, sir. No one realizes how gentle we are."

Mr. Lobster thought over what the mouse had said.

"Is the owl your enemy?" he finally asked the mouse.

"Oh, a terrible enemy, sir."

"Then I shall be your friend, for I have no affection for the owl." Mr. Lobster felt that he was being very kind.

"Oh, be my friend, sir!" squeaked the mouse. "I have never had a friend, only a few relatives. And let me stay here in peace in my house until the owl goes to bed. I will do anything I can for you."

"Very well," said Mr. Lobster, "I am your friend, and you may stay here. I think, since you got here first, that is only reasonable, anyway. But tell me one more thing, if you will pardon my curiosity. I believe Mr. Badger told me the owl goes out only at night. Is it also true, then, that he goes to bed in the morning?"

"Oh, yes, sir."

"That settles it," said Mr. Lobster. "I knew that he couldn't be as wise as he thinks he is, for he is most discourteous. And if he goes to bed in the morning, then he is plain foolish."

With that comforting thought Mr. Lobster settled down to wait the long night through. He knew that he would not sleep a wink. He was too worried about getting home in the morning. The dampness and coolness of the night would not last forever. So he was very nervous and twitchety, folding and unfolding his tail, creaking in all his joints just from sheer worry, and, when all is said, having a perfectly miserable night.

Of course, the night had to pass, for the world must roll on, and the sun must have its day. And in the first light of the early day Mr. Lobster crawled out of the hole in the stump, hoping that now he would be able to see his way home or meet someone who could direct him to Mr. Badger.

The mouse came out, said, "Thank you, sir," and scampered off to find a small breakfast.

Mr. Lobster found that he was alone. There were just as many trees in the woods as there had been the night before. And no sign of a path, and no sign of the Ocean. He had no idea which way to go, or where the tallest tree was.

"I am just as lost as I was last night," he said to himself. "This trip has turned out to be a dreadful mistake."

He did not hear any birds, for at this time of the morning the birds were busy getting their breakfasts. He looked around for some passing creature, but there were no creatures. So he just crawled unhappily along, feeling worse by the minute.

Mr. Lobster did not know that the woods creatures had already spied him, and that they were all so frightened at seeing a lobster in the woods, and such a great big lobster, that they were keeping well hidden, watching Mr. Lobster from safe distances.

"What a lonesome place," thought poor Mr. Lobster. "Lonesomeness is one of the very worst things I know. Being lost is another. And here I am both lonesome and lost!"

He crawled and crawled, and the sun grew brighter and brighter. The dew on the grass and leaves was dried by the sun, taken up into the air so that it could fall again the next night, and the air of the woods became warm. Mr. Lobster felt his shell beginning to get dry.

And he was still lost.

He tried to hurry, but he could hurry only when he was swimming; and he couldn't swim on land no matter how hard he tried.

"It is all up with me now," he said sadly. "I am lost and alone, and all my wisdom is doing me no good at all. Evidently you have to have different kinds of wisdom for different places."

So he stopped to rest, feeling that there was no use in struggling further, and looking around, he was amazed to find that he was right in front of the hole in the stump where he had spent the night.

"After all my crawling I haven't gotten anywhere!" he moaned. "What a strange place a woods is, and how dreadful!"

Just then the mouse came scampering toward the hole in the stump. Seeing Mr. Lobster, the mouse stopped, trembling all over so that even his long tail was all aquiver.

"Don't be afraid," said Mr. Lobster, "and please don't squeak. I couldn't stand it now. I am lost. Soon I shall be nothing but a dried-up shell. I shall be gone."

"I was afraid you had changed your mind, sir," said the mouse, "and had decided to eat me. You see, I am not used to kindness. But can't I do anything for you, sir, if you are lost?"

Mr. Lobster looked at the tiny creature. He was a dormouse, a very pretty creature with large ears and a pure white chest, and an extra long tail.

"I fear not," he said. "You are too insignificant."

"I have beautiful relatives, sir," said the mouse.

"Have you any relatives that know Mr. Badger or Mr. Bear?" asked Mr. Lobster, with only a very little hope.

"Well, not exactly, sir," replied the mouse, "but perhaps my cousin, the squirrel, could help you. He could climb a tree and see where your friends are, and perhaps he would tell them your trouble."

"I am getting drier every second," said Mr. Lobster, "and if I get all dry then I am done for. And I shall get all dry if I don't get home. And I don't know the way home."

"How awful!" exclaimed the mouse, who was, like all

"I AM GETTING DRIER EVERY SECOND," SAID MR. LOBSTER.

mice, a kind and considerate creature. "If you don't mind, sir, I can't spread the news unless I know your name."

"I am Mr. Lobster."

In an instant the mouse was gone, and Mr. Lobster was alone again. He just stayed where he was, feeling drier and drier, and unhappier and unhappier. He really had little faith in the mouse. The creature seemed too small to be of any good.

Just before the very worst happened, the mouse came scampering back.

"Good news, sir!" he cried. "I have told my cousin, and he climbed a tall tree and saw Mr. Badger in one place and Mr. Bear in another, and he told the birds of your plight, and the story is spreading all through the woods."

Indeed, the mouse had been as good as his word. Soon there was the greatest chatter, and birds began coming to perch in trees and look at Mr. Lobster, all of them very much excited. There were robins and finches and thrushes. There were sparrows and wrens and bluebirds. Two blue jays were talking very loud. One crow came and took a good look at Mr. Lobster and immediately flew away to tell all his friends, the way crows always do. The trees were full of birds, and they made a babel of noise, without stopping for an instant.

Mr. Lobster was more miserable than ever at being the object of so much attention. He felt altogether too conspicuous.

"I am not sure that it is true that misery loves company," he said wisely but sadly to himself, "but it certainly draws a crowd."

And then who should come but Mr. Badger, running just as fast as his legs would carry him. And right behind him came Mr. Bear.

"My poor friend!" cried Mr. Badger. "To think you came up here to see me, and came to this! I will save you!"

All the birds made a great outcry then.

"Hold on to my tail!" exclaimed Mr. Badger. "I will drag you from here to the Ocean!"

"Too late," moaned Mr. Lobster. "I am almost fainting, and I could not hold on tight enough for such a ride."

"Then what shall we do?" cried Mr. Badger.

"Let him ride on my back," said Mr. Bear. "Mr. Lobster saved my life once, and now it is my turn to save his. You are both heroes already. Now I shall be a hero."

Mr. Bear came up close to Mr. Lobster so that he could climb on. Alas, Mr. Bear's back was so high up from the ground that Mr. Lobster did not have the strength to climb up.

"It is no use," said Mr. Lobster, and he sighed so deeply that all the birds sighed too, making a sad little sound trembling among the leaves of the trees.

"I could climb on Mr. Badger's back," said Mr. Lobster, "but that is the best I can do. I am nearly dry."

"Oh, dear," cried Mr. Badger. "I could pull you easily, but I could never carry you on my back."

Everything seemed lost and hopeless. Even the birds were silent.

But just then, when Mr. Lobster was sure that he was going to faint and that everything was all over, there was a rush of wings. A new bird came flying with the speed of a bullet. It was the permanent partridge, the most cunning of all the birds.

"What is all this hubbub and chatter I've been hearing?" he asked. "Is there trouble?" Oh, he was a fine-looking bird, and he stood on the ground, unafraid of anything, and he spread out his tail and raised up the ruff on his neck, so that he looked magnificent.

Mr. Badger quickly told him the whole story of Mr. Lobster's unhappy trip to the woods.

"Well, well," said the permanent partridge. "It is a very good thing I came along. I should say let Mr. Lobster climb up on Mr. Badger's back, and then let Mr. Badger climb up on Mr. Bear's back, and then let Mr. Bear run down to the Ocean as fast as he can."

And that is just what happened.

Poor Mr. Lobster was now so dry that he scarcely knew what he was doing, but he managed to climb on Mr. Badger's back and wrap his long claws around Mr. Badger's neck.

And then Mr. Badger, groaning under the heavy load, but being as brave as any hero, climbed up on Mr. Bear's back and wrapped his arms about Mr. Bear's neck.

Mr. Bear started.

It was an exciting and strange sight—the strangest the woods had ever seen.

Mr. Bear ran fast.

All the birds flew along beside him, chirping and calling out encouragement until he got to the end of the woods.

Mr. Lobster cried out to Mr. Badger, "Faster! Faster!"

And Mr. Badger called out to Mr. Bear, "Faster! Faster!"

And Mr. Bear, who was really three creatures at once, ran so fast that he didn't have any breath left even for a single growl as he went.

It was a wild and terrible trip, and there was danger every minute that Mr. Lobster or Mr. Badger might fall off. But they didn't. And when Mr. Bear reached the beach he bravely walked right into the water, so that Mr. Lobster could let go of Mr. Badger and fall right into his own Ocean without doing another thing.

Mr. Lobster did let go at once. He fell with a splash that soaked Mr. Bear and Mr. Badger, and both of them ran for the beach.

And so Mr. Lobster was saved.

The Very Strange End
of a Long Voyage

MR. LOBSTER recovered his health very soon after he was restored to salt water, and he went gladly home.

After the desperate adventure in the woods he felt that he had gathered about all the knowledge any lobster could possibly hold. When he counted up all the things he had learned since he had first gone ashore, they were so many that the number amazed him. And so it seemed quite foolish for him to seek after more knowledge.

He rested for some days after Mr. Bear and Mr. Badger saved his life, but it wasn't long before he was out crawling around again, pruning some of the seaweeds in his garden, looking for pleasant creatures, and feeling very much like his old self. It was while he was taking a long crawl that he met the sculpin, whom he had not seen for some weeks.

Mr. Lobster said to the sculpin, "I want to tell you the things I have learned by going ashore." And he told the sculpin everything that he could think of, not leaving out even the mouse.

The sculpin was forced to listen, because he was always polite, but he was so envious that he almost ceased being Mr. Lobster's friend right then and there. And when Mr. Lobster had finished his speech, the sculpin looked him right in the eye.

"That all sounds very well," he said, "but pray remember that all those things will do you no good the instant you are dead!"

"Me dead! Me gone!" exclaimed Mr. Lobster. "Why do you have to say such unpleasant things, when I have just been telling you what a wonderful summer I have had?"

"The truth is sometimes unpleasant to those who are reckless," said the sculpin in his most important and dignified manner. "Still, it is the solemn truth that if you persist in your wanderings you will come to a sudden, and probably very disagreeable, end. Then you will be dead and gone."

"I suppose you want me to stay at home all the time." Mr. Lobster did not like the idea of the sculpin's giving him advice, but in his own heart he had recently thought a good deal about staying home. The affair in the woods had made him think deeply. In fact, he was just going to say that he thought of staying home for a time; but now the sculpin had said it first, and so Mr. Lobster wanted to do just the opposite.

"I can be as independent as Mr. Badger," he said to himself.

The sculpin frowned, and when he frowned his dignity became very impressive, and he became so homely that he was positively unique.

"I should think," he said, "that at your age of sixty-eight it was time you settled down."

"We shall see about that," said Mr. Lobster.

"Yes, we shall see," said the sculpin.

Mr. Lobster did not wait to see any more of the sculpin that day. Just to show the sculpin that his age was nothing to worry about, he tail-snapped away at such a rate that the sand flew up in a cloud, and there was a stream of bubbles a yard long behind him—and good big bubbles, too.

Now Mr. Lobster was always bold and fearless when he talked with the sculpin, but when he was alone with himself he was not always so sure of things. And so it happened that when he did begin to go ashore again he did not take any long walks away from the beach. He stayed right near the Ocean so that he could crawl into the water any minute.

"I still have to go ashore," he explained to himself, "even if I don't go very far, because my curiosity is not cured. I should think that it would be quite cured after that horrible adventure, but it isn't. I must ask Mr. Badger about that."

When he asked Mr. Badger, that wise and fearless creature smiled.

"Of course it is not cured," he said. "The only cure for curiosity is finding out, and you have not found out everything yet."

Mr. Lobster thought that over for a minute to be sure that Mr. Badger was not having a joke.

"Why, I can never find out everything," he said then.

"Of course not," agreed Mr. Badger.

"Then I shall be curious as long as I live!" exclaimed Mr. Lobster, partly in wonder and partly in delight.

"Exactly!" cried Mr. Badger. "It is a wonderful thought, you see. I know because I am just as curious as you are. You know, I once used to go out only at night, as most respectable badgers do, but I was so curious about what went on in the daytime I changed my habits entirely. I am so curious that the very first morning I wake up and find that I am not curious I shall know I am dead."

"And so shall I, I suppose," said Mr. Lobster. "I certainly hope I never wake up and find myself dead!"

Mr. Lobster was serious about that, but for some reason Mr. Badger laughed and laughed, as he did when he heard a good joke.

"You want to be careful each morning before you wake up," he said. And he laughed again.

Of course, now that Mr. Lobster's terrible experience

in the woods was a thing of the past, Mr. Badger looked
back upon it with a great deal of pleasure.

"Never think seriously about the disasters of the past,"
he said. "Think only of the pleasures. You had the narrowest escape of the whole summer, and you are lucky,
indeed. That should be a joy to you as long as you live if
you think of it as you should."

And Mr. Bear, who came down to the beach almost
every day now, also looked back upon Mr. Lobster's escape with a good deal of pleasure.

"I am very grateful to you," he said to Mr. Lobster, "for
having such a narrow escape. It gave me a chance to save
a life. You two were always saving each other's lives and
being heroes. Now I have some claim to distinction
and honor. Now we are all heroes."

Mr. Badger laughed at that. He loved to tease Mr. Bear
and make him growl.

"You are not so much of a hero as you think," he said.
"I was the one who saved Mr. Lobster's life. I carried him
on my back, you may remember. You simply carried me
on your back, and I didn't need any saving. Why, if I had
not been right on the spot, Mr. Lobster would be right
there in the woods now."

Mr. Lobster shuddered at the thought.

Mr. Bear gave a good hard growl.

"How dare you say such a thing!" he demanded. "If I
hadn't been there, you wouldn't have accomplished a
thing, and Mr. Lobster would never have been saved!"

Mr. Lobster interrupted.

"Mr. Badger is only joking," he said. "Of course, you saved my life. I would have been lost but for your great strength and courage. You both saved my life, and you are both heroes."

"Well, I certainly think I am," said Mr. Bear, and after that he was more friendly than he had ever been before.

For a good many days the three good friends and heroes were content to walk on the beach together or go fishing along the river to get a supper for Mr. Bear. It seemed as if their adventures of the summer were all over, for there were now only a few days left before the glad season would be ended and autumn would come to color the hills.

Mr. Bear was well satisfied with the life he was leading, for he was getting plenty to eat without hard work, and he was a known hero. Mr. Lobster also felt that life was pleasant indeed.

But Mr. Badger was restless.

"Nothing is happening," he said.

"And a very good thing it is, too," said Mr. Bear quickly. "Making things happen doesn't always turn out the way you expect it to."

"Yes, that is why I like making things happen," said Mr. Badger. "You never can tell what will be the end of what you start. You just wait—one of these days I am going to have a great idea."

Mr. Bear gave a low, unhappy moan.

"I dread thinking of it," he said. "I shall hate to see that day."

Mr. Lobster didn't feel that way at all, for he was curious about what Mr. Badger's newest idea would be.

For a day or so Mr. Badger said nothing. Then there came a day when the sun was bright and the Ocean had a lovely sparkle because the sunshine danced upon the wide blue water. All the trees and grass moved in a light breeze—just enough of a breeze to cool your finger if you wet it in your mouth and held it up in the air. A few clouds which had been freshly washed and were much whiter even than snow were out sailing in the sky, every one of them sailing from the land out over the Ocean and then far and far until they were out of sight.

The three friends were walking, and Mr. Badger was watching the white clouds.

"I have observed," he said, "that the clouds go right out to sea like ships. I am sure there must be some land beyond the Ocean, even if we can't see anything."

"What is the use of thinking about something we can't see?" asked Mr. Bear.

"Because I have an idea," answered Mr. Badger. "Yes, at last I have another idea! It is even more than stupendous!"

"Oh, please tell us at once!" begged Mr. Lobster. "I have been curious for days."

"Just a minute, please," put in Mr. Bear in a great hurry. "Would you mind waiting until I have started home and have walked far enough so that I can't hear you?"

"You will regret it if you don't listen," said Mr. Badger.

"I am afraid I shall regret it much more if I have anything to do with it," answered Mr. Bear.

"At any rate," said Mr. Badger, "it is very impolite to walk away when a person is about to express an idea. Of course, if you want to be impolite..."

Mr. Bear hesitated. He considered it perfectly proper to be cross, being a bear, but he wanted always to be considered highly civilized, and he knew that highly civilized people were always polite.

"I agree with Mr. Badger," said Mr. Lobster. "Besides, we have to listen to other people's ideas to get knowledge."

"All we get from Mr. Badger's ideas is into trouble," said Mr. Bear crossly, "but I suppose I shall have to listen. Go ahead and do your worst."

The three friends stopped walking and sat down on a sand dune from which they could look out over the Ocean.

"Here is my idea," said Mr. Badger. "If there is another land and another beach on the other side of the Ocean, why shouldn't we see it? We have had delightful times this summer, with our narrow escapes and our picnic. But we have never traveled. Now there is a big sailing boat tied up to the wharf in the river, and it came sailing in from the Ocean, from way out farther than we can see, where the clouds go. So it must have come from somewhere. I say, let's hide aboard that ship and travel to the other side of the Ocean!"

"And stay there?" asked Mr. Lobster. He was curious at once, but he also thought instantly of his fine home.

"Oh, no," answered Mr. Badger. "Travelers never stay

anywhere. They haven't time. We can see the other end of the Ocean and then return when the ship comes back here to our river."

"If you will excuse me," said Mr. Bear, "I think I would rather just hibernate. It's about time I got ready, and I might be late if I traveled."

"What do you mean by that?" asked Mr. Lobster. "What do you do when you hibernate, as you call it?"

Mr. Bear looked proud.

"Hibernating," he explained, "is a very superior arrangement. It means eating a good big dinner and then going to sleep and sleeping through all the cold and stormy winter weather. Anyone who is really wise hibernates, and I shall soon make my plans for this winter's sleep, as I see that the end of the summer is here."

"How wonderful you are!" exclaimed Mr. Lobster.

"Of course," agreed Mr. Bear.

"Pooh!" said Mr. Badger. "We shall get back here in plenty of time to hibernate. That is no excuse."

"Well, anyway," said Mr. Bear, "it is a very foolish idea, this business of going across the Ocean. And it sounds dangerous. I haven't forgotten the first time I went out in a boat. That was your idea, too."

"I thought that you were a hero," said Mr. Badger.

"I am!" Mr. Bear gave a low growl.

"Heroes are not afraid of dangerous ideas. That is the difference between heroes and ordinary people." Mr. Badger pretended to be very serious. "And a hero would go on such a voyage in a minute. I am sorry to have to say this, Mr. Bear, but I am afraid that all those who do not go on this trip can't be heroes."

Mr. Badger looked around, very much pleased with himself.

"Now," he said, "I shall take a vote to see who is going. I am a hero. So of course I am going. And how about you, Mr. Lobster?"

Mr. Lobster really had not made up his mind to go. It seemed to him a much longer and possibly more dangerous trip than even his long walk to the woods, and he would never forget how that turned out. And yet he was very curious. And he knew that he could never give up being a hero. So he said:

"I vote to go."

"And you, Mr. Bear?" Mr. Badger's beady eyes twinkled. He knew that Mr. Bear could never refuse now no matter how much he wanted to. And he knew that Mr. Bear would be furious at being tricked that way, which pleased mischievous Mr. Badger a good deal.

"All right," said Mr. Bear. "You know very well I am a hero, and now probably I shall be a dead hero. But I will go. Somehow I always lose out in every argument with you, but some day I'll have my turn."

Mr. Badger made all the plans and gave all the directions to Mr. Lobster and Mr. Bear. The next day, which was the day set for the start of the great voyage, Mr. Lobster was so curious about the other side of the Ocean, and so excited, that he could hardly wait for the time to come when he was to go ashore. But he ate a tremendous dinner, just as Mr. Badger had told him to, and when the tide was right he went ashore and met Mr. Badger and Mr. Bear.

The three friends waited on the beach until the sun had set and the night was dark. Mr. Bear grumbled and growled a little. He even trembled, but he said that was only because the night was cold.

Mr. Lobster trembled in his shell, but as no one could see what went on under his shell, he did not have to explain.

Mr. Badger was in the best of spirits, as he always was when something was about to happen.

"This is the greatest adventure of the summer," he said.

Very slowly and very carefully they walked across the bridge and approached the ship like three thieves.

"We must be cautious," whispered Mr. Badger, "for we haven't exactly been invited on this ship, and I think it would be just as well if we take care not to be seen."

"I knew it," said Mr. Bear. "There is always something shady in your schemes."

The crew of the ship were all ashore, and no one saw the three friends, although Mr. Bear kept looking around as though at least a dozen enemies were following.

"I don't like doing things by night," he complained. "I make it a rule to stay at home after dark."

Mr. Lobster thought that was a good rule himself. He was sure that he wasn't afraid, for he knew that he was a hero; but he did think it would be pleasant to be home at such a dark time.

THEY APPROACHED THE SHIP LIKE THREE THIEVES.

Fortunately there was a little more than half a moon shining; so they could see fairly well.

"Right this way," said Mr. Badger cheerfully.

They went along the wharf, climbed aboard the ship, and looked around.

Mr. Bear and Mr. Lobster were lagging behind. For some reason they did not feel in a hurry.

"Right this way!" cried Mr. Badger again.

There was nothing to do but follow. So Mr. Bear and Mr. Lobster followed Mr. Badger through a little door and down some steps, which were very hard for Mr. Lobster because he had to go down backwards, hanging on with his tail.

Mr. Badger led the way to a dark little cabin which had just one round window. Then he shut the door, and they all waited.

After a while Mr. Bear said, "I suppose we shall have to stay in this miserable dark little place all night."

"Oh, more than that," answered Mr. Badger. "It may take us days to get to the other side of the Ocean. That is why I told you to eat a big dinner today."

"Days!" exclaimed Mr. Bear in terror. "And with no food! I am going straight home. I am sick of being a hero, and I resign if I have to go hungry."

Mr. Bear would have walked right away then and there, but just at that moment there was a great shuffling of feet on deck, and the noise of pulling and hoisting and casting off lines.

"Too late to go now," said Mr. Badger.

Mr. Bear gave a low sad growl.

"I am already hungry just at the thought of days without food," he said. "I have even forgotten what I had for my dinner."

Mr. Badger looked out of the round window, which was very near the water.

"We're off!" he cried.

And so the voyage was started.

In some ways the voyage started out to be anything but a great success. After the night melted away and the sun rose up over the Ocean the three friends looked out of the little round window and saw nothing but water, with no land anywhere in sight. That was a little fearful. And then, besides, Mr. Bear was hungry, and when he was hungry he was unhappy, and when he was unhappy he growled.

"I am starving," he said.

He walked back and forth and back and forth most miserably, the way bears always do when they are unhappily kept in a small place. And to make matters worse, someone on the ship cooked fish every few hours, and the smell of the frying fish came down to Mr. Bear and made him furious.

"I am going to get some of that fried fish!" he declared.

"If you do," warned Mr. Badger, "you will probably be thrown overboard and have to swim to shore."

At the thought of such an impossible swim Mr. Bear collapsed.

And then, in the middle of the afternoon, although there was no sun in the little cabin, Mr. Lobster began to feel dry.

"There you are!" said Mr. Bear angrily. "You are starving me to death and drying up Mr. Lobster. Your ideas are certainly fine for your friends, aren't they?" He growled hard.

"I will tend to that," said Mr. Badger, who was never at a loss for ideas.

He opened the little round window. The next minute the ship rolled, and the water came pouring in the window, flooding the cabin. It was delightful to Mr. Lobster and refreshed him at once, but Mr. Bear got soaking wet, and he hated water almost as much as he hated work and hunger.

"I give you fair warning!" he cried. "There's nothing so cross as a wet bear!"

Mr. Badger was soaking wet too, but he laughed.

"That's a good joke on everybody but Mr. Lobster," he said. "That's the way it goes when you are off on an adventure. There must be many hardships to travel so that you appreciate your home when you return. I wonder what will happen next."

"I know," said Mr. Bear.

"What?" asked the curious Mr. Lobster.

"Something else unpleasant," answered Mr. Bear.

Mr. Badger closed the window, and it was arranged that after that when Mr. Lobster got dry Mr. Bear could open the door and go outside and wait while the window was opened again. But he must look out first, for they must not be seen.

They traveled thus all the first night, all the first day, and all the second night. Mr. Bear got hungrier and hungrier and vowed that although he had been willing this once to try just one more of Mr. Badger's ideas this was positively the last time. All that he wanted now was to hibernate.

"I look forward to sleeping all winter more than I ever have before," he growled. "I will know when I go to sleep this time that at last I am safe from Mr. Badger."

On the morning of the second day the ship stopped sailing. The three friends rushed to the window to look out and see the other side of the Ocean. But when they looked, there was nothing to see but water everywhere. The ship had stopped in the middle of the Ocean.

"I never want to see water again," said Mr. Bear. "If we don't get somewhere tomorrow, I am going to do something desperate."

Even Mr. Badger and Mr. Lobster were hungry. Mr. Lobster felt hollow under his shell, but he didn't care to mention it because he had voted for the voyage.

"Perhaps this is another mistake, though I should think I couldn't make a mistake every time," he said to himself. "Besides, if the worst happens, I can crawl out through the window and drop into the Ocean. But I am a hero and must not desert my friends."

There was a great deal of noise on the ship all that day. "I think they are fishing," said Mr. Badger. "Afterwards we shall move on."

Just before nightfall the ship started moving again. There sprang up a fine strong wind, and the brave ship dashed along, driving through the waves so that the water splashed up on the little window all the time.

They sailed all that night and all the next day. Mr. Lobster was very hungry. Mr. Badger was even hungrier, but as the voyage was his idea, of course he could not say anything. In fact, if the truth were told, the three adventurers were all pretty miserable now, for it looked as though the voyage would never end. Mr. Bear was growling practically all of the time, which got on Mr. Lobster's nerves, and Mr. Badger was unusually silent.

Once Mr. Badger did speak a little sadly.

"It seems a pity," he said, "that sometimes things planned just for pleasure end just the other way."

"That is particularly true of your ideas," said Mr. Bear unkindly.

"We must be brave and unafraid," said Mr. Badger. "A badger is never afraid."

"Probably you are not hungry," said Mr. Bear.

"I am hungry," admitted Mr. Badger. "And I confess that this voyage is taking a little longer than I expected. The Ocean must be very wide."

"Well, I am going to look for food," said Mr. Bear. And with those words he opened the door of the cabin and walked out, slamming the door behind him.

Mr. Badger and Mr. Lobster waited for Mr. Bear to return.

"Do you think he is lost?" asked Mr. Lobster anxiously, after a long time.

"I don't know." Mr. Badger sighed. "But he may be in trouble anyway, and he is our friend and we are both heroes; so it is our duty to go and look for him."

"Do we have to?" asked Mr. Lobster.

"Yes, we have to," said Mr. Badger.

Mr. Lobster didn't say anything out loud, but he knew that he had learned something. "Sometimes," he said to himself, "being a hero is very uncomfortable. It is not so easy as it looks."

Mr. Badger opened the door, and they both went in search of Mr. Bear. Almost immediately they heard a muffled growling, a growling that was angry even when muffled. They hurried toward the sound.

There was Mr. Bear stuck in a very small doorway. It was so small that he had been able to get only his head and shoulders through. There he stood, apparently with no head at all, kicking with his hind legs and growling terribly. The growls, of course, came from the dark place where he had his head, which Mr. Lobster and Mr. Badger could not see.

Mr. Badger couldn't help chuckling at the ridiculous sight.

Mr. Lobster was frightened.

"He is probably choked!" he cried.

"Oh, I guess not," said Mr. Badger. "He can still growl

all right. Just listen to him! Let's see if we can pull him out."

Mr. Badger grabbed Mr. Bear's right hind leg. Mr. Lobster could grab in only one way; so he fastened his big claws on Mr. Bear's left hind leg.

"Now pull!" cried Mr. Badger.

They pulled for dear life. Mr. Bear let out the most awful growl they had ever heard.

"Pull again!" commanded Mr. Badger. "One, two, and three!"

This time they pulled even harder than before, and with a ferocious roar Mr. Bear came unstuck and sat down, and Mr. Badger went flying into one corner and Mr. Lobster went flying into another. Then they all got up and hurried back to their cabin.

"Who had hold of my left hind leg?" demanded Mr. Bear.

"I did!" exclaimed Mr. Lobster, pleased with himself because he had pulled so hard.

"Well, it was kind of you and all that," said Mr. Bear, "but those claws of yours grabbed right through to the very marrow of my bone, I should think by the feeling. I shall be lamed for life."

"I am very sorry," said Mr. Lobster.

"I am sorrier," said Mr. Bear, and with that he went over to the corner of the cabin and licked his wounds.

Afterwards he was a little more friendly, and he explained that he had smelled fish and had put his head in the little door and tried to reach a fish.

"Of course I couldn't reach," he said. "It has been my experience in life that everything is just an inch too far away."

Mr. Lobster and Mr. Badger said nothing. They were all so hungry now that conversation lagged.

However, the voyage was not going to last forever after all. In the dark of the night the ship nosed gently up to a wharf. There was a great deal of hustle and bustle, and for more than an hour a great deal of unloading and banging around. Then the crew went ashore, and all was quiet.

"We're here!" exclaimed Mr. Badger. "We have come to the other side of the Ocean. As soon as I find out where we are I shall know whether I am a bandicoot or a wallaby or a brock!"

"Thank goodness!" exclaimed Mr. Bear. "It doesn't matter to me what you are as long as we get something to eat."

"What shall we do?" asked Mr. Lobster, who was now so curious to see the other side of the Ocean that he could hardly wait another minute.

"Follow me," said Mr. Badger.

So they followed Mr. Badger to the deck of the ship, then to the wharf, and then to the bank of the river near by.

It was a very dark night, with no moon or stars shining. Mr. Badger had been living by daylight so long that even his eyes could not see very well. Mr. Lobster and Mr. Bear had no idea where they were. But they could see the river in front of them, and land on the other side. And Mr. Badger spied a boat.

"You see," he said, "here is a river somewhat like our own river at home. Of course, there are rivers everywhere. But this one looks wider and darker than ours. And over there is probably a beach, though I am sure it will be different from ours. We must row over in that boat."

"We must eat, you mean!" put in Mr. Bear.

"Not now," said Mr. Badger. "You can never think of comfort when traveling. The first thing is to see the place you have come to, no matter what happens."

Mr. Bear growled at that.

Mr. Lobster was so curious he was perfectly willing to wait a little longer for food.

"It is really wonderful!" he exclaimed.

"We are having a wonderful adventure!" said Mr. Badger.

Mr. Bear only growled.

Of course Mr. Bear had to give in and do what the others did; so he rowed the boat across the river, and they all got out and walked across the sand in the dark. There, sure enough, was a beach, although they could see only a few feet of it, and there was an Ocean.

Mr. Lobster immediately crawled down to the water and had a good swim.

"It tastes just like our Ocean," he said when he returned to his friends.

"Of course," agreed Mr. Badger. "It is the same Ocean, but this is the other end of it." Mr. Badger was a happy creature, for his voyage was a success. He said now, "Just wait until the daylight comes, and then we shall see all the wonders of this strange place."

Mr. Bear was grumbling a bit, but the three friends sat down in the dark to wait for the morning. After all, it seemed that Mr. Badger's idea had been a good one.

They had been waiting only a short time when Mr. Bear heard a noise from across the river.

"That sounds like a noise on our ship!" he exclaimed in alarm.

"It can't be!" cried Mr. Badger.

They hurried across the sand, stumbling in the dark. They saw lights on board the ship, and then, before they could even get into their boat to row across the river, they saw their ship begin to move away from the wharf. Down the river it went, out into the Ocean, and finally out of sight altogether.

It was gone, and they were left!

"Do you know what that means?" cried Mr. Bear.

"What?" asked Mr. Lobster.

"We are left here forever! We shall never get home!"

At that thought Mr. Lobster trembled all over. He would never see his lovely home again!

It was the bitterest blow the three friends had known in all their adventures. They were so dismayed that not even Mr. Badger could say a word.

In sad silence they walked back to the beach to wait for the morning, and in sad silence they sat for a long time. Finally Mr. Badger got up courage to say one thing.

"I hope this turns out to be a beautiful place," he said.

"There is no place as beautiful as home," said Mr. Lobster.

"Please do not speak," said Mr. Bear. He forgot to growl.

And so they were all sad and forlorn when the great sun came up and the world and all the Ocean before them grew light. And then they began to look around.

First Mr. Bear made a queer sound, and then Mr. Badger made a queer sound, and then Mr. Lobster made a queer sound.

For they were on their own beach, and not on the other side of the Ocean at all!

"The ship came back!" said Mr. Badger.

"Well," said Mr. Bear. "That was a fine voyage, wasn't it? We landed right where we started."

"All travel should end where it starts," said Mr. Badger.

"Well, I dreaded the thought of the voyage home, to tell the truth," said Mr. Bear. "I admit that this is a very happy ending after all. Now I can go and eat a tremendous dinner, and I shall not be too late to hibernate."

"It is the best joke of the summer!" said Mr. Badger. "That is the happiest kind of ending to our adventures!"

Mr. Lobster said very little. The friends said good-by to each other and decided that the summer had been very pleasant. Mr. Badger and Mr. Bear walked away together like the best of old friends.

Mr. Lobster hurried to the Ocean and then swam and crawled as fast as he could to his own home.

"I didn't satisfy my curiosity about the other side of the Ocean," he said to himself, "but I did get safely home. And home is the happiest ending of all."

THOSE INTREPID EXPLORERS, MR. BEAR, MR. LOBSTER AND
MR. BADGER.

Mr. Lobster
Faces the Winter

IT WAS a cold day along a certain river that winds through the meadows and comes down to meet the sea near a big cliff. All the meadow grasses and cat-o'-nine-tails were brown. The blackbirds and long-legged herons were gone, and all the small birds that make their nests in the deep grass. Only the tough old crows, shiny black and bright-eyed, flew over the river country. They didn't want cold weather, but they weren't going to leave home, even if it snowed and froze.

Near the sea and along the beach the gulls were just as busy looking for small fish and flying on white and gray wings as though it were summer time. For the gulls, like the crows, stay in the north in the winter time. But one old gull, who had seen a good many years and who had been studying the sky for some time, said to some young gulls who were near: "I feel very sure by the feel of the water on my toes this morning that we are going to have a hard winter."

"What is it that will be hard about it?" asked a very young gull who had never seen a winter.

"Everything," replied the old gull, "but especially the water in the river. And when the water becomes hard nothing comes floating down, like fish or turnips or other dinners, and so it is hard work to find food. Also, when the water is hard you can't dive into it. Altogether that makes a hard winter."

The young gulls decided to land on the clam flats and talk the matter over, and they went off with a good deal of noise.

Up on the hills and in the woods, where such creatures as Mr. Bear and Mr. Badger and the owl and the dormouse and the permanent partridge lived, a cold wind was blowing. It made a wintry sound in the sky, and a dry rattly rustle in the bushes and trees. The pine trees knew that they would be green, no matter how cold it got, so they didn't care. The other trees were already red and yellow and brown, so that the sunshine made them beautiful; but they shivered. And the bright-colored leaves, tired of holding on to their branches, and cold in the chill wind, let go and fell to the ground.

In all that shore country, which is a very special country where things are different from city and town things, only the old ocean was unchanged. There it was, as blue as blue and reaching away forever to the edge of the sky. And when you looked at it you were glad that even if winter were coming the great water would still be there, and its waves would still come rolling in on the sandy beach. But if you put your foot in the water, or your hand, then you would know that something had happened since summer.

Now Mr. Lobster, who was known far and wide as The Curious Lobster, lived in that ocean. And he was therefore in it all over; so he was sure that something had happened.

Mr. Lobster was in his home under two big rocks at the bottom of the ocean not very far from shore. When he woke up on this particular day his long feelers shivered a little.

"I believe," he said to himself, "that we are going to have the turn of the seasons. This house has been a very handy place because it is easy for me to get from here to shore, where I love to go, and it does not take me long to get from shore to home. And home should be a place not too difficult to reach. Home is too important to be far away. But I am afraid that I am living so near the shore that the change of seasons will bring cold water here, and I hate water that's too cold. A wise creature always prepares for necessary changes, and since I am wise I must think about preparing. I may even have to move for the winter."

It occurred to Mr. Lobster that he could think just as well if he were walking, and he might meet a pleasant creature, such as a small fish, which would serve for breakfast. So he left his home and his seaweed garden and crawled along the bottom of the ocean.

As he crawled he realized that he was quite hungry, and he began to look carefully about for dabs, flounders, perch, or stray clams. In fact, he looked so carefully and thought so hard about breakfast that he forgot all about the coming of winter and preparations for moving.

He made several very fast rushes, and he tail-snapped backwards with amazing speed for a lobster sixty-eight years old when he thought he saw a shark, so that, generally speaking, he felt unusually strong and well. And when he had met several pleasant creatures—to be exact, two dabs and two small flounders, he felt even better.

Just at the moment when he felt that it was not necessary to look for any more breakfast along came his old acquaintance the sculpin, looking extremely sulky, which made his ugliness even uglier than ever—and that is saying a good deal. For an instant Mr. Lobster had hopes that the sculpin was too cross to speak to him, because Mr. Lobster did not enjoy speaking with cross creatures. But the old fish came right up and, without the slightest courtesy, not even a good-morning greeting, said:

"Well, Mr. Lobster, it is a wonder you are not walking around on dry land this morning." The sculpin had never gotten over the fact that Mr. Lobster had learned to go ashore, and whenever he thought about it he was angry because he could not go ashore, too. So the tone that he used now was not a pleasant one.

"Good morning," said Mr. Lobster, who was too wise to be discourteous. "I am afraid I shall not be going ashore again for some time."

"Afraid, indeed!" If the sculpin had had a nose he would have sniffed. As it was, he blew several impolite bubbles. "May I ask why, if you don't mind talking with one who merely remains in the ocean where he is supposed to remain—and where you should remain?"

The sculpin did not say this in a humble tone. On the contrary, he was trying hard to be superior.

"I beg your pardon," replied Mr. Lobster, "but I also consider the ocean my home. The mere fact that I have had many delightful times ashore with my friends this summer does not change my feeling about home. Home is the same, no matter where you go. The reason I shall not go ashore any more is that it is cold weather there now, and my friends, Mr. Badger and Mr. Bear, are no longer there to meet me."

"Ah, so they have gone away." The sculpin was actually pleased that Mr. Lobster's land friends were gone.

"Well, you might say so," said Mr. Lobster.

"I might? Now what do you mean by that?"

"They are not really gone," explained Mr. Lobster. "They are hibernating."

"Oh!" The sculpin was immediately unpleasant again —more unpleasant than ever. For he didn't know what Mr. Lobster meant, and if there is anything superior

"AFRAID, INDEED!" THE SCULPIN BLEW SEVERAL IMPOLITE
BUBBLES.

creatures dislike, it is to find out that there is something they don't know. So he scowled terribly; but he remained silent, as he did not want to ask Mr. Lobster to explain, which would reveal his ignorance. And then he waved his huge fins and sailed away without a sound. As he went, he stirred up a good deal of sand in Mr. Lobster's face, apparently on purpose.

Mr. Lobster, now that he was alone again, dismissed the sculpin from his mind. He realized that he had not been thinking about preparations for winter at all.

"It's strange," he said to himself, "but when I am very hungry I find it hard to think about anything but eating, even if there are other important matters to be considered. I wonder if that's so with all creatures." And that thought made him curious to know what other creatures thought about it, and he wished that he could ask Mr. Badger, who always had an answer for any question. It made him sad to think that he would not see Mr. Badger again until spring.

While he was still being curious and somewhat sad, the sculpin came swimming back. He had decided that he would have to ask Mr. Lobster, after all.

"What is hibernating?" he demanded.

"Hibernating is sleeping," answered Mr. Lobster politely, just as if the sculpin had also been polite. Mr. Lobster always pretended that other people were polite, for he had discovered that if only one person is impolite there is not much trouble caused by it, but if two people are impolite things are very difficult.

"Then why didn't you say 'sleeping' in the first place?" snapped the sculpin.

"But it means sleeping all winter," said Mr. Lobster.

"What! Night and day?"

"Yes."

"And not ever eating?"

"Not eating a thing."

"Then it is absurd, and I don't believe it. If you did that you'd be gone."

"Well, Mr. Badger and Mr. Bear do it all winter," said Mr. Lobster.

"Then they're gone, aren't they?"

"Not really gone," replied Mr. Lobster, "because they told me that they would be back in the spring of the year."

"Nonsense, I should say!" This time the sculpin blew bubbles of satisfaction and superior knowledge. "You will see that they won't ever come back. You can't go all winter without eating and not be gone."

Mr. Lobster straightened out the joints in his tail and shell so that he looked as big and important as possible. He was somewhat angry himself now.

"I am sorry to disagree with you," he said calmly, "but my friends are both heroes, and heroes always tell the truth, and Mr. Badger and Mr. Bear both promised me that they would return. Besides, they have tried hibernating before, and they have always come back. So I guess they will this time."

"Anyway, the whole thing is absurd!" The sculpin was

surrounded by bubbles, and they weren't pleasant bubbles either.

"Nothing a hero does is absurd," declared Mr. Lobster.
"And now I think I shall be going home."

He gave an extra hard tail-snap, which left the sculpin
yards away, and then turned and started for home.

As soon as he started he realized once more that he
must think about moving. First his breakfast and then the
sculpin had driven that really important matter from his
mind. And he knew very well by the feeling of his shell
and joints that the water was getting colder and that soon
it would be altogether too cold for him. There was no
doubt now that he must move out into deeper water for
the winter. It was the one thing he had failed to consider
in the spring when he had moved into the home where
he now lived.

When he saw the two big rocks, which were such sure
protection, and the lovely seaweed garden, which was
such a delight to the eye, a feeling of real sorrow settled
upon him. He was suddenly unhappier than he had been
for a long time, a most unusual feeling for him to have
just after a good breakfast. In fact, it was an unusual feeling for him to have at any time, for he was so curious
that he was always trying to satisfy his curiosity. Of
course that kept him busy and got him into adventures,
and he usually had no time to be unhappy. As he had said
to himself more than once, "In order to be really unhappy you have to sit down and think about it, and I
haven't time to do that, and I am too wise to do it, even

if I did have time." Which is just one of many things which show how wise Mr. Lobster was.

But now he was unhappy, and there was no denying it. "I love my home," he said to himself, "and now I've got to move out. I wonder if there is anything worse than moving out of home. If there were only some way to avoid it..."

He went slowly past his seaweed garden and settled himself down inside his home to think. For a good many hours he thought and thought very patiently and very thoroughly. And then, when it seemed as though there were no more ideas left to think about, he had a wonderful thought.

"Hibernating is the thing!" he exclaimed. "If I hibernate I'll be asleep, and I won't know whether the water is cold or not. And I won't have to leave home, because I can hibernate right here."

And immediately he was happy.

"Tomorrow," he told himself, "I shall go out and look for several pleasant creatures. Then, when I have eaten well, I shall come home and hibernate until spring. I shall be the first lobster ever to do such a thing. I wonder what it will be like. Already I am curious about it."

The next day the water was even colder than before, but Mr. Lobster pretended that he did not notice it at all. He spent most of the day looking for pleasant creatures. Then, when the green daylight under the ocean began to fade, he hurried home. First he placed stones and sand in front of the entrance of his home to make a wall, so that it could be plainly seen that he did not wish to be disturbed. Then he climbed over into the most comfortable corner of his home, squddled down into the sand, and prepared to sleep.

All was dark.

"I shall hibernate until the water is warm and Mr. Badger and Mr. Bear come out again," he said to himself confidently. And with that happy thought he went to sleep.

In the morning, when the sunshine coming down through the green water revealed his house and his wall and his seaweed garden as plain as could be, just as it did every bright morning, Mr. Lobster thought that he must be awake. A lobster, you know, never closes his eyes, even when he sleeps; so he could not help seeing things. In fact, at first, when he saw all the things he knew so well, he was greatly worried.

"No," he said to himself, "I am not awake. I cannot be awake. I am hibernating, and so I must be asleep."

And he did not move at all.

When the light grew brighter, and he could see each little leaf in his seaweed garden, and see how brown they were, now that cold weather had come, he said to himself: "I am asleep. I am asleep. I am hibernating for the winter."

And he did not move at all, because he knew that if he moved he would be awake.

In the afternoon he had a feeling in a certain place under his shell, a kind of hollow feeling that he had known many times before.

"I am not hungry," he told himself very firmly. "I cannot be hungry because I am asleep. And oh, how pleasant it is to be asleep for the entire winter. How pleasant to be in my own home instead of having to move."

He had to say those words to himself a good many times, because the feeling under his shell was really not pleasant at all. Moreover, it seemed to be an unusually long day, so long that he began to wonder whether he could possibly sleep all winter long.

But finally the light faded and darkness came, and gradually everything was gone but the night.

The second day was even longer than the first, and much harder.

In the first place, not very long after the light came, several small fish just the right size for breakfast went swimming past Mr. Lobster's front door. When he saw them the hollow feeling under his shell immediately became much worse than it had been the day before.

"If I did not know I was asleep," he said to himself, "I should think I was good and hungry. But those fish must be just a dream. All that I see must be a dream, but I do wish it wouldn't be so dreadfully real. I wonder what Mr. Badger does when he hibernates, and if he gets hungry while he is asleep, and if he has such dreams . . . Dear me, dreams can be so troublesome."

In truth, Mr. Lobster was not happy, and not to be happy in your own home is to be miserable. So Mr. Lobster was miserable.

And then, to make things still worse, the water was

much colder than it had been before, and the cold began to creep in between the joints of Mr. Lobster's shell. His feelers were almost numb, and no matter how tightly he curled his tail, he grew colder and colder all over.

By the time night came he felt that he had passed the longest and coldest day of his life.

"I hope," he said to himself, "that the beginning of hibernating is the worst, and that from now on it will be pleasant. How can it be so uncomfortable to be asleep?"

He was still firmly resolved to hibernate, but as he lay still and shivered in the darkness he was just a little afraid. He wondered if he might not starve or freeze before spring. It was a dreadful thought. But still he did not move at all.

A Serious Mistake
Is Corrected

SOMEHOW THE long cold night passed. When morning came, and Mr. Lobster saw that all was the same as
the day before and the water colder than ever, he began
to despair. He again thought of the dangers of starving
and freezing if it should be true that he was not really
asleep.

"I suppose I must be patient," he thought. "It always
takes time to learn new things."

So he still lay without moving. And he wondered just
how much colder the water would feel in his dreams,

and how hungry he could dream he was, and how very real and unpleasant dreams could be.

While he was going over these things in his mind he saw a familiar face looking over his wall and peering into his home. There was the sculpin.

"Good morning," said the sculpin. "So you are still here, although a codfish told me yesterday that all the lobsters had moved into deep water for the winter. Do you mind telling me just why you are hiding?"

Somehow the tone of the sculpin's voice and the superior look on his ugly face just at the moment when Mr. Lobster was suffering from cold and hunger made Mr. Lobster angry, and he answered before he remembered that he was asleep.

"I am not hiding!" he exclaimed. "I am hibernating!"

"What nonsense!" replied the sculpin scornfully. "Do you take me for a complete fool? If you are hibernating, you are asleep. You said so yourself. And if you are asleep, how can you talk? Pooh! I thought that this hibernating business was all a lie. Now I know it!" And with several bubbles of superiority and disgust the sculpin turned and swam away.

Mr. Lobster was left feeling completely miserable.

"I am not asleep at all," he said to himself. "The sculpin is right. And I am not hibernating either. All I am doing is starving and freezing. I have made a terribly serious mistake, for I should have been in deep water days ago."

He slowly uncurled his tail and moved his legs and began to crawl out of the sand.

"This is a great disappointment," he went on, "but the only thing to do when you have a disappointment is to think about something else. I shall think about having breakfast right away. I am two days late for it already."

So he left the home he loved and started to look for dabs and flounders. He did not go north toward the mouth of the river, nor west toward the shore. He did not go south toward Cape Cod, which was also shore. Very bravely, and without looking back, he started for deep water, which was east, toward the middle of the ocean. He knew that this time he was leaving his home for a long time.

He was sad as he crawled along the bottom of the ocean, even though he tried to think only of his breakfast and of the next spring when he could return to his home and go ashore and see his friends. Even after he had met several pleasant creatures, and the hollow feeling under his shell was gone, he still kept thinking of his home and his serious mistake.

"The water is now so cold I may not be able to get away," he said to himself. "I am probably in danger. And I have certainly had a complete failure....Well, I must not think of the past, and my failure is already in the past. A wise person does not think of the past except to remember pleasant things. Now what shall I remember?" Then he began to think of happy things like the picnic he had had with Mr. Badger and Mr. Bear, and how Mr. Badger had called him a hero. Soon he forgot to be unhappy, and was crawling along at a very good speed.

It was difficult for Mr. Lobster to be unhappy very long, anyway, not only because of his wisdom, but because he was so curious as he traveled that he was careful to see everything he passed; and that kept him always interested. And when you're interested, you are happy.

He passed beautiful gardens of seaweed, big boulders and caves, and two old wrecks of boats that had sunk many years ago. There were starfish and crabs and huge sea snails moving about. There were many fish, too, some of them so big that when he saw them he kept very still until they had passed by, but most of them friendly cod and haddock who were glad to stop and pass the time of day with him and wish him a pleasant winter.

Although he knew that the water was bitter cold and that he must keep moving as fast as possible, he did not allow himself to worry or to be afraid.

"I am doing the best I can to correct my mistake," he said to himself. "After all, this is really a very fine ocean that I live in."

At night, cold and tired, but satisfied that he had traveled a long distance, he rested under a large boulder covered with periwinkles and barnacles. In the morning he started out again very early, still going into deeper and deeper water. All the time he was getting further and further away from the daylight, and he knew that in another day or two he would be down deep where it would be dark and warm. There he would spend the winter.

The second afternoon the going was harder than the day before, because the bottom of the ocean was hilly,

and he found that he was getting tired from his steady
crawling. So, although he knew that he ought not to rest
very long, he stopped beside a large area of seaweed and
just lay there looking around.

He had been there only a short time when a huge
round form came drifting down through the water, wav-
ing its flippers in lazy fashion until it rested on the bottom. At first Mr. Lobster was fearful because of the size
of the creature, but when it came near him he saw that it
was an enormous sea turtle, and he knew that turtles
were usually friendly.

"Good afternoon," he said.

"Yes, yes, indeed," agreed the turtle. "You are Mr.
Lobster, I believe. I've seen a good many of your relatives, but you are the biggest I've seen yet. Very fitting,
indeed. Very fitting that we should meet."

"Thank you," said Mr. Lobster. "And you are the biggest turtle I have ever seen."

"Only the simple truth, the simple truth," murmured
the turtle. "I love to have people speak to me frankly, and
of course I am well aware of my size. You don't see many
like me, they all say. But I don't let that go to my head,
and I don't boast about it. In fact, when people flatter me
I just pull my head and flippers in and refuse to have
anything to do with them. Nothing like being a turtle;
you can always go away without moving. Yes, it's a lovely
afternoon. I've just been floating around for a while on
top of the water. I'm going south, you see; always go
south for the winter; and I'm just browsing about a bit

before I go. Never do anything in a hurry, I say. What do you say?"

"Oh, I agree," said Mr. Lobster. "That is, unless there is danger."

"Danger, did you say?" asked the turtle. He waved one flipper in a negligent fashion, then scratched his neck for a moment, and went on. "I don't know the meaning of the word. Are you out for a little crawl, Mr. Lobster, or are you exploring?"

"I am going into deep water for the winter."

"I see. I see. Pity you lobsters don't go south. Personally, I'm spending the winter at Bermuda this year. Nothing like an island, I say. An island or exploring—they're practically the same thing, of course. That's why I thought you might be out exploring this afternoon. Good afternoon for exploring."

Mr. Lobster was somewhat confused, not only by what the turtle was saying, but because the turtle talked so fast.

"I am afraid I don't understand," he said. "Did you say an island and exploring were the same thing?"

"Oh, yes, yes, indeed. Practically speaking. That is, they accomplish the same thing, you know."

The turtle was so good-natured and easy-going, and not in the least bit superior in manner, that it was impossible to be angry with him, even if he did speak as though he thought he knew everything.

"Perhaps," said Mr. Lobster, "I am exploring, as I am looking for a new home for the winter."

"Not what I meant at all, not at all!" exclaimed the turtle. "Exploring isn't looking for things half so much as it is an excuse for getting away from things. Explorers are always looking for places where there aren't any other people. Just like an island. When you find an island, no one can bother you. What kind of a place do you want for a home?"

"Well, I think a kind of cave under a rock," answered Mr. Lobster. "I have just had that kind of a home, and I was very happy there. I should be traveling now, but I stopped to rest because I was tired."

"Easy, very easy." The turtle was lazily scratching himself again. "Don't you worry a bit about it. I know some excellent places not very far from here. Wouldn't take us more than a day or two at the most. Besides, I'm in no hurry. There's no sense in hurrying, no sense at all. So you just go ahead and rest all you want; and we'll start in the morning. Nothing like a good rest when you feel the need of it. I often rest for days at a time. Keeps me from feeling my age. I'm two hundred and twenty now, and you'd never know I was more than a hundred. Well, I'll take a nap myself now. I'll see you in the morning."

With those words the talkative turtle pulled in his head until it was out of sight, tucked in his flippers, and looked just like an old shell with nobody at home in it.

Mr. Lobster was a bit out of breath just from listening; he had never before met a creature who talked so much. Also, he was tired from his long crawl. So he took the turtle's advice and spent a quiet night right where he was, although he dreamed that the turtle was talking very fast and that he couldn't understand a word that was being said.

In the morning he ventured along the borders of the seaweed to look for breakfast. When he returned, the turtle had put his head out and was looking around.

"Good morning, good morning," he said by way of greeting. "Thought you must have gotten lost. Looked all around and didn't see a sign of you."

"I've been getting breakfast," explained Mr. Lobster.

"Good idea. Very good idea. Personally, I don't bother about breakfast. I often go for weeks at a time without eating. Personally, I'm tired of it. Been eating the same things for over two hundred years, you see. Are you ready to travel? Call it exploring for you if you want to; won't be for me, of course, because I've been there before. I'll show you around this part of the ocean."

"I am all ready to go," said Mr. Lobster, "but I am afraid I shan't be able to go as fast as you can."

"Oh, I've thought of that. There never was a lobster who could travel as fast as I can—if you don't mind my saying so. But what's the use of hurrying, as I may have said before. Hurrying is all right if you do it just for fun, but it's terrible if you have to. Hard on the nerves. You wouldn't think I had any nerves, to look at me, but I'm positive I have; so I've always been careful not to arouse them." The talkative turtle reached out one flipper, then another. "I feel fine," he said. "Now you just climb up on my back, and hook your claws onto the edge of my shell.

Hang on as hard as you want to—you can't hurt my shell. Jump on!"

Mr. Lobster obeyed at once. He had never ridden on a turtle's back, and he was curious to see what it would be like.

"Are you ready?" asked the turtle.

"All ready," answered Mr. Lobster.

"Here we go, then. First I'm going up to the surface of the water, if you don't mind. Take a look at the weather, you know, and get some fresh air."

And with that the turtle's great flippers began to move, his neck stuck out straight, and he went up through the water so fast and so straight that he was nearly on end. If Mr. Lobster hadn't been holding on tightly he would have fallen off backwards. At the surface of the ocean the weather was cold, but the sky was blue and the sun shining brightly. While Mr. Lobster just looked around, the turtle took several deep breaths.

"Beautiful day, beautiful day," he said. "I do delight in fine weather. Hang on now, and we'll start for your cave."

He went down faster than he had come up, and when he was near the bottom he pointed his head toward the east and began swimming along so fast that Mr. Lobster's feelers were blown out behind him, and the water rushed past him as though he were flying through it. It was all a strange experience for Mr. Lobster, who, for all his great age and wisdom, was what you would call a rather slow traveler.

THE TURTLE SWAM SO FAST THAT MR. LOBSTER'S
FEELERS WERE BLOWN OUT BEHIND HIM.

Whenever they came to a great rock or a hill the turtle pointed his head up and they sailed up over without the slightest effort. Mr. Lobster realized that such obstacles would have delayed him seriously if he had been crawling along the bottom in his usual fashion. For some time after they started he was so busy hanging on to the edge of the turtle's shell that he scarcely had a chance to look around, but as soon as he got used to the speed he began to enjoy the experience tremendously.

"It is just the way the birds sail through the air," he said to himself, remembering how he had watched the sea gulls when he had been ashore. "I suppose that I am the first lobster ever to travel this way. It seems to me there is always something new to learn, and I do hope I never get too old to enjoy new things."

The turtle, without slowing up in the least, turned his neck around so that he was facing Mr. Lobster and said, "Easy, isn't it? Just hang on and go where you want to without any trouble. Nothing like it, I say. Nothing like it."

"I thought you said you didn't believe in hurrying," remarked Mr. Lobster.

"Hurrying? Who said I was hurrying? This is just the way I go when I am wandering about. What I call cruising speed, you know. You lobsters don't know anything about speed, if you don't mind my saying so. Would you like to have me hurry?"

"No, thank you. I'm afraid I would not have any breath left if you went any faster," said Mr. Lobster quickly.

"Just a little dash of speed?" asked the turtle.

"Oh, no, thank you!"

"Well, if you insist. But some time I would like to show you some real speed. Just for fun, you know. I wouldn't think of hurrying except for fun. Have to think of my nerves, you know. Never know when they'll kick up if you're not careful."

So they went on and on at the same speed until late in the afternoon, when the turtle slowed up considerably and began to look around as though he had entered a region he had known before.

Soon he called out to Mr. Lobster.

"I know where we are now," he said, "and we are coming to a fine cave." He went up over a tremendous rock, then down to the bottom on the other side and stopped. "Have a look around," he said. "If you don't like this one I'll show you some others. No hurry, you know. No hurry at all. We'll wander about for another day or two if you'd like to, and I'll show you all the caves in the neighborhood."

Mr. Lobster straightened out his feelers in front of him for the first time since he had started his ride. Then he crawled down from the turtle's back and looked around him. Sure enough, there was a small cave under the big rock they had just come over. He crawled to the entrance, explored it with his feelers very carefully, then turned around and backed in. He always preferred to back into a strange cave. Then, if there wasn't room enough to turn around after he got in, he could still crawl out easily and see what he was doing. The dangerous thing was to have to come out of a cave backwards, because he never knew what kind of fish might be waiting around a cave entrance.

When he found himself inside this cave he was pleased to see that it had a smooth, sandy floor and just enough room for him to turn around in comfortably. And there were rock walls on all sides, which made it seem safe. He decided at once that he could be nearly as happy here as he had been in his other home near shore. So he went out to the turtle again and told him that the cave was all right.

"That's fine, that's fine," said the talkative creature. "Though I did sort of hope we could wander about a bit more. I find I like your company, if you don't mind my saying so. But if you're satisfied, I might just as well start for Bermuda. The weather looked cold, and I guess there's no use hanging around in these parts any longer."

"I am very grateful to you," said Mr. Lobster with his customary courtesy. "You have been very kind to me, and you have done me a great service."

"Glad you feel that way, of course," said the turtle, "but don't let it worry you. Pleasure for me to meet you, you know. I've enjoyed the little trip myself. And any time you're out exploring or happen to be around an island, look for me and maybe we'll meet again. Don't forget—there's nothing like exploring and islands!"

With that last bit of advice he started off. Soon he was out of sight, and Mr. Lobster realized that he was alone again, that not even the sculpin could bother him here, and that his winter in deep water had really begun.

After being with such a friendly creature as the talkative turtle Mr. Lobster felt somewhat lonely, although he had been accustomed to living alone for years and years. He knew that the winter would seem very quiet and unexciting after his summer with Mr. Badger and Mr. Bear.

"Oh, well," he said to himself, "a fact is a fact, and no getting around it. So there's nothing to do but settle down and wait for spring."

And that is just what he did.

Three Good Friends
Meet Again

THERE IS very little to be said about Mr. Lobster's winter, for life in the dark, deep part of the ocean, where his new cave was, turned out to be very quiet and unexciting. Mr. Lobster explored the territory surrounding his cave, discovered where the small fish and sea clams lived, and did some traveling. But mostly he preferred to spend a restful winter, waiting for warm weather and the time when he could return to his home near shore. He did make one new friend, a large old horseshoe crab who had lived in those parts for many years, but as the crab was a born wanderer and often disappeared for days or weeks at a time, they did not see each other very often.

But winter, like all the other things of nature, cannot stay forever. It must change and give way to spring, so that life can begin again, and all things and creatures under the sun and in the great waters can feel the new year and be glad and eager to grow and move and have new experiences.

So a day came when even deep down in the ocean there was a feeling of change in the water. It would be impossible to say whether Mr. Lobster felt it first in the joints of his shell or in the ends of his long feelers. He did not know himself. Perhaps it was just a pleasant feeling that stole over him, a feeling that it was time for something to happen, something that would have a happy ending. Perhaps things under the ocean smelled different and new, the way the earth does when spring comes. Anyway, the minute Mr. Lobster woke up on this morning and crawled to the entrance of his cave he felt certain that it was time for him to move, and he was happy. He was immediately eager to return to his real home.

Of course he started at once. For several days he crawled along the bottom of the ocean, traveling not nearly so fast as he had on the talkative turtle's back, but going steadily toward the west, where the shore was. And finally, late one afternoon as the light was fading, he saw a familiar sight which gave him the greatest joy. There were the two big rocks where his real home was.

There was the seaweed garden with new green leaves sprouting and everything looking fine and fresh.

For several minutes he just stayed still, gazing at the place he loved.

"Coming home is such a wonderful feeling," he said to himself. "So wonderful that I can't describe it. I can only feel it."

Then he entered his home, cleaned out a few old leaves of seaweed that had drifted in during the winter, and began one of the happiest nights of his life.

"I am glad now that I didn't hibernate after all," he thought, "because if I had, there wouldn't have been any returning. And returning is what starts everything off right again. It sort of makes old things new, you are so glad to see them again."

The next morning he went for a long crawl, looking over all that region which he knew so well, and getting even more pleasure from it than if it had been a brand new place he had never seen before. There were the hills and hollows where he had looked for breakfast many a time, and there were patches of seaweed and old shells that were almost as pleasant to see as old friends.

Thinking it over as he returned home, he said to himself wisely: "Old things and places newly discovered are better than really new ones because there are memories to go with them. I am sure that is why I like this place better than any other, for there is nothing more pleasant than happy memories."

For a few days he spent his time near home. This was the season when he usually shed his shell and grew larger, and he was waiting for the feeling that would tell him he must hide away until he had a new hard shell that would be sure protection. It was always easy to tell when the time had come, for he would feel like growing bigger, and when a lobster grows bigger he must get out of his old shell or else there is no way for his body to grow. When a lobster gets so big that he stops growing, he does not shed his shell again, because there is no need to.

This year Mr. Lobster knew that he was so big and so old that it would not be strange if he did not grow any more but kept his old shell for the rest of his life. But he wanted very much to have at least one more new shell, for he had not forgotten the large red spot on his old shell caused by his terrible experience before Mr. Bear became his friend.

"And besides," he thought, "I do so much want to be sixty-nine years old. That will be a perfect age, and yet I can't really say I am a year older unless I shed my shell; so if I don't shed now I shall be only sixty-eight forever. And sixty-nine is the age of wisdom and serenity."

So he waited patiently, although he was anxious to go up the river and find Mr. Badger and Mr. Bear.

After almost a week he was delighted one morning to wake up and feel like growing. He knew exactly what to do. He lay very quietly in the darkest, softest corner of his home and began first with his two big pincher claws.

Slowly and carefully he drew those in toward his body, pulling them right out of the shells that covered them and not moving the heavy shells at all. Next he drew up all his feet the same way. When that was done the shells of his big claws and little claws were absolutely empty.

For several minutes he rested. Then he folded up his tail as tightly as possible and humped up his back so that his back shell and tail shell were very tight, like a piece of clothing that is too small. When they were as tight as could be, he just bent his back and spread his body and all his muscles, making them as big as possible.

Crack! The old shell split right down the middle of his stomach, clear to the end of it, and he pulled out his tail and crawled out of the old shell and over to the other side of his cave. The old shell was left behind on the sand, looking almost like another lobster there.

"Now," he said to himself, "I am sixty-nine years old. I am very happy."

Of course, now that he had no shell at all he dared not leave his home, for a lobster without his shell has no protection from large fish or other unpleasant creatures that might be hungry. So Mr. Lobster remained hidden in his home while his new shell, which was at first as soft as skin, grew hard.

It was several days before he was ready to go out. His new shell was a beautiful dark blue-green, without any red spots, and with only a suggestion of orange at the very edges. Mr. Lobster was indeed handsome, for a new shell is always perfect and shiny, and this shell was the

best and shiniest he had ever had. And besides, although
there were quite a few red lobsters in the ocean, he had
always preferred to be a green one; so he was proud of
his fine color.

He knew right away what he would do. First he would
enjoy a pleasant crawl from his home to the place where
the tide flowed into the river. Then he would go in with
the tide, just as he had the summer before, and go ashore
to find Mr. Badger and Mr. Bear.

When he had almost reached the place where the tide
began, he felt a movement behind him in the water, as
though someone were coming along in a great hurry. He
stopped to look around, and there was the sculpin, that
old fish who thought that he was the most important and
superior creature in that part of the ocean.

"I believe it is Mr. Lobster," said the sculpin in a not
exactly friendly tone. He was looking hard at Mr. Lobster's beautiful new shell.

"Good morning," said Mr. Lobster cheerfully. He was
perfectly aware how magnificent he was, and well
pleased with himself to be in such excellent condition
when the sculpin came along.

Poor sculpin! Of course, he was wearing his same old
skin. He had had it for years, and each hard winter had
made it look a little worse. So you can't blame him if he
felt somewhat unhappy and cross at the sight of Mr. Lobster's gorgeous new shell.

"It's just like every other morning as far as I can see,"
said the sculpin.

"I have just gotten a new shell," said Mr. Lobster, "and I am about to go in with the tide and travel up the river."

The sculpin blew a bubble about the size of a loud grunt. Or perhaps it was a snort.

"I wouldn't put on airs if I were you," he said.

"Pardon me, but I am not doing anything of the kind," said Mr. Lobster briskly. "I hope it is not wrong for me to enjoy a new shell while it is still new. I believe in taking simple pleasures as they come, and enjoying them to the full. Also, I am now sixty-nine years old, and I take some little pleasure in that."

"I call that bragging," protested the sculpin. "However, if you persist in going ashore on dry land this year as you did last, it is likely that you will never have another year to brag about."

"Pardon me again," said Mr. Lobster, and he spoke with considerable firmness, "but bragging is not what you say. It is how you say it. And I never say things in that unpleasant and superior manner. Now I must be going."

"Are you going ashore?"

"Yes, I believe I am."

"Will you never learn to stay in the ocean where you belong?" The sculpin spoke angrily.

"Let us be friendly," said Mr. Lobster politely. "My curiosity will not allow me to stay in one place, you know. And my curiosity has brought me the greatest happiness. If we can be friends, I shall tell you all about what I discover ashore this year."

With those words he began to crawl away from the

sculpin. Soon he felt the flow of the tide and knew that he was started for the river.

He had made so many trips up the river the summer before that now he felt like an old hand at traveling with the tide. And how happy he was! He was back in the part of the ocean he loved; he had his own home again; and he was sixty-nine years old and beautiful to behold.

"I suppose very few people have so many things to be happy about as I have," he said to himself as he went along. "And on top of everything I am on my way to see Mr. Badger and Mr. Bear. This is one of the times when everything is just perfect. I shall always remember this day, if there comes a time when I am discontented. A good day should always be stored away for future use."

When he had gone so far up the river, a distance which he knew by his feelers must be right, he went to the top of the water very cautiously and looked out with just one eye. What he saw delighted him. For there on the bank were two familiar figures, Mr. Badger and Mr. Bear. They were looking intently down the river and did not see him at all.

Mr. Lobster felt a sudden trembling in the joints of his new shell. He was excited.

But instead of swimming over and speaking to his friends at once, he thought that he would surprise them. Mr. Badger always appreciated jokes and surprises. So he sank under water where they could not see him and then crawled along the bottom of the river until he was directly under the bank where Mr. Badger and Mr. Bear were sitting. Then he came to the surface very slowly and lay still, being so close to the bank that Mr. Badger and Mr. Bear did not know he was there.

For a moment he lay there listening.

"The tide is almost full," said Mr. Badger, "and yet I see no signs of Mr. Lobster."

"This is the third day we have waited here," said Mr. Bear. "And I feel worse every day. I was really very fond of Mr. Lobster."

"Well, aren't you still fond of him?"

"You can't be fond of anyone who isn't any more." Mr. Bear's tone was sad. "It's always that way. All good things have to end."

"That's nonsense!" exclaimed Mr. Badger. "Good things are always beginning. Thinking of the end just spoils things. I always think of the beginning."

Mr. Bear sighed unhappily.

"Sometimes," he said sadly, "even the beginning is bad. Now here is this summer beginning without Mr. Lobster, and that is very bad."

"That's nonsense, too!" Mr. Badger spoke sharply. "There isn't any beginning to anything worthwhile until something good has happened. So this summer simply has not begun."

Mr. Bear was silent.

Mr. Lobster thought that it would be mean to keep his friends waiting any longer. So he made a great splashing with his tail, and then he tried to make a sound like one of Mr. Bear's growls.

"What was that?" exclaimed Mr. Badger.

"Trouble probably," said Mr. Bear. "It sounded just like trouble. I'm going home."

Then Mr. Lobster spoke.

"Good day, Mr. Badger. Good day, Mr. Bear."

And he floated out where they could see him.

"Mr. Lobster!" cried Mr. Badger happily. "Playing a trick on us, as I live! Good for you! I knew you would come back! I knew it! Do come ashore!"

Mr. Lobster swam over to a low part of the bank and crawled up to the meadow beside Mr. Badger and Mr. Bear. The bright sun shone on his new shell, and he looked very imposing and bigger than ever before. He could not help feeling just a bit proud of his first appearance of the year before his two friends.

"A brand new shell!" exclaimed Mr. Badger.

"Yes, and I am sixty-nine years old now." Mr. Lobster tried to speak with due modesty.

"And a great deal bigger, too," said Mr. Badger quickly. "It's a good thing I did not have to pull you out with my tail this time. I never could have done it. Never. Well, I've never been happier in my whole life than I am at this moment. Now there is a beginning to the summer."

Then Mr. Badger looked over at Mr. Bear and went on talking, this time to Mr. Bear.

"You are always so gloomy if things don't happen just at the minute you want them to," he said. "I told you Mr. Lobster was not gone. Mr. Lobster is too much of a hero to be gone. I don't believe he ever will be gone."

"MR. LOBSTER!" CRIED MR. BADGER HAPPILY.
"I KNEW YOU WOULD COME BACK!"

Mr. Badger had been talking so fast and so happily that neither Mr. Lobster nor Mr. Bear had had a chance to get in a word.

And now Mr. Bear gave a growl.

"If you would stop talking, I would like a moment of peace," he said crossly. "Of course, I am not important at all, but I would like to tell Mr. Lobster that I am glad to see him too."

"Why, you are the biggest hero of us all, you know," said Mr. Lobster to Mr. Bear, "and I shall never forget that last summer would have been my last and I never would have been sixty-nine or had a new shell if it had not been for you."

Mr. Bear looked happier. Praise was sweet to him, and praise from a creature as wise as Mr. Lobster was especially pleasant to hear.

"There!" he said to Mr. Badger.

"There, indeed," said Mr. Badger, and then he chuckled. "But you did insist on being miserable every day that Mr. Lobster did not appear."

"I believe in facing facts," said Mr. Bear seriously. "And it was a fact that Mr. Lobster was not here."

"A fact is something you can't change," observed Mr Lobster.

"Very true," agreed Mr. Badger, "but there are just as many happy facts as unhappy ones. So I believe in facing the happy ones and turning my back on all the others. If I just don't happen to think of a specially happy fact, I make a wish and think about that."

"Well, I learned one fact last winter," said Mr. Lobster, "and that was that I did not succeed in hibernating. But tell me, did you have a pleasant winter, Mr. Bear?"

Mr. Bear sighed rather wistfully.

"Oh, yes," he answered. "I dreamed all winter of fried fish and honey."

"I dreamed of adventures," said Mr. Badger. "Heroic adventures! It is a wonderful way to pass the time when everything is cold and the world is covered with snow."

"Snow?" said Mr. Lobster. "I've never heard of that before. Would you mind explaining?"

"I am glad to say I have never seen any snow," put in Mr. Bear. "I understand that it is very cold and not good to eat; so evidently it is perfectly useless."

"I saw some once," said Mr. Badger. "One spring when I woke up early I found it in the deep woods. I walked in it and got my feet cold because they sank right in. I should say snow is a kind of white mud."

"White mud!" exclaimed Mr. Lobster. "I didn't know there was such a thing. And does it cover all the earth?"

"That's what the permanent partridge told me. He never hibernates; so he has seen a great deal of snow. Someone puts it down in the winter and takes it away in the spring."

"It must take a lot of work," remarked Mr. Bear, feeling glad that he did not have to do it.

"It must be a mystery," observed Mr. Lobster. "Like the tide and the wind. The older I get the more I realize that there are many mysteries in the world; and I like to think about them."

The three friends were silent for a moment, thinking of mysteries.

Then Mr. Bear spoke up:

"I must begin to think of my supper."

"The tide has turned, and I must return home," said Mr. Lobster.

"Let us all meet on the beach tomorrow," said Mr. Badger.

With that happy thought the friends parted. Mr. Lobster went home to the ocean with the ebbing tide, and all the way he was thinking of snow and being curious about it and at the same time being perfectly happy because he had found his friends.

"There is nothing else like meeting old friends, as I must have said before," he said to himself. "If you have a home you love and true friends who are glad to see you, you have everything, it seems to me. No wonder I am happy."

Mr. Lobster
Has an Idea

AFTER THEIR reunion the three friends passed many happy days on the beach, walking and fishing and enjoying the fine summer weather. Mr. Lobster stayed on shore longer and longer each day until he was just as used to being out of water as he had been the year before. This year it was not as much of an adventure to go ashore because it was not a new experience, and an adventure has to be new. But Mr. Lobster had more confidence than he had had the year before, so he enjoyed every visit with Mr. Badger and Mr. Bear.

On his way home Mr. Lobster usually met the sculpin,

who still considered Mr. Lobster's travels foolish and dangerous but made an effort to be as pleasant as possible.

"It is a good thing for the sculpin to be polite even when he feels cross," said Mr. Lobster to himself. "It strengthens his character and makes other creatures respect him. But I am very curious at times to know what he is thinking about me."

One day the sculpin said:

"It strikes me that you are having a very quiet summer. You are never late getting home, and you seem to have no narrow escapes. Surely all your adventures are not over, are they?"

"I don't know," answered Mr. Lobster. "You really never know about an adventure or a narrow escape until it happens."

"Well, I hope that if you have one you will live through it so that you can tell me about it," said the sculpin in a most serious manner. "I have always felt that when things are especially quiet it is a sign that something is going to happen."

"Not something unpleasant, I hope."

"That depends." The sculpin spread all his fins and tried hard to look wise. "It depends on whether you do dangerous things, such as leaving the ocean, the only really safe place there is."

"I see," said Mr. Lobster. "You still disapprove of my going ashore, don't you?"

"Since you have asked me, I must say I do," replied the sculpin, "but please do not think that I am being disagreeable. As I have said before, it is the duty of a friend to give advice."

"Thank you," said Mr. Lobster. "I am sorry that I can't take your advice if it would make you happier. But I feel that I have not learned all about things ashore yet, and I have not nearly satisfied my curiosity. I am sure that if you are patient I shall have something interesting to tell you. Things have always happened in the past, so I suppose they will keep on happening. How unfortunate it would be if nothing happened!"

With these words, which were the sentiment of Mr. Badger as well as Mr. Lobster, he crawled away home, looked over his seaweed garden, and prepared for a night of contentment and thinking about the morrow.

The next day when he saw Mr. Badger and Mr. Bear he remembered the sculpin's words.

"We are having a very quiet summer," he remarked.

"Too quiet," said Mr. Badger at once. "In fact, I have been thinking for the past few days that we had better have an idea. I am getting restless."

"I'm not," said Mr. Bear, "and before you say anything more I say that this is one of the best summers I have ever had. There has been plenty of food and no danger or hard work. I call that perfect. If you have an idea, there will probably be trouble. You know your ideas are risky."

"Of course they are," agreed Mr. Badger. "What is the use of thinking of ideas unless they may lead to adventures? And how can you have adventures that aren't risky? Now answer me that!"

"My answer is, don't have any ideas." Mr. Bear gave a very small growl.

"A creature as smart as I am can't help having ideas," Mr. Badger said, chuckling. "All smart creatures have ideas. You had better look out if you don't have any. It is a bad sign."

"I confess that I have ideas," Mr. Lobster remarked, "but I haven't any good ones just now."

"Well, I have one!" exclaimed Mr. Badger triumphantly. "It just came to me."

"Tell us!" Mr. Lobster was eager.

"Don't tell us if it's dangerous!" protested Mr. Bear.

"It is probably not dangerous at all," Mr. Badger said calmly. "It is only a small idea to keep us busy until someone thinks of a bigger one. My small idea is this: let us all separate for two or three days and each one make a secret search for something new, something we haven't seen before, or something handy for an adventure. We shall see who brings back the strangest and best thing."

"Can it be anything at all?" asked Mr. Lobster.

"Certainly."

"It sounds silly to me," said Mr. Bear. "It just means that I shall have to spend all my spare time hunting. That will keep me busy, and it is work."

"But you will do it, won't you?" begged Mr. Lobster. "I am already curious to know what you and Mr. Badger will bring. I am sure that it will be something I have never seen before, and that will increase my knowledge."

"Yes," agreed Mr. Bear. "At least it isn't dangerous; so I

will do it. Only you must remember that if trouble comes of it Mr. Badger is to blame."

"Good!" said Mr. Lobster happily. "And now I suppose we must part for three days."

"Wait a minute, please," said Mr. Bear. "As long as this isn't a picnic we don't have to bring our things to a hard place, do we? Let us bring them to the meadow."

"I agree to that," said Mr. Badger.

So it was all settled in a most friendly manner, and Mr. Lobster started for his home.

With three days for searching, Mr. Lobster was determined to find something exceedingly interesting to take ashore; and he began a careful search of the bottom of the ocean, hoping that he would come upon something really new and surprising. His travels were interesting because he always liked to see new places, but, although he spent all the first day searching, the result was very disappointing as a search for new things. He found a huge piece of whale bone, a great anchor lost from a ship, and several of the strange things made of slats in which he had once seen another lobster pulled up through the water. He tried to move each one of these objects, but they were all too heavy for him. With all his strength, he could not even budge them. And most of the movable things, such as seaweed and shells and strange stones, seemed too unimportant to take ashore.

He thought of consulting the sculpin, but as the sculpin disapproved so strongly of going ashore at all it seemed hardly possible that he would be interested in giving any help in the matter.

"I guess I shall have to go ashore on the beach by the cliff, where we have not been this year," Mr. Lobster decided. "The winter storms may have washed something interesting ashore."

So the second day he went ashore on the loneliest part of the beach, first making sure that there were no dangerous-looking creatures in sight. Then he crawled along the beach under the great overhanging cliff, searching the sand and going amongst the rocks, being very careful to look over every inch that he covered.

For a long time he saw nothing but driftwood and stones and a few cans, such things as might be found on any beach. But as he approached the end of the cliff, where the beach ended at the river mouth, he climbed up on a rock to get a better look around, and he spied a large dark object between two boulders. When he hurried over to examine it, he found that it was a large coil of rope in excellent condition. Of course rope was not exactly a new thing, for there had been a short piece tied to the boat in which he and Mr. Badger and Mr. Bear had gone fishing the summer before; but this was a fine piece thirty or forty feet long.

"Surely this will be handy for something," Mr. Lobster said to himself. "It just couldn't help being useful on an adventure, for instance. I shall take it into the ocean and then up the river."

When he took hold of the rope with his big claws he found it most awkward and heavy to move, and he realized at once that it would be impossible for him to drag it all the distance along the bottom of the ocean and the bottom of the river to the meadow.

"I must pull it the way I pulled the boat," he decided.

So he crawled over it and under it and in amongst the coils until he found an end which he could pull. When he pulled on that good and hard the rope unwound, and soon Mr. Lobster was crawling down the beach with the rope like a long tail behind him, and the end of it fast in one of his big claws.

It was slow, hard work, but by keeping at it steadily he succeeded in getting it to the mouth of the river by the end of the afternoon. There he put two big stones on the end so that it would not drift away. Then he went home.

The next day, which was the third and last, and the day on which the three friends were to meet in the afternoon, Mr. Lobster started with the tide to pull his rope up the river. This also proved to be very slow work, for every little while the far-away end of the rope, a long distance behind him, would get heavy; and whenever he went back to see what was the matter there were whole crowds of crabs hanging on and having a ride. Every time he crawled back and scolded them the crabs scurried away, but soon after he started pulling again the rope would once more get heavy, and he would know that the crabs were riding again.

Mr. Lobster was patient with the crabs, who were distant relatives of his, and he kept his temper; but he was rather tired and cross when he finally reached the place where he was going ashore.

"If you ride any further," he told the crabs, "you will find yourselves on dry land, for that is just where I am going."

Then he took the end of the rope in his claw once more, gave a mighty tug, and swam to the bank of the river. There he climbed up a low place in the bank, still holding fast to the rope, and got the end of it safely up on the meadow. Then, still holding it, he decided to rest and wait for his friends.

It was a beautiful day, bright with sunshine, and soon Mr. Lobster was startled by something which flashed and sparkled some distance away in the grass of the meadow. He had never before seen anything like it. Watching closely, he saw that it moved, but it was so bright that it quite dazzled his eyes so that he could not tell the size or shape of what was coming.

"If Mr. Bear were here, he would say it was trouble," he said to himself, "and perhaps it is. But I am curious to know what it is, and I shan't move until I know. Perhaps it is a new kind of creature."

He squddled down in the grass, trembling just a little in his joints, but still watching. As the flashing brightness came nearer, he could see a huge figure behind it, and a noise came over the meadow, a strange noise.

Mr. Lobster began to think that perhaps, after all, he had better return to the bottom of the river, but then he

"IF YOU RIDE ANY FURTHER," HE TOLD THE CRABS,
"YOU WILL FIND YOURSELVES ON DRY LAND."

thought that there was something familiar about the noise. It was muffled and strange, but it was very much like Mr. Bear's worst growls.

Sure enough, behind the bright object came Mr. Bear himself. He was holding the bright object in his teeth, holding his head up to keep the object from bumping along the ground. He growled every step he took, and he squinted so that it looked as if he were making a funny face.

When Mr. Bear saw Mr. Lobster, he stopped at once and set his burden down.

"There now!" he exclaimed proudly. "Did you ever see anything like that? I guess that will be a surprise even to Mr. Badger. I've practically ruined all my teeth getting it here, and I'm nearly blind from the sun."

The object was a glass jug full of a clear liquid, so that the whole thing shone when sunshine struck it.

"What is it?" asked Mr. Lobster.

"I don't know," Mr. Bear answered, "but it is mysterious and new, and it will certainly come in handy. Look. It is as hard as a rock, and yet you can see right through it. Isn't that strange?"

"I never knew there was such a thing," observed Mr. Lobster.

He crawled over and touched the jug with his feelers and big claws.

"It is amazing!"

"It is stupendous!" came a brisk voice behind Mr.

Bear. There was Mr. Badger, looking especially pleased with himself but not carrying a thing.

"Is stupendous more than amazing?" asked Mr. Lobster.

"Much more," answered Mr. Badger.

Mr. Bear was swelling with pride.

"Look carefully," he said. "It is not only stupendous, but it is handy. It is filled with water. Whenever you get thirsty you can drink without having to search for water."

"You have done well," said Mr. Badger. "What did you bring, Mr. Lobster?"

Mr. Lobster pulled the end of his rope and crawled across the meadow until the whole rope was in sight.

"It is not stupendous, I am afraid," he said modestly, "but I thought it might be useful. I also thought it was fine until I saw Mr. Bear's wonderful object."

"Don't feel bad about it," put in Mr. Badger. "A long rope is just what we shall need some time."

Mr. Bear gave a low growl.

"What about you, Mr. Badger?" he demanded. "You had this idea of bringing things, and now you haven't brought anything at all."

"Oh, yes, I have!" Mr. Badger chuckled. "I have brought the most wonderful thing of all. Just wait a minute, if you please."

He turned and hurried across the meadow and disappeared in the long grass, where it was higher than his head. In a few minutes he reappeared, walking slowly backwards and pulling something. When he reached Mr.

Bear and Mr. Lobster they saw something new to all of them. It was a large cart with four strong wheels, a stake at each corner, and a long wooden handle by which Mr. Badger was pulling it.

Mr. Bear and Mr. Lobster watched the wheels turning. They were both fascinated, and so surprised that for a moment neither could speak.

Then Mr. Bear growled.

"Just my luck," he said in a tone of disgust. "When I bring something stupendous you bring something even better. I suppose this is more than stupendous."

"Yes," answered Mr. Badger, so pleased that he couldn't help chuckling at Mr. Bear, "I guess this is colossal!"

"What does that mean?" asked Mr. Lobster.

"A colossal thing is the biggest of all," said Mr. Badger, "and also the most important."

"I thought so," said Mr. Bear, who was still disgusted.

"But what is it?" asked Mr. Lobster, whose curiosity was not nearly satisfied.

"I call it a land boat," answered Mr. Badger. "It isn't big enough for all of us to ride in it at the same time, but we can take turns."

"What makes it go?"

"It can go down-hill all by itself," Mr. Badger said. "It just goes, but it isn't alive. I bit it to see. Isn't that marvelous?"

"Anything will go down-hill," put in Mr. Bear in a rather disagreeable tone. "If it would go up-hill by itself, then I would say it was really marvelous."

"Nothing goes up-hill by itself but the wind," answered Mr. Badger sharply, "and you can't see the wind. Therefore it is plain that anything you can see can't be expected to go up-hill by itself. And for myself, I prefer things I can see."

"So do I," agreed Mr. Lobster. Then he looked over to Mr. Bear and said, "But I think your mysterious object is very wonderful. You know, I worked hard to bring my rope here, and if I am not cross at Mr. Badger I think you ought not to be."

"All right," Mr. Bear agreed, "but some time I am going to do something more remarkable than Mr. Badger. He is always so pleased with himself. I want to be pleased with myself."

"I just have a happy nature, that's all," said Mr. Badger in a kindly tone. "And I have found out that it keeps me happy if I think of pleasing things about myself and pleasing things I have done. For mistakes do not make happy memories, but pleasing things do."

"How true," agreed Mr. Lobster. "And I would like to say that I think my rope is best because it may be the most useful, and Mr. Bear's object is best because it is the most mysterious, and Mr. Badger's land boat is best because we can ride in it. So we all have brought the best thing."

That remark made them all happy, and Mr. Bear walked all around the cart, looking it over very carefully. Mr. Badger examined the jug, amazed that he could see through it although it was hard. Mr. Lobster was very busy coiling his rope so that it would be ready for use.

While he was busy with his coiling, he was trying to think of something to do with the things they had gathered, and for some reason or other he remembered the talkative turtle. Possibly the end of the rope looked like the turtle's tail. Anyway, thinking about the turtle, Mr. Lobster remembered about exploring, and immediately he knew that he had discovered the very thing for the three friends to do for an adventure.

"I have something important to say," he said to Mr. Badger and Mr. Bear. "Usually Mr. Badger has the ideas for adventures, but this time I think I have one."

"Good for you!" exclaimed Mr. Badger. "Then when we have narrow escapes I won't get all the blame for them. What is your idea?"

"Do you want to hear, Mr. Bear?" asked Mr. Lobster politely.

Mr. Bear pondered a moment.

"Will you use my mysterious object?" he asked.

"Oh, yes, we shall use everything we have."

"Well, I know Mr. Badger won't be happy unless something is happening." Mr. Bear gave a low sigh, for he loved peace and comfort, and he was inclined to be lazy in warm weather. And he felt certain that anything Mr. Lobster and Mr. Badger agreed upon would be disturbing.

"Very true," said Mr. Badger. "It's high time we started something."

"I suppose I want to hear, then," said Mr. Bear. "I trust that your ideas are not so dangerous as Mr. Badger's—such as stealing boats."

"Then," said Mr. Lobster, pausing so that what he said would have due importance, "I say that we go exploring. I met a turtle last winter who recommended exploring, and I have been curious about it ever since. I want to see what it is like."

"Exploring is like an extra long picnic," explained Mr. Badger. "It lasts for days and days. And it is just the thing for an adventure! Mr. Lobster, it is the best idea I ever heard mentioned!" Mr. Badger was indeed enthusiastic.

"What shall we explore?" asked Mr. Bear. "What shall we search for?"

"Oh, that doesn't matter," said Mr. Badger at once. "As long as you are exploring, it doesn't matter whether you accomplish anything or not."

"The turtle said the object of exploring was to get away from things," said Mr. Lobster.

"I don't want to get away from anything," said Mr. Bear.

"You see new places too," added Mr. Lobster.

"Are they better places than the ones we have already, though?" Mr. Bear was being quite serious.

"That is the best part of exploring!" exclaimed Mr. Badger. "If the place you find is better than the one you leave, then you are happy without coming home. If the new place is worse, then you're glad to come home. So you're sure of being happy either way it turns out. Exploring is perfect."

"If we go exploring, do we come home nights?" asked Mr. Bear.

"Of course not. Not for days and days."

"Well, I prefer to come home nights," protested Mr. Bear. "Any other arrangement is bound to be uncomfortable."

"Who ever heard of an explorer who was comfortable!" exclaimed Mr. Badger. "Why, exploring is just like a narrow escape. You do it so that you will have something to remember and talk about afterwards; and what would an explorer have to talk about if he were comfortable? He might just as well stay at home."

Mr. Bear was silent.

"You will have your object with you, Mr. Bear," said Mr. Lobster. "Then you can have a drink of water if you get thirsty."

"I am usually hungry," said Mr. Bear ungraciously.

"Explorers find food," Mr. Badger was saying. "They eat anything. And if you want to, we can take our fish lines with us and catch fish."

"I suppose I shall have to go," said Mr. Bear not very happily.

"We shall go in my land boat!" said Mr. Badger. He was delighted.

"Exactly," agreed Mr. Lobster.

"I object to that." Mr. Bear growled a little. "I saw Mr. Badger pulling that thing, and he had to go backwards."

"We can use my rope," said Mr. Lobster. "Then we can go frontwards."

There was nothing left for Mr. Bear to object to or argue about, although deep in his heart he suspected that the whole business of exploring would turn out to be very dangerous and uncomfortable.

"Very well," he said. "I will go."

"Let us start tomorrow," suggested Mr. Badger.

"I am going home and have a good meal," said Mr. Bear. "No knowing when I'll get another, once we get started."

Then they put Mr. Bear's jug and Mr. Lobster's coil of rope in the cart, and Mr. Badger pulled the cart over into the long grass.

"Tomorrow morning we shall all meet here," he said when he returned.

And so the three friends parted.

The Explorers
Meet with Disaster

EARLY IN the morning Mr. Lobster started for the shore. On the way he encountered the sculpin and said good-by to him, explaining that he was going exploring and might not return for some time.

"Not even at night?" asked the sculpin.

"Oh, no," answered Mr. Lobster.

The sculpin spread all his fins.

"Then I may as well say 'Farewell,'" he said in a gloomy tone. He blew a bubble the size of a long, sad sigh. "We say 'Farewell' only to people we don't expect to see again," he added.

"Then I shan't say it," replied Mr. Lobster. "For I am planning to return. I hope you are happy while I am gone. And please don't worry about me."

"Very unfortunate. Very unfortunate, indeed," said the sculpin.

Mr. Lobster hurried away from the depressing fish and went so fast up the river that he arrived at the meadow at the same time Mr. Badger got there. Mr. Badger had his fish line with him.

Mr. Bear came along very slowly a few minutes later, also carrying his fish line. Mr. Badger pulled the cart out of the long grass, and the three friends made ready to start their exploration.

First Mr. Lobster, with his big claws, cut a piece from his rope, and Mr. Badger, who was most clever with his paws, tied it around one of the stakes at the front of the cart and then made a loop in the other end so that the result was a simple kind of harness. Then he put the handle back over the cart, climbed in, and took hold of it.

"Now we are ready," he said. "The person who rides can steer this just like a water boat, but this boat steers from the front. And the one who pulls it can just put his head through the loop. We shall carry the extra rope and the fish lines and Mr. Bear's object along for future use. I didn't sleep a wink all last night thinking it all out."

"I am afraid this business is your idea now," remarked Mr. Bear. "That makes me worry about its safety."

"But Mr. Badger is the best planner, we must admit," said Mr. Lobster.

"We shall see." Mr. Bear growled softly, but Mr. Lobster paid no attention to that. He considered it wise to pretend not to hear everything that went on.

Mr. Badger had gotten out of the cart and was busy loading it.

"Who is going to pull the land boat?" asked Mr. Lobster.

"We shall take turns," answered Mr. Badger. "First, Mr. Bear can pull you and me. Then, when he is tired, we can pull him."

Mr. Bear still looked rather doubtful, but he said nothing.

So Mr. Badger stood beside the cart, and Mr. Lobster climbed onto his back and then into the front of the cart under the handle. He was so excited that he trembled in every joint of his bright new shell. "I suppose," he said to himself, "that I am the first lobster ever to ride about on land. It will be another new experience, and more new knowledge. Truly, this will be the most remarkable year of my life."

Mr. Badger had climbed into the cart and seized the handle.

As Mr. Bear put his head through the loop in the rope he looked over his shoulder and said, "Take good care of my object."

Then they started.

For Mr. Lobster it proved to be a delightful experience. From the cart he could look all around and see more of the meadow than he had ever seen before. Mr. Badger steered so well that the cart rolled ahead very smoothly. Mr. Bear was so strong that he could walk right along, pulling his two friends, without any real hard work.

After a time, however, when they had traveled a considerable distance up the river, Mr. Bear looked over his shoulder and said, "Isn't it time for me to ride now?"

"Certainly," agreed Mr. Badger.

So everyone changed places. Mr. Bear sat up straight in the cart, one paw resting on his beloved jug, and looked like a king. Mr. Badger put his head into the loop of rope, and Mr. Lobster took hold with one of his big claws.

Everything was fine until they started, and then, alas, Mr. Bear proved to be so heavy that Mr. Badger and Mr. Lobster could just barely move him. In fact, the cart moved so slowly that it seemed to all three of the explorers that they were not getting anywhere at all.

"Can't you go any faster?" asked Mr. Bear.

"You weigh too much," said Mr. Badger. "I am afraid that if we are going to accomplish anything, you will have to do all the pulling, Mr. Bear."

"I might have known it," groaned Mr. Bear. "I have to do all the work. However, I shall do it for a while until we see how this exploring turns out. If it is nothing but work, I vote we return home."

"Wait until we discover something," said Mr. Badger.

The three friends changed places again, and once more Mr. Bear did the pulling.

At noontime Mr. Bear suggested that they all stop for a rest; so they paused on the bank of the river. Mr. Lobster was able to find two clams, and Mr. Badger and Mr. Bear fished and each caught a fish for lunch. Mr. Bear preferred his fish fried, but he knew there was no use saying anything about that now. And Mr. Badger, although he could and did eat fish, would have preferred a fine piece of meat; but he also said nothing. Mr. Lobster was perfectly happy, for he was not hungry and was contented to wait until suppertime for his next meal.

During the afternoon Mr. Bear became restless. The explorers were still traveling across the meadow, going further and further up the river; but now there seemed to be very little new about it. When they finally came to a wide creek, Mr. Bear stopped.

"Now where shall we go?" he asked. "I refuse to go through water."

"We must go along the creek to the woods," said Mr. Badger. "Then we can go over that hill we see from here and down the other side to the meadow again."

"Are we going through the woods?" asked Mr. Lobster. "I should like to do that."

"Explorers go everywhere," answered Mr. Badger gaily.

So Mr. Bear pulled the cart across the meadow to the edge of the woods. Of course, Mr. Bear and Mr. Badger had been in woods many times, so this was not a new experience for them. But Mr. Lobster had never been in the woods except the terrible time when he had been lost there, and then he had been so frightened and had gotten so dry that he had not enjoyed the woods at all. Now he looked about him with the greatest pleasure.

As they entered the woods a crow came flying from somewhere and landed in a tall tree and looked down on the explorers. Mr. Lobster saw the bird and was immediately curious.

"I wonder what that crow can see from there," he said.

"I couldn't see a thing from there," said Mr. Badger, and he gave a shiver. "If I were up as high as that I would be so frightened I am sure I would shut my eyes tight."

"It does my heart good to know there is one place you don't want to go," remarked Mr. Bear.

"Well, I don't know how to climb trees, and I can't fly," retorted Mr. Badger, "and I am too wise to want to go where I know I never can go. I prefer to want to do things I know I *can* do sometime—like having adventures and exploring."

"That's just an excuse," said Mr. Bear. He was pleased with himself because he thought that for once he had put Mr. Badger in his place.

But nobody could put Mr. Badger in his place for long. He always managed to have the last word himself.

"Cheer up," he said to Mr. Bear brightly. "When you are as wise as I am, you will understand all that I do about life." And he chuckled, which made Mr. Bear furious, as Mr. Badger knew it would; and Mr. Bear growled.

Mr. Lobster was listening and thinking things over. "I guess it would be common sense for me not to want to get to the top of a tree," he said to himself, "but I just can't help being curious about it. I want to know what it

is like to be high up in the air. Just for once. I don't know
why it is, but curiosity keeps right on, even when it is not
common sense. There's nothing to be done about it."

By this time they had reached the top of the hill. The
crow had been following them, and he had called to his
friends; and now there were about twenty crows sitting
in the tops of the trees, watching the three explorers.
Crows are not very friendly or trusting; so they did not
come down to earth but talked the matter over among
themselves high overhead. They made quite a chatter.

Mr. Badger knew that the birds were interested in
what was going on.

"I think our boat will go down this hill by itself," he
said, looking down the hill to the river. "We shall show
these crows how explorers travel."

There was a clear space between the trees on the hill,
and it looked as though it would be a simple matter to
steer the cart down the hill and out on the smooth
meadow.

"Give me the rope," said Mr. Badger to Mr. Bear, "and
watch us go. I shall steer right for the bank of the river."

Mr. Lobster felt himself trembling at the thought of
flying down the hill, but he had no time to consider
what was the wisest thing to do. For Mr. Bear had already
given Mr. Badger the rope, and the cart had started
moving.

"Hang on!" cried Mr. Badger. "Here we go!"

The cart went faster and faster, and the faster it went
the more it rattled and banged and shook. Mr. Lobster

found himself bouncing around so that it seemed as if his shell would be shaken to pieces. And the wind blew past him so that he felt as though he were out in a gale.

"Is this like flying?" he managed to ask Mr. Badger.

"Better!" shouted Mr. Badger, who was very busy with the steering. "It isn't so far to fall if anything happens."

Just then something did happen. The cart hit a bump, and Mr. Lobster bounced straight up in the air and came down on top of Mr. Badger. He would have tumbled right off Mr. Badger and out of the cart, but quick as a wink he grabbed hold of Mr. Badger with both his big pincher claws and held on with all his strength.

"Ouch!" yelled Mr. Badger. "Ouch! Let go!"

"I can't! I'll fall off!" cried Mr. Lobster.

The cart dashed out of the woods onto the smooth meadow and headed straight across the grass for the river, with Mr. Badger groaning piteously and Mr. Lobster holding tighter and tighter.

Nearer and nearer they came to the river, but still Mr. Badger steered straight ahead.

"Look out!" cried Mr. Lobster. "The river!"

Mr. Badger gave a pull on the handle. The cart gave such a sharp turn that it went up on two wheels almost at the very bank of the river.

"O-o-ouch!" shrieked Mr. Badger.

Fortunately the cart did not tip over. Slowly it came to a stop. Mr. Lobster let go of Mr. Badger and fell out of the cart onto the soft meadow grass.

Mr. Badger climbed out.

"Wonderful!" exclaimed Mr. Badger, "although you nearly finished me! Wasn't that a narrow escape?"

"It was for you," said Mr. Lobster, "for you nearly went over the bank into the river. Why didn't you turn before?"

"To tell the truth, I didn't even see the river," admitted Mr. Badger. "When you grabbed me with those awful claws of yours, I shut my eyes, and I didn't open them until you shouted. Thank you for shouting."

"Thank you for letting me hold on to you," said Mr. Lobster. "I would have fallen out but for you."

"I suppose you are welcome." Mr. Badger sighed. "But if you ever have to grab me that way again, there's no telling what will happen."

At this point Mr. Bear, who had run down the hill, came puffing up.

"Is my object safe?" he demanded.

Mr. Bear's object and the fish lines and rope were still in the cart.

"Certainly," said Mr. Badger. "Everything is safe, and so are we. Did you see the wonderful ride we had? I've never traveled so fast in my life!"

"I heard you yell, and it didn't sound like joy," said Mr. Bear.

"That was my fault," said Mr. Lobster. "I was forced to grab Mr. Badger. Now I feel that I have had a great experience and that I am wiser than before, as I can say that I have ridden fast on land."

"We are both wiser than before," said Mr. Badger. "What a pity Mr. Bear wasn't with us."

"I suppose that now I am not so wise as you and Mr. Lobster," said Mr. Bear, "and I shall never hear the end of it."

"Well, hardly," said Mr. Badger in a superior manner. "You can't expect to be as wise as we are unless you do what we do."

"Do you mean that I have to come flying down the hill the way you did?" asked Mr. Bear with horror in his voice.

"Certainly," Mr. Badger answered.

Mr. Bear gave a low growl.

"Be sure and steer around when you get to the river bank," said Mr. Lobster, "if you decide to try it. We very nearly went right off the bank."

"Would you do it again?" asked Mr. Bear.

"Just now I feel that I would not care to go again," replied Mr. Lobster frankly. "You see, I feel that there are some experiences it isn't necessary to have but once."

"Remember," said Mr. Badger, "that you can't gain wisdom without courage."

"I wonder whether it would be courage or foolishness, though," observed Mr. Bear. The more he thought of it the more terrified he was at the idea of flying down the hill; but at the same time he could not think of letting Mr. Badger get the best of him.

"That is something you never can tell until afterwards," said Mr. Badger.

"Well, I am going to be as wise as you are. I know that!" exclaimed Mr. Bear. And he took the loop of rope from the front of the cart, put his head through it, and started for the hill.

"Wait a minute!" cried Mr. Badger. He ran over and took the rope and fish lines and Mr. Bear's object out of the cart. "Now you have all the room you need. Mr. Lobster and I will watch you."

"Good luck!" called Mr. Lobster. Then, feeling a little dry, he slipped into the river for a few minutes while Mr. Bear pulled the cart across the meadow to the woods. When Mr. Lobster climbed back to the meadow, with Mr. Badger's help, Mr. Bear was just disappearing into the woods.

"Now for the fun," said Mr. Badger. "There is really no danger, because Mr. Bear won't have to shut his eyes from pain as I did; but I'll bet he gets a surprise when he finds out how fast he comes."

"I trust that he thinks his surprise is a pleasant one," said Mr. Lobster. "An unpleasant surprise makes a whole day miserable."

"It is time for him to be starting," observed Mr. Badger.

They were both watching the top of the hill, where the crows still sat in the tree tops.

Suddenly the two friends heard a roar from the woods, and all the crows flew up out of the trees and came flying down the hill toward the meadow.

"They are following Mr. Bear!" exclaimed Mr. Badger excitedly. "And that means trouble. Crows never chase after anything but trouble. And listen to that roar!"

Mr. Bear was roaring indeed. He had forgotten that he

was much heavier than Mr. Badger and Mr. Lobster, and he had gone clear to the top of the hill. As soon as he started his ride his great weight made the cart go faster than he had ever dreamed of going. So he started roaring with surprise and fright.

"Here he comes!" cried Mr. Lobster.

Mr. Bear and the cart shot out of the woods at lightning speed. He was sitting upright, all his hair blown out straight behind him, his paws around the steering handle, and his mouth wide open with the most fearful sounds coming from it. And right over his head and right behind him came the whole flock of crows, cawing and yelling with delight because Mr. Bear seemed to be running away from them.

It was a strange and wild sight.

The cart came flying across the meadow, all the noise and Mr. Bear and the crows with it, and headed straight for the river.

Mr. Badger and Mr. Lobster were too excited to speak.

In spite of his terror, Mr. Bear was steering very well, and probably everything would have gone all right—but just as the cart came rushing up to Mr. Badger and Mr. Lobster it hit a small bump. Mr. Bear let out a groan and pulled hard on the steering handle; and he pulled with such great strength that the handle came off the cart and Mr. Bear fell over backwards in the cart, his four feet sticking up in the air.

The cart kept going straight for the river.

"Jump!" yelled Mr. Badger.

THE CART REACHED THE BANK OF THE RIVER
AND WENT SAILING INTO THE AIR.

Mr. Bear couldn't jump because he was on his back. He tried to sit up, but it was too late. The cart reached the bank of the river, went sailing into the air, and then fell with a great splash into the water.

All the crows gave shrieks of delight and flew pell-mell back to the woods.

Mr. Badger and Mr. Lobster rushed to the river bank.

Mr. Bear had gone completely under water, cart and all. When he came up, he was trying to growl and spit out water at the same time, which made the strangest sounds. He was floating on the cart and splashing all his feet and making a terrific commotion so that the water was flying everywhere.

"Help!" he managed to shout.

"Lie still!" yelled Mr. Badger. "Stay in the boat!"

There was a small island of mud in the middle of the river, just a clam flat, and the cart and Mr. Bear were drifting toward it.

"I'm floating away!" Mr. Bear shouted. "Help! I'm in water!"

He struggled and splashed all the more.

"Be calm!" called Mr. Badger.

Mr. Bear lifted up his head and growled horribly.

"How can I be calm when I'm floating in water and never coming back?" he demanded. "I'm going to be gone!"

Then the wheels of the cart struck bottom in the shallow water near the island. Mr. Bear made another struggle and fell out of the cart into the water, and the cart floated away down the river. Mr. Bear groaned fearfully, but then he found that his feet were on bottom, and he ran through the water as fast as he could go until he was on the island. There he stood, wet and trembling, the unhappiest looking bear in the world.

"You're safe!" cried Mr. Badger joyfully.

"Safe!" Mr. Bear snorted. "How can I be safe when I am surrounded by water?"

"Can you swim ashore?" asked Mr. Lobster, who for some moments had been too horrified to speak.

"I don't know how to swim."

"Try it," advised Mr. Badger. "It is easy."

Mr. Bear made a low, unhappy sound.

"Oh, no," he said. "I wasn't made to swim. Only fishes and things born in the water are supposed to swim. Besides, I hate being in water!"

"What shall we do?" asked Mr. Lobster.

"Build me a bridge!" exclaimed Mr. Bear. "A bridge is the only safe way to cross water. Oh, why did I ever make friends with Mr. Badger? He causes me more trouble as a friend then he did as an enemy. It was his idea to ride in that land boat, and every idea he has makes trouble for somebody, usually me."

"You broke the handle, and you have lost my colossal land boat," said Mr. Badger sadly, "but I shall have to forgive you."

"You will have to build me a bridge!" declared Mr. Bear in an angry tone. "I demand a bridge!"

Mr. Badger and Mr. Lobster looked around. There was

not a bit of wood in sight. There was nothing on the meadow which looked like material for a bridge. And over beyond the hill they had come down so fast, the sun was setting. The day was nearly done.

"Well," said Mr. Badger, "Mr. Lobster and I will look for a boat or a bridge, but the night is coming now, and it will be impossible to search until the morning. You must be patient and wait till then."

"I have never been very patient, even at my happiest moments," said Mr. Bear. "And now how can I be patient at the unhappiest moment of my life?"

No one could answer that question. Mr. Lobster and Mr. Badger were both silent, and Mr. Bear was so miserable he could only make low moans. It was a most desperate and unhappy situation.

"I shall go to the woods for the night," said Mr. Badger, "and shall return and save you the first thing in the morning. Have no fear. I shall have an idea."

Mr. Bear only moaned a little louder.

"I shall sleep at the bottom of the river," said Mr. Lobster.

"Probably that is where my bones will lie," muttered Mr. Bear.

It was a sad parting, the saddest parting the three friends had ever had.

As Mr. Lobster slipped into the water, he thought: "I am afraid it turned out to be a most unpleasant surprise for Mr. Bear, although I cannot understand how anyone can think that water is anything but delightful. Life is very strange, indeed. I guess that no matter how wise a person is, he doesn't know how a surprise will turn out, for even a wise person can't know everything, no matter how hard he tries. I must remember that and not be too proud of my wisdom."

He found a deep hole under the bank of the river, and, although he was deeply worried and unhappy over Mr. Bear's plight, he finally managed to spend a fairly comfortable night.

As soon as the sun was brightly shining the next morning, so that its rays came down through the water, Mr. Lobster climbed slowly up the bank of the river to the meadow.

Mr. Badger was already there.

"Look!" said Mr. Badger.

Mr. Lobster looked.

There was no island. The tide had come in and covered it. And there was no Mr. Bear. There was only water.

Mr. Bear's
Terrible Night

THE TWO friends had a strange feeling, as if it could
not be true that Mr. Bear was nowhere in sight and the
island covered with water. For a few minutes they kept
on looking at the river, hoping that somehow Mr. Bear
would reappear, and trying to think that perhaps they
had come to the wrong place. But it was no use. It *was* the
right place, and there was no island, and no Mr. Bear.

"He is gone," said Mr. Badger.

"We must search," said Mr. Lobster. "Nothing is gone
until you have searched for it without finding it. It must
be the same with people."

"How wise you are. Perhaps there is hope. Let us start at once."

So Mr. Badger and Mr. Lobster started walking along the bank of the river. It was an unhappy walk, and neither Mr. Lobster nor Mr. Badger cared to say anything about exploring. In fact, they were so silent as they went along that Mr. Lobster realized that he had never known Mr. Badger to stay quiet for such a long time.

"It is a beautiful day," Mr. Lobster said, trying to make a little pleasant conversation.

"I really haven't noticed," said Mr. Badger. And even after that he didn't try to notice.

Mr. Lobster decided not to attempt any more conversation.

Slowly they followed the winding river, keeping on the bank so that they could search the water as well as the meadow. When they came to a creek, Mr. Badger would run along it until he found a place where he could jump to the other side. Mr. Lobster swam across all the creeks.

When they had traveled for what seemed an endless and totally unhappy distance without seeing any sign of Mr. Bear, they stopped for a few minutes of rest.

"I am becoming more and more wretched," said Mr. Badger. "I wish now that I had never found the land boat. It was all my fault."

"I wouldn't say that," protested Mr. Lobster. "It is best, when something unfortunate happens, to call it an accident. Then nobody is to blame."

"Don't you think it was my fault?"

"No, I do not." Mr. Lobster spoke positively. "Mr. Bear broke the handle himself, and that caused the accident. Either Mr. Bear was too strong or the handle was not strong enough. It certainly had nothing to do with you."

Mr. Badger sighed with relief.

"I feel very much better. Thank you very much, Mr. Lobster," he said with great feeling. "Since you are so wise, of course you are right. I always believe every word you say. This has been a hard morning for me, for I am by nature so happy and carefree that when I am miserable I am extra miserable thinking of how happy I used to be."

"We have not finished our search yet, you know," Mr. Lobster said. "So Mr. Bear is not gone yet. Why don't you go to the woods and look down from a hill? Perhaps then you could see far enough to see Mr. Bear."

"A brilliant idea!" exclaimed Mr. Badger. "You wait here, and I will go at once and hurry back and tell you what I see."

Mr. Badger trotted off.

Mr. Lobster, left alone, slipped into the river to get wet. For some time he crawled aimlessly along the bottom. When two small flounders just the size of a lunch came swimming by he did not try to catch them. He was too busy thinking about the unfortunate end of the exploring and about Mr. Bear to be able to eat.

When he climbed out on the bank again Mr. Badger was returning from the woods as fast as he could run.

"There is something big and black lying on the

meadow right by a tall tree without any leaves," he said, panting. "We must hurry along. It may be Mr. Bear."

They started again. Mr. Lobster could not go as fast as he wanted to because he could never travel by snapping his tail when he was on land. But he made his eight legs go as fast as possible, and together they headed in the direction where Mr. Badger had seen the tree without leaves.

"There it is!" cried Mr. Badger after a short time. "Right near the river and sticking up out of the meadow!"

Mr. Lobster tried to go faster.

"There's Mr. Bear!" shouted Mr. Badger.

Sure enough, there was Mr. Bear curled up on the soft grass of the meadow fast asleep. And the tree without any leaves was the mast of a sailboat which was floating in a little creek behind Mr. Bear.

"Mr. Bear!" called Mr. Lobster and Mr. Badger at the same time.

Mr. Bear opened his eyes and yawned. Then he saw Mr. Badger, and he managed to give a low growl.

"Well! So it is you," he said in a sleepy voice.

"Are you all right?" asked Mr. Lobster anxiously.

"Oh, yes," answered Mr. Bear in a contented manner. Then he remembered to be cross, and he growled again at Mr. Badger. "But no thanks to you and your precious land boat," he said crossly. "What a terrible night I had! You will be the end of me yet! I always get the worst of everything." He was trying to look very miserable, but actually he looked sleek and well-fed and comfortable.

"Perhaps I owe you an apology," said Mr. Badger, "but I did not know the handle on my land boat was not strong."

"Apologies are always too late," said Mr. Bear severely.

"I am sure it was not Mr. Badger's fault," said Mr. Lobster kindly, hoping to restore friendship without any more cross words.

"And Mr. Lobster is so very wise," added Mr. Badger hopefully.

Mr. Lobster, being modest, said nothing more.

"Well," said Mr. Bear, "I suppose that if Mr. Lobster says it was not your fault I can believe it."

"By all means!" said Mr. Badger eagerly. "It was all an accident, and explorers are bound to have accidents."

"Accident!" Mr. Bear snorted. He was wide awake now. "I call it a catastrophe!"

"Goodness! What is that?" asked Mr. Lobster.

"A catastrophe," said Mr. Badger, who loved to explain, "is an accident that happens to a great many people at the same time, or else it is just a single accident of tremendous size."

"Oh," said Mr. Lobster. "And Mr. Bear is tremendous; so this was certainly a catastrophe, wasn't it?"

"Certainly," agreed Mr. Badger.

"Well, now we are all together again, and we can be happy once more," said Mr. Lobster. "And I am curious to know what happened. Will you please tell us, Mr. Bear?"

Mr. Bear looked actually happy. For once he was the

most important of the three friends, and for once Mr.
Badger would have to let him do most of the talking. He
stood up, looked calmly around, and then glanced with
pride at the sailboat floating in the creek.

"By the way," he said in his most important manner,
"that is my boat. And it is better than any land boat you
have to pull."

"How did you get it? What happened last night?"
asked Mr. Lobster, whose curiosity was making him
tremble with eagerness to hear every word of Mr. Bear's
story.

"You are right about the boat," said Mr. Badger. "It is
much more colossal than mine."

Mr. Bear gave a sound of approval at Mr. Badger's
words. Then, settling himself comfortably in the soft
grass, he began.

"It was a terrible night," he said. "I walked back and
forth on that miserable island, which was not nearly big
enough for a creature my size, for hours. I was hungry
and unhappy. And I was surrounded by water. How I
suffered—thanks to that awful ride in Mr. Badger's land
boat. While you both were sleeping happily, I was suffering."

"Oh, we weren't happy at all!" exclaimed Mr. Badger.

"Please do not interrupt," said Mr. Bear sternly. "As I
was saying, while you were sleeping happily, I was suffering. While you were safe on dry land, I was in the
greatest danger."

Mr. Badger did not dare interrupt again.

Mr. Lobster, who had the softest heart under his hard shell, felt even sorrier for Mr. Bear than before.

"For hours I remained in that hideous plight," Mr. Bear went on, when he saw that they were listening carefully to each word. "And then, sometime in the darkest and most dangerous part of the night, the island began to get smaller and smaller. It was sinking in the river."

"Pardon me for speaking," put in Mr. Lobster, "but perhaps the tide was coming in and covering the island."

"When the island began to sink," continued Mr. Bear, just as though no one had spoken, "I realized that the end had come. So my suffering and peril increased every minute. And there was no one to help me."

He looked sharply at his friends to be sure they understood, and both Mr. Lobster and Mr. Badger trembled with sympathy and looked very distressed and said, "Do go on."

Mr. Bear was pleased at the trembling and again continued. "Finally, there was no dry land left on the island. I was not only surrounded by water. I was standing in water. First it covered my feet; then it came higher and higher. I am sure no one has been in a more terrible situation. But then, just when I was about to be gone, this fine boat came floating down the river, and it came so near that I was able to climb aboard. It was a great struggle, but I saved myself."

"How clever and brave you are!" exclaimed Mr. Badger tactfully.

"Yes, indeed," murmured Mr. Lobster.

"WHEN THE ISLAND BEGAN TO SINK," CONTINUED MR.
BEAR, "I REALIZED THAT THE END HAD COME."

"So I drifted down the river," Mr. Bear said. "And someone had left a large package of fried fish on the boat, and I ate all of them. It was necessary for me to eat them, for I had been starving all the time I was on the island. When the boat drifted into this creek, I came ashore. I was so exhausted that I fell asleep."

Mr. Bear could not pretend any longer that he was miserable. He was really so satisfied with himself that it was perfectly plain to Mr. Badger and Mr. Lobster.

"Perhaps you fell asleep because you were so full of fish," remarked Mr. Badger, who saw that Mr. Bear was in fine condition and had had a large meal. Mr. Badger's usual good spirits had returned, and there was a twinkle in his eye.

"Such suffering as mine is nothing to joke about," said Mr. Bear. But he looked so full and comfortable that it was impossible for him to impress Mr. Badger.

Mr. Lobster was too wise to say anything to spoil Mr. Bear's story, but he thought to himself : "Mr. Bear had a fine supper, and Mr. Badger and I haven't eaten a thing. Mr. Bear has been sleeping comfortably for hours while we have been looking for him. I know now that the persons who do the worrying suffer more than the person who has the adventure. I shall remember that and not get lost and cause my friends suffering."

He looked over to Mr. Bear. "You have had a hard time, indeed," he said, "and Mr. Badger and I are delighted to find you safe and well. Now I should like to look at your boat a little more closely."

"So should I," said Mr. Badger. "We must do something with it."

"Please remember that it is my boat," said Mr. Bear.

"And please remember that we all used my land boat," replied Mr. Badger. "No friend is ever selfish. That is one of the ways you know friends."

"I shall not be selfish," said Mr. Bear, "but I must protect myself against your ideas. You are both welcome to look at my boat."

It was a sailboat, which is the most beautiful kind of boat there is. It was more than twenty feet long and painted white, with a forward deck big enough for even Mr. Bear to stand on, and a cockpit big enough for all three of the friends. On the deck was a large anchor fastened to a large coil of rope. The sail, which was new and neat, was furled on the boom. Everything about the little vessel was shipshape and clean.

"A sailboat!" exclaimed Mr. Badger joyfully. "I have always wanted to go skimming over the water in a boat like this."

"Boats mean work," remarked Mr. Bear. "I remember how I worked when we went fishing. I did all the rowing."

"But sailboats go without rowing," explained Mr. Badger eagerly. "All you have to do is sit still, and the wind blows you along. It is like going down-hill all the time, but of course not so fast. I could spend the rest of my life sailing."

"I prefer to spend the rest of my life on dry land," said Mr. Bear.

"Anyone who has spirit loves to sail," insisted Mr. Badger.

Mr. Lobster was afraid that Mr. Badger and Mr. Bear would have an argument about boats. Also, Mr. Badger's words interested him. Mr. Lobster had ridden on a turtle and on Mr. Bear's back and in a land boat and in a rowboat. But he had never skimmed over the sea in a sailboat. So naturally, since he was always curious about new things and eager for new experiences, he wanted to sail in Mr. Bear's boat.

"I should like to try sailing," he said. "I think we might try it to see whether we like it. Then we can decide. Certainly it is unwise to dislike a new thing before you try it."

"Your wisdom is perfect, Mr. Lobster," said Mr. Badger.

"You think his ideas are perfect because they agree with yours," said Mr. Bear.

"Of course," assented Mr. Badger readily. "That's the best way to tell a perfect thing. How can anything be perfect if it doesn't agree with you?"

Mr. Bear was sure Mr. Badger was wrong, but he didn't know what to say. It seemed to him that Mr. Badger had an answer to everything, and Mr. Bear kept hoping that someday he would be able to say something so brilliant that it would leave Mr. Badger in stunned silence.

"Where could we go?" asked Mr. Bear of Mr. Lobster.

Mr. Lobster was very quiet, thinking as hard as he could. He was afraid Mr. Badger would have an idea first, and Mr. Bear would surely disagree with it.

"I am sick of this river and the meadow," Mr. Bear went on. "There's too much trouble here. I want to get away from it all."

They were almost the very words the talkative turtle had used, Mr. Lobster realized. "I know!" he answered. "The turtle told me that when he wanted to get away from things he went exploring; so why can't we continue our exploring in your boat? We can explore the sea. I am sure explorers do not have to stay on the bottom of the ocean or on land."

"But what is there to explore on the sea?" asked Mr. Bear. "It is nothing but water, and water looks just the same and just as wet and dangerous, no matter where it is. What did the turtle find?"

Mr. Lobster was not eager to answer that question, but he always told the truth. So he said, "Islands."

"Islands!" exclaimed Mr. Bear in horror. "Never! Imagine going to all the trouble of exploring and running all kinds of risks just to find islands, which are dangerous and always surrounded by water! Never!"

"But there are big islands with trees and caves which are perfectly safe," declared Mr. Badger.

"From my experience an island is never safe," insisted Mr. Bear.

It looked as though the three friends could not agree. Mr. Lobster and Mr. Badger were eager to sail away exploring for islands, but Mr. Bear was firm. And the sailboat was Mr. Bear's.

Mr. Lobster said to himself: "It is always wisest to

make important decisions when one is not hungry or tired or cross. Perhaps we all shall be happier after a good supper and a good night's sleep at home."

So he said to Mr. Bear and Mr. Badger:

"Let us all go home and think the matter over, and let us return to this place day after tomorrow. Then we can take a vote."

It was agreed to do what Mr. Lobster suggested, although it was a long distance from home for each of them.

Mr. Bear examined his boat to make sure that it would not float away.

"I don't see why you want the boat, if you don't want to sail the sea in it," observed Mr. Badger.

"I just like to own it," answered Mr. Bear. "I like to know it is my property." He hoped that would silence Mr. Badger.

"Property is a nuisance," said Mr. Badger cheerfully. "I don't own anything except a fish line, and I am one of the happiest creatures in the world."

Mr. Lobster thought that Mr. Badger was right, but he didn't say a word. He slipped into the water and started down the river, resolved to have several good meals before he settled down in his home for the night.

A Mystery at Sea

WHEN THE three friends met again on the meadow the sailboat was still safe in the creek, and Mr. Bear and Mr. Badger were on the friendliest terms. Everyone was happy. The sun was shining brightly. The sky was summer blue. It was a perfect day for the beginning of a pleasant adventure.

"We shall now vote to see whether we shall go exploring the sea for islands—large, safe islands," announced Mr. Badger. It was Mr. Lobster's idea, of course, but Mr. Badger was so enterprising that every time the three friends started on a new plan he made himself the leader.

Somehow, no matter who started things, Mr. Badger was running them without the others knowing just how it came about. "I just want to say," he went on now, "that as we vote we must remember that we are friends and heroes."

"Are we heroes because we were last year?" asked Mr. Bear.

"'Once a hero always a hero' is my motto," replied Mr. Badger.

"How shall we vote?" asked Mr. Lobster, who was pleased to be reminded that he was a hero.

"I have here three black stones and three white stones," said Mr. Badger. "Here is one white stone and one black stone for each of us." And he gave Mr. Bear and Mr. Lobster each their stones, keeping the last two for himself.

"I thought it all out last night," he continued, "and gathered the stones this morning. It is a perfect way to vote without any argument or unpleasantness. If you vote to go exploring for islands, go over behind that tuft of grass and leave your white stone. If you vote not to go, leave your black stone there. After we have all voted, we shall count the stones and see whether black or white wins. As it was Mr. Lobster's idea to go exploring for islands, he should vote first. As the stones are my idea I shall vote second, if no one objects. As the boat is Mr. Bear's, he can vote last, which is most important."

Mr. Bear had been about to object to being last, but Mr. Badger's final words were so pleasing to him that he said nothing. As long as he was important he was content.

Mr. Lobster was eager to vote.

"Shall I go now?" he asked.

"Yes, the time has come for us to know our fate," answered Mr. Badger.

Mr. Lobster crawled as fast as he could over to the tuft of grass and dropped his white stone, which he had carried in his right claw. The black stone he hid where no one would see it. Then he returned.

Mr. Badger took but a minute to vote. Then he returned and waited with Mr. Lobster.

Mr. Bear walked more slowly to the tuft of grass, and he gave a low growl when he got there. But he returned without saying a word.

"Now we can look," said Mr. Badger.

They all hurried over to see the vote.

Behind the tuft of grass lay three white stones.

"How glad I am!" exclaimed Mr. Lobster happily.

"A perfect vote!" declared Mr. Badger.

Mr. Bear sighed, not exactly unhappily, but with a sound that meant it was no use complaining.

"When I went to vote there were already two white stones there," he said. "So I knew there was no use leaving a black one, and I left a white one, too."

"It was a fine thing for you to do," said Mr. Lobster.

"This will be our greatest adventure!" said Mr. Badger joyfully. He was so delighted he could hardly keep from dancing. "We are friends and heroes, and explorers of land and sea. I claim that we are all remarkable!"

Mr. Bear agreed with that, naturally, and he looked unusually happy, even though he was about to go exploring again.

Mr. Lobster was thinking, and he said to himself: "How true it is that if you want people to do something it is best to praise them first. I learn a good deal from Mr. Badger, even if I am older than he is."

Mr. Badger thought that he had managed things very well.

"I have thought of something," said Mr. Bear. "If we are going to sail the sea I want to take my object with me. I may get thirsty."

"And my rope," said Mr. Lobster.

"Mr. Bear and I will get everything," said Mr. Badger. "Come on, Mr. Bear."

While they were gone Mr. Lobster went in the river and got thoroughly wet and caught three small flounders and a perch. When Mr. Bear and Mr. Badger returned with the jug and the rope and the fish lines everyone was ready to start.

Mr. Badger had never sailed a boat, but he loved to experiment, and he was unusually smart. In a few minutes he found out how to hoist the sail and tie the halyards around the cleats. Then he took hold of the sheet, which is not a real sheet at all, but the rope with which the sail is pulled tight so that the wind will fill it and it won't flap, and sat in the stern where he could steer.

Once more he was running things, which made him contented and happy.

Mr. Bear took his place in the cockpit.

"As I don't have to row, I suppose I don't have to ride backwards in this boat," he said. And that made him happy.

There was a very short rope at the stern of the boat which trailed in the water. Evidently it had been broken when the boat drifted away from its rightful place. Mr. Lobster went into the water and took hold of the end of that rope, and Mr. Badger pulled him aboard.

"That rope will save my tail from destruction, I do believe," said Mr. Badger. "I approve of acts of friendship and helpfulness, and I am also a hero; but I should be miserable if I had to pull Mr. Lobster up with my tail every time he wanted to get wet. Probably I should lose my tail, and then I should no longer be a badger. Every badger must have a tail."

"What would you be?" asked Mr. Lobster instantly.

No one could answer that question. Mr. Lobster had hit upon a mystery, which is something that can never be explained, for anything that is explained is no longer a mystery.

The jug and rope and fish lines were on the cockpit floor. Mr. Bear pushed the boat into the river. Mr. Badger pulled in the sheet so that the sail was stiff in the breeze. The little boat heeled over and started for the sea.

"Hooray!" cried Mr. Badger. "We're off on the greatest adventure yet!"

Mr. Lobster felt that it was one of the most important moments of his life.

Mr. Bear was so proud of his boat that he forgot about danger and being surrounded by water.

So it was a very happy beginning in every way.

When they reached the mouth of the river, Mr. Badger steered straight for the open ocean. The bow of the boat pointed for the far horizon, where the blue sky came down to the blue sea, and it looked as if you could easily sail right off the sea into the sky.

Mr. Bear noticed that immediately and began to worry a little. He enjoyed sailing very much, he found, but he preferred to have some land fairly near at hand.

"Are you going to keep on in this direction?" he asked Mr. Badger when they had been sailing for some time.

"Certainly," answered Mr. Badger. "This is the way the wind is blowing, so we shall go this way."

"I don't see any land ahead of us," observed Mr. Bear. "I don't believe we shall come to anything but sky. And suppose we just come to the edge of the ocean?"

"Don't worry," said Mr. Badger confidently. "If we come to the edge of the ocean without finding any land, I shall steer along the edge until we do find some."

The next time Mr. Bear looked astern, the land they had left had disappeared entirely; so there was nothing to be seen on all sides but water and sky.

"I still don't see any islands," he said.

"You must be patient," advised Mr. Badger. "An island

is practically always a surprise. You don't see it until you're almost there."

It was hard for Mr. Bear to keep his worries to himself, but he decided to be quiet for a while and think about what he would do if they did not come to an island, and whether there was a good chance of finding honey on islands.

Mr. Lobster was not worried at all. He knew that he could drop overboard any time he wanted to and land in his own ocean. He had a strange feeling almost like homesickness when they sailed over the very place where he had his home on the ocean bottom, and he almost asked Mr. Badger to stop a moment while he went down to look at his home once more before he left for such a long time. But he decided that would only mean one more departure, and he was enjoying the new experience of sailing so much that he really hated to stop.

So they sailed on and on.

The breeze grew stronger, and the little boat went faster, skimming over the sea just as Mr. Badger had dreamed of doing. And he discovered that by pulling the sheet tight and pulling the tiller toward him he could make the boat tip over on its side and fairly dash along, with spray flying and the water rushing past, so near the edge of the cockpit that it looked as though it might come in over the side at any moment.

Unfortunately, when he made the boat tip, Mr. Bear lost his balance and rolled along until he hit the side of

SKIMMING OVER THE SEA JUST AS MR. BADGER HAD
DREAMED OF DOING.

the boat with a bang. He let out a loud growl. Then he looked up and saw the water almost at his very nose.

"You are sinking my boat!" he cried.

"Oh, no, there's no danger," said Mr. Badger.

Mr. Lobster was hanging on with both big claws and saying nothing.

"I thought this was better than a rowboat," said Mr. Bear unhappily, "but at least a rowboat doesn't lie on its side."

"We are going faster this way," Mr. Badger explained. He loved the excitement and the flying spray. "We shall reach our island sooner."

Mr. Bear crawled back and balanced himself as well as possible, which was not easy for him, as he was not graceful. He tried to duck the spray, for he hated getting wet, but he did not succeed at all, and soon he began to growl softly. As he got wetter and wetter he growled more loudly.

"Did you say something?" asked Mr. Badger pleasantly.

"I am saying a good deal to myself," answered Mr. Bear.

Mr. Badger, who knew very well what the trouble was, eased the tiller a bit, and the boat was again on even keel. The spray stopped flying, and Mr. Bear felt better and safer.

"Personally," he said in a most serious manner, "I prefer comfort to speed."

"I prefer excitement," said Mr. Badger.

"I believe," said Mr. Lobster, "that speed is for escaping and such emergencies. If you go too fast, you don't have time to see things and think about them, and I think seeing and thinking are most important, for they lead to wisdom. Also, speed is not very peaceful, and I love peace."

When anyone sixty-nine years old and as wise as Mr. Lobster speaks words of advice, of course it is not polite to contradict. So Mr. Badger, who was polite, even if he did love a joke, said nothing; and he did not again make the boat tip.

The afternoon passed very pleasantly, although Mr. Bear was nearly wearing his eyes out looking for islands and seeing none at all. Mr. Badger didn't seem to be looking at all, or even caring whether they saw islands or not.

Finally Mr. Bear asked:

"Do you see any islands, Mr. Badger?"

"Not a one," answered Mr. Badger cheerfully.

"You don't seem worried about it."

"Oh, no," replied Mr. Badger. "Exploring wouldn't be any fun if you discovered what you were searching for too soon."

Mr. Bear just kept on looking.

After a time the ocean began to grow smaller and smaller, and the sky seemed to come closer and closer. The sun, which had been low over the water far behind the boat, was gone. First the darkness was just a great distant shadow on the sea. Then it began to fill the air, and all the sea and sky were dim and veiled and beautiful.

Then, without anyone's being able to see it come or know exactly how it happened, the miracle of night had taken place; and there was no sea, no sky, only a single faint star and great darkness. And then another star, and finally all the company of stars making beauty in the blackness.

The three friends were silent for some time while this wonder worked about and over them. Then Mr. Bear spoke.

"It is night, and we are nowhere," he said.

"I will let the sail down, and we can float here," said Mr. Badger.

"But we have sailed all day and we are nowhere," insisted Mr. Bear.

"You are always somewhere as long as you are alive," said Mr. Badger. "We would not be real explorers if we did not stay out all night. Staying out all night is what makes exploring special."

"I see," said Mr. Bear, who did not like the idea of being out at night at all. "This business is going to be more than I counted on."

"It always is," said Mr. Badger. "That is life."

"I am hungry," said Mr. Bear.

"We shall fish," said Mr. Badger.

Mr. Lobster had been unusually happy. For the first time in his life he had seen the coming of the night when he was not deep under water. He said to himself: "Mr. Bear and Mr. Badger do not mention the coming of night. It must be that they have seen it so often they have forgotten how wonderful it is. Perhaps we forget many wonderful things just because we see them often. If I am ever unhappy or not interested in what is going on around me, I shall remember wonders that happen every day—like tides and sunshine and darkness and clouds and wind."

It was a happy and comforting thought. Mr. Lobster was content to say very little until he felt that it was time for him to go into the water for the rest of the night. Then he took hold of the end of the short rope at the stern, and Mr. Badger let him down into the water. There he hung, cool and comfortable.

Mr. Bear and Mr. Badger decided to wait until morning to fish, even though they were both hungry. Mr. Bear talked more about it than Mr. Badger, probably because he was bigger and so, of course, hungrier. Also, Mr. Bear was one of those persons who mention their discomforts and miseries; so it was impossible for Mr. Badger to keep him silent, no matter what he said.

Finally Mr. Badger took a drink from the jug and curled up in the cockpit. The gentle rocking of the boat pleased him, and the adventure of sleeping out at night far from his home pleased him, and he was not afraid of anything. So he was soon fast asleep.

Mr. Bear was nervous and restless. All day he had stayed in the cockpit. Now that the sail was down and the boat was gently drifting, he began to walk back and forth. He muttered to himself at first, making quite a little noise, but when he saw that Mr. Badger was asleep he stopped. He decided that it was no pleasure to mutter unless there was someone to hear him. Mr. Bear would never admit that he was afraid because he knew that if he did Mr. Badger would say he wasn't a hero; but now he was badly worried. When everyone else is asleep it is just as lonesome as if they were not there, and Mr. Bear felt that he was all alone now. And he worried about islands. He wondered if there were any islands in that ocean.

After a time he decided to walk on the deck, just to get out of the small cockpit. It was very dark, and Mr. Bear was clumsy, and the further he went along the deck the narrower it became. The first thing he knew he was on the very bow of the boat, with water all around him— black, deep water, as all water looks at night; and the deck was so narrow he didn't dare try to turn around for fear he would fall overboard. So he started to go backward. He couldn't see where he was going, and he didn't go straight, so that soon he was on the very edge of the boat. The boat began to tip. Mr. Bear was really frightened then, and he gave a backward and sidewise jump and tried to turn around

There came a horrible rattle and a scraping noise in the darkness. The boat tipped further and further. And then there was a tremendous splash. Water flew all over Mr. Bear. But the boat was level again.

Mr. Bear gave a fearful growl and jumped into the cockpit so heavily that the whole boat shook.

When the boat tipped so far, Mr. Badger was rolled right out of the corner where he was sleeping. His head hit the floor with a crash, waking him up in a most unpleasant manner. And just as he awoke he heard the great splash. Then Mr. Bear came tumbling down into the cockpit. All in all, it was enough to frighten anyone.

"What is it?" he cried out. "What is happening?"

"Disaster!" cried Mr. Bear. "We are lost! Things are falling from the skies! Another one and we are gone! Haul in Mr. Lobster!"

Mr. Badger hauled in Mr. Lobster.

"What is the matter?" asked Mr. Lobster at once. "I heard a fearful splash. Did Mr. Bear fall overboard?" It was so dark now that Mr. Lobster could see scarcely a thing.

"I'm here," said Mr. Bear from the darkness, "and I wish I were home. Someone is dropping things from the sky. One more and we are lost."

"I don't hear anything now," said Mr. Lobster. "Perhaps there won't be another one."

"There always is," groaned Mr. Bear. "I feel it in my bones that something is wrong. That's why we haven't seen any islands."

"We must wait," said Mr. Badger.

"Do you call this exploring pleasure?" demanded Mr. Bear. "I haven't slept a wink tonight, and now we are waiting for things to fall on us."

"We are waiting to see whether this is an adventure," said Mr. Badger. "Think of it—here we are in the black night miles and miles from home, miles and miles from land. Isn't it exciting?"

"Please don't remind me," begged Mr. Bear. "Please don't say another thing about home and land."

"Well, I don't hear any signs of danger," said Mr. Badger. "I guess all danger is past." He sighed as though he were a little disappointed.

Everything was still and dark. No one knew what had made the mysterious splash. But after waiting and listening for some time longer, the three explorers decided to go to sleep again. So Mr. Lobster was let down into the water once more, Mr. Badger curled up in his corner, and Mr. Bear settled himself as well as possible, knowing that he would stay awake all the rest of the night listening for another splash.

But all the rest of the night there was not a sound but the gentle lapping of the water at the sides of the boat.

Mr. Lobster
Saves the Day

AT LAST the darkness began to go away from the ocean, and Mr. Bear could see over the water. And the water grew wider and wider. The black sky became gray, then white. At last the edge of the sky seemed to burn and glow, and the sun rose.

Mr. Badger woke up and hauled in Mr. Lobster.

"Well, it was a safe night after all," said Mr. Lobster cheerfully as he looked around and saw that the boat and Mr. Badger and Mr. Bear were still there.

"Perfectly safe," said Mr. Badger. "Evidently one of the

stars just went out and fell in the sea, and we heard the splash."

"I say it was a close call," said Mr. Bear. "It was so close that I got wet. And now I am good and hungry."

"I was afraid you would remember that," said Mr. Badger, sighing.

"As if anyone could forget anything so important as eating," said Mr. Bear, shocked at Mr. Badger's words. "Sometimes, Mr. Badger, you are positively foolish."

"It would be better if you could forget eating for a time," said Mr. Badger. "For the sad fact is that you will have to go hungry until we discover an island."

"You said we could fish!" exclaimed Mr. Bear with a growl. "There's got to be some limit to this exploring. It may be necessary to skip supper and stay out on the water all night, but I'm not going to skip all my meals. That wouldn't be exploring; it would be starvation."

Mr. Lobster was hungry, too, but hunger did not upset him.

Mr. Badger looked very serious.

"I was not joking," he said. "I remembered after I lay down to sleep last night that although we brought our lines with us we have no bait. And we are out so far on the ocean I suppose there are no small clams here."

"No, there aren't," said Mr. Lobster, "and I am afraid I can't catch fish big enough for you."

"I knew it," said Mr. Bear miserably. "There is always

something wrong, and this is just about the wrongest thing possible. We must start for home."

"We can't turn back," said Mr. Badger. "No explorer ever turns back until he discovers something."

"I resign from being an explorer," growled Mr. Bear. "I am going home, and this is my boat. I have discovered that I am hungry, and that's enough for me."

"We may be quite near an island by now," said Mr. Lobster at this point, "and we know we are a long way from home. Why don't we hoist the sail and go ahead full speed?"

Everyone realized that it was a dangerous situation to be out on the ocean without any land in sight and not a bit of food to eat.

Mr. Badger didn't say a word, but he sprang to the halyards, hoisted the sail, pulled his sheet tight, and gripped the tiller. The little boat started.

Mr. Badger, being clever, was an excellent helmsman, and all the day before he had steered the boat on a straight course. Today, however, a strange thing happened. When the boat felt the morning breeze gently pushing like an invisible hand, and started, it went straight for only a short distance. Then it began to turn to the left. Mr. Badger tried to steer to the right, but the boat wouldn't go there. It just sailed around to the left until the sail began to shake and flap. Then the sail swung over to the other side and filled with wind again, and it seemed as if everything were all right again. But again the boat went straight for only a short distance, and then the same thing happened. Something was wrong.

Mr. Badger could not understand it, and he thought he understood almost everything. He was deeply worried.

Mr. Bear was annoyed by the flapping of the sail and all the fuss Mr. Badger was making over the sheet and the tiller.

Mr. Lobster thought it best not to mention things he was worried about; so, although he observed that all was not as it should be, he kept silent, watching the water.

Up in the bow Mr. Bear was looking everywhere for islands and thinking a good deal about food. He thought of fried fish, and then he looked all the harder. He thought of honey, a whole tree filled with honey. And he wanted to be the first one to see an island so that he could shout the news of his discovery, which he knew would make him important. But as he saw nothing but water, no matter which way he looked, there was nothing to shout about.

They were all silent for a long time, and poor Mr. Badger was as busy as could be. Almost all the morning passed that way, and no one was really happy.

At last Mr. Bear, growing irritable because he saw no islands and was very hungry, spoke up.

"It seems to me you are a pretty bad boat steerer," he said to Mr. Badger.

"The wind is tricky this morning," said Mr. Badger. "It must have changed since yesterday."

Mr. Bear growled and muttered something about starvation and why anyone with a good home should ever want to be an explorer.

Just then Mr. Lobster, who was still watching the water, saw something. It was a block of wood with a piece of seaweed on it, and it was floating past the boat. He was sure that they had just passed the very same block of wood a few minutes before. He said nothing, but he kept watching the water with the greatest care, and in a few minutes he saw the same block of wood for the third time.

"Look!" he exclaimed. "Do you see that piece of wood? Do you see the seaweed on it?"

Mr. Badger and Mr. Bear looked, and both of them saw it. The block of wood went past the boat and out of sight in the waves.

"Now wait," said Mr. Lobster.

They all waited several minutes. Then Mr. Bear cried out:

"There it is!"

Sure enough, the same block of wood came floating along.

"It is a mystery," said Mr. Lobster.

"Something is terribly wrong, I'm sure of that," said Mr. Bear.

"We are sailing around in a circle," said Mr. Badger. "That is why the boat acts so strangely. After all my work this morning, we are going no-where."

Then Mr. Bear growled.

"You said yesterday that we couldn't be nowhere as long as we were alive," he said. "And now we are going nowhere. Does that mean we're not going to be alive?"

"I don't know. I really don't know," said Mr. Badger. For once in his life, he was baffled.

"Starvation!" growled Mr. Bear. "That's what it is. And you called it exploring and adventure. I don't believe there are any islands! They have all sunk!"

"We must be brave," said Mr. Badger.

It was a desperate situation. Mr. Bear had drunk almost all the water in the jug. And they were going nowhere.

"I have such bad luck," groaned Mr. Bear.

Then there followed the unhappiest silence the three friends had ever known.

Mr. Lobster was thinking hard. In all his life in the ocean he had never known any tides or currents that went round and round in circles. And he had never known the wind to blow in circles when he had been ashore. Therefore he was sure that something must be wrong with the boat. And somebody would have to do something at once or all would be lost.

So he spoke up.

"Sometimes just being brave is not enough," he said. "You have to be wise, too. And I think it would be wise if we examined everything carefully. Does anyone see anything wrong with Mr. Bear's boat?"

They all looked but everything seemed all right.

"I see nothing," said Mr. Lobster finally. "So if you will let the sail down, Mr. Badger, and let me go overboard I will swim under the boat and all around and make an examination there."

Mr. Badger let Mr. Lobster into the water by the short rope, and Mr. Lobster began swimming. When he got around by the bow of the boat he was surprised to see another rope going down into the water. He decided to investigate that at once; so he followed it, sinking deeper and deeper under the water. Finally he was on the bottom of the ocean, and there was the rope, and it was tied to a big anchor.

"There," he said to himself. "That was the splash we heard last night. Mr. Bear knocked the anchor overboard. No wonder we have been sailing in circles. I have solved the mystery, and now it is only a fact."

He hurried back to the boat, and Mr. Badger pulled him in.

"We are anchored," he said. He was tremendously pleased with himself. "It explains the splash. As soon as we pull the anchor in, we can sail on."

They all looked at the forward deck of the boat. The anchor was gone and its rope was tied to a cleat on the deck. No one had noticed it before.

"You are wonderful," said Mr. Badger. "You have saved us."

They all got hold of the anchor rope and pulled as hard as they could. The anchor would not budge. They tried and tried, but it was no use.

Mr. Badger tried to untie the knot in the end of the rope, but it was too tight.

Mr. Bear groaned unhappily. He knew who had knocked the anchor overboard, and he was too wretched and ashamed to growl or say a word.

"I will cut the rope," said Mr. Lobster.

"A boat is not complete without an anchor," said Mr. Badger, "but I suppose we must cut the rope. I hope you don't mind losing your anchor, Mr. Bear."

"Not at all," said Mr. Bear meekly. "I never use anchors anyway."

So Mr. Lobster dropped overboard and went down to the bottom of the ocean again. There he went to work with his big claws and soon cut the rope. Then he returned to his friends.

Mr. Badger then hoisted sail and took the tiller. The boat started once more, and this time the three explorers were really on their way.

"Mr. Lobster has proved himself a hero again," said Mr. Badger. "And he is the wisest one of us all."

"Yes, indeed," agreed Mr. Bear, who was still very meek, and who seemed to be so busy looking for islands that he did not turn around.

Mr. Lobster, pleased and happy, was thinking things over, as he always did when something had happened. "I have learned something," he said to himself, "from this experience. Very often when things go wrong we blame luck, and strangely enough we find out that the whole trouble was caused by something we did ourselves. I wonder if Mr. Bear realizes this, too."

But, being considerate, he said nothing to Mr. Bear.

MR. LOBSTER WENT TO WORK WITH HIS BIG CLAWS
AND SOON CUT THE ROPE.

They had not been sailing very long before Mr. Badger began to chuckle to himself as he steered. Mr. Bear, who couldn't think of anything to chuckle about, turned around in amazement.

"Would you mind telling me what there is to laugh about?" he demanded rather unpleasantly.

"A joke," answered Mr. Badger. "Whenever things are not going just right I like to think of a joke, and I've just thought of a good one."

"Tell us," begged Mr. Lobster.

"It is this," said Mr. Badger. "Three heroic explorers skimming over the sea in search of islands and just sailing round and round in circles for a half a day and not going anywhere at all. It's one of the funniest things I ever heard of. What a joke on us!" And he laughed out loud.

Mr. Lobster thought that, come to think of it, it was a joke.

Mr. Bear snorted.

"You didn't think it was a joke when it happened," he said severely.

"That doesn't matter," said Mr. Badger happily. "Lots of things are unfortunate when they happen, but after wards you can see something funny in them, too. It is a pity to remember just the unfortunate part, but it is a joy to remember the funny part. I'm always going to remember this morning as a joke."

"Will it be a joke if we don't discover any islands?" asked Mr. Bear.

"We shall see later," answered Mr. Badger. "Anyway, not finding any islands is unpleasant to talk about. So I shan't bother my head with it."

"Well, I am coming to believe there are no islands in this ocean," said Mr. Bear. "And I have drunk almost all my water, and I am starving. I must be starving, because I haven't eaten all day long."

"The turtle said there were islands," put in Mr. Lobster, trying to cheer up Mr. Bear.

"Maybe they are in another ocean."

"How can there be other oceans?" asked Mr. Badger. "Why, it is a wonder to me there is room enough for this one, it is so big. There just can't be another, can there, Mr. Lobster?"

"This is the only ocean I know," replied Mr. Lobster, "but I am sure there are many things I do not know yet. There are so many wonders in the world I sometimes feel that I am only beginning to learn about them. Perhaps there are many oceans. I do know that the turtle lives in this ocean, though, because I met him here. So I am sure that the islands he discovers are here, too."

"There!" exclaimed Mr. Badger. "You really need not worry, Mr. Bear."

"I disagree with you," said Mr. Bear firmly. "When there is no food in sight and no dry land anywhere to be seen, I have to worry. I have practically nothing else to do."

Mr. Lobster thought to himself: "How very true! If Mr. Bear were only busy he would not have time to worry. I think not being busy is sometimes the hardest thing of all."

Out loud he said: "Why don't you take turns steering your boat, Mr. Bear? I am sure Mr. Badger will teach you."

At first Mr. Bear didn't like the idea of having Mr. Badger teach him anything, because he was afraid Mr. Badger would be very superior about it. But Mr. Badger, like a good teacher, was so polite that he consented.

The rest of the afternoon passed without trouble. Mr. Bear steered most of the time, which kept him too busy to growl or worry. He almost forgot that he was hungry.

But one true fact remained that nothing could conceal or change. There were no islands anywhere in sight. And everyone was looking hard now. The water in Mr. Bear's jug was gone. Soon Mr. Badger and Mr. Bear would be thirsty. And still there were no islands. Each one of the three friends was thinking one thought, but not one of them cared to mention it.

Mr. Lobster said to himself: "There are some things too serious and important to be mentioned. They are the things one keeps in his own heart, and they may be great sorrows or great joys. Sometimes silence is a most excellent thing. I shall remain silent now."

When the darkness began to gather they were still silent. The breeze was strong, and the boat was sailing beautifully, sailing straight ahead toward the place where the dark sea and the darkening sky met. And that place came nearer and nearer.

When all was completely dark, and the night was upon them, Mr. Badger took his turn at the helm.

"I think we had better leave the sail up all night," he said. "That is, if Mr. Lobster does not mind staying all night in the boat. In the morning perhaps we shall be there."

"I shall be glad to stay here," said Mr. Lobster readily.

So it was agreed to sail in the dark, and the little boat kept skimming along.

There Is a
Stealthy Rustle

SO THEY sailed through the long dark night. The sound of the water rushing by and the feeling of the endless motion of the sea were different and strange when nothing could be seen. The sail was pale, like a place where the darkness had faded. And the boat made small sounds of creaking and moving, as if it were alive and could feel the great waters under it. These were the sounds no one noticed in the day time, for at night in boats and houses many little noises come out like mice, only to disappear when it is light again.

The three friends all experienced the wonderful and strange sensation of moving through darkness with only the stars overhead, and the whole world lost and invisible, so that they all felt like wanderers. And, because at night the feeling of adventure is strongest, they all felt like adventurers. And, because they were waiting and silent, not knowing where they were going, they all felt something like mystery, something not to be explained or understood.

At last the stars began to grow dim.

"Someone is putting out the lights in the stars," said Mr. Badger. "Soon it will be day."

Mr. Bear immediately sat up and began to look around, trying to see through the dimness of the fading night; but for some time he could see nothing except water and the white sky of very early morning.

Mr. Lobster had been out of water all night, and, although the night had been cool and he had not been uncomfortable, now that the day was come he began to think of getting wet again. He wondered if Mr. Bear and Mr. Badger would mind stopping while he went down to the bottom of the ocean and looked for some breakfast; but, as it would be selfish for him to eat while his friends were hungry, he decided to say nothing about it.

"No food. No water," sighed Mr. Bear. "Lost on the sea and starving."

"Something will happen," said Mr. Badger.

They had all been brave all night, and no one had complained. It had been a long voyage, and every one of

"LOOK!" MR. BEAR EXCLAIMED. "A DISCOVERY! LOOK
OVER THERE!"

them was hoping that soon it would be over. They were hoping so hard that no one could think of a joke now, not even Mr. Badger.

Suddenly, after a long silence, Mr. Bear cried out.

"Look!" he exclaimed. "A discovery! Look over there!"

There was a dark spot on the water, far ahead of the boat.

"An island!" shouted Mr. Badger. "An island as sure as I am a badger and a hero. We are successful explorers! We are about to discover something!"

Soon Mr. Lobster could see. There was not only one island: there were two, one a very small one with low bushes growing on it, and the other a large island with tall trees.

"Saved!" exclaimed Mr. Bear. "And I discovered them! Doesn't that make me something, Mr. Badger?"

"It makes you a great explorer," said Mr. Badger.

"Don't steer for the small one," said Mr. Bear. "Small islands sink. Steer for the big one. I want an island that won't sink, and one where there's plenty of food."

"I have never been on an island," remarked Mr. Lobster. "I am terribly curious."

After sailing and sailing, while Mr. Bear grew more and more impatient, they could see the beach of the large island, and Mr. Badger steered for a small harbor.

"As we have no anchor, we must run in where the water is quiet and let our boat rest on the sand," said Mr. Badger.

When they were entering the harbor itself, which was really only a small cove, Mr. Bear climbed up on deck so as to be the first one ashore. He walked out to the point of the bow, all ready to jump.

Mr. Badger saw him there, of course, and a gleam of mischief came into his eyes.

"Hold on everybody!" he shouted.

Then he suddenly steered the boat straight for shore, without letting down the sail or letting go of the sheet. There was a terrific bump, which sent Mr. Lobster sliding across the seat; and Mr. Bear let out a great growl. Of course there was nothing for Mr. Bear to hold on to. He tried to jump from the boat to the dry beach, but it was too far. Splash! The water flew everywhere. Mr. Bear howled with rage. Mr. Badger laughed.

Mr. Bear had to run through water to get to shore.

"Is that the way you handle a boat?" he demanded angrily.

"The wind pushes the boat, you know," said Mr. Badger innocently. He was busy letting down the sail and furling it neatly.

"I am going to look for breakfast and lunch and supper," said Mr. Bear. And he started off for the woods without waiting for his friends to go ashore.

When he was gone, Mr. Lobster said to Mr. Badger, "I am afraid you did that on purpose."

"I am afraid I did," answered Mr. Badger, pretending to look ashamed and not succeeding at all. "Somehow there are times when I cannot help doing mischievous things. I guess it is because I am an independent badger. And I do love to hear Mr. Bear growl when I know it's nothing serious."

"Well, I suppose you will never change your ways," said Mr. Lobster.

"I hope not," said Mr. Badger. "I am so happy as I am."

Mr. Lobster crawled over to the side of the boat. "I think I shall drop into the water now," he said. "I must look for food before I explore the island, for now I am as hungry as I am curious, which is saying a great deal. Shall we meet here later?"

"Yes," agreed Mr. Badger. "I shall find Mr. Bear and we must all meet here and discover the island together. I shall pretend I have not seen anything in the meantime."

So Mr. Lobster dropped into the water and began crawling over a new part of the bottom of the ocean; and Mr. Badger went ashore.

Mr. Lobster found the bottom of the ocean near the island a delightful place. There were rocks and seaweed and, best of all, many pleasant creatures such as flounders, sand-dabs, and perch. He crawled up several small hills and looked under all the big rocks for caves until he found one where he could spend his nights while he and Mr. Badger and Mr. Bear were exploring the island. And while he was crawling about he made some fast tail-snaps and rushes, so that the hollow place under his shell was no longer troubled by hunger and he felt that life was very good indeed. Also he kept a sharp lookout for unpleasant creatures, such as big fish and sharks, but he did not see one.

When he was satisfied that everything was safe and pleasant, he returned to the cave which he had chosen and began to clean it out and make it neat. There were some old seaweed leaves and several empty shells in it, and these he pushed or carried outside and buried some distance away.

"I cannot be anywhere for a long time without having a home there," he thought; "so I shall call this my exploring home. Of course it is only temporary, but even temporary things should be neat. It is so much more pleasing to the eye. People who shut their eyes can put up with anything, I suppose, but as I never shut my eyes, I could never be happy in an untidy place. How very strange it must be not to see anything in the day time— just as though it were dark night. I must ask Mr. Bear and Mr. Badger sometime if it is night whenever they close their eyes."

With such curious thoughts he kept his mind busy until his new home was entirely satisfactory. Then he crawled ashore to meet Mr. Badger and Mr. Bear.

"I trust that you are feeling better," he said to Mr. Bear.

"Oh, yes, I am passing well," answered Mr. Bear. "But I would like a good big fried fish—or a tree full of honey."

"You must remember," put in Mr. Badger, "that if you ate the same things here that you have at home it wouldn't be exploring. Explorers always eat strange food, and the best explorers eat things they simply hate."

"I am already a great explorer, for you said so," replied Mr. Bear, "and I discovered this island. And I intend to eat whatever I please."

Mr. Lobster wondered if Mr. Badger would disapprove of the delicious small fish he had just eaten. He thought it best not to ask any questions.

Instead, he said, "Let us start exploring the island."

"By all means," agreed Mr. Badger. "This is the greatest time of all. We shall walk all around this island this very day."

So they started. Mr. Badger and Mr. Bear walked slowly so that Mr. Lobster could keep up with them, and Mr. Lobster crawled just as fast as his eight legs would carry him. They walked for a time on the beach, but Mr. Bear remarked that it looked just like any other beach, so he didn't see any use in walking there.

"In fact," he added, "I would never know I was exploring."

"You are wrong as usual," said Mr. Badger. "This beach goes all around the island, I am sure; so it is a round beach. Our beach at home is a straight beach."

But they left the beach and went into the woods and continued on their way. This pleased Mr. Bear and especially pleased Mr. Lobster, for he still had not had nearly enough of woods and trees. He crawled through the old leaves on the ground and over weeds and enjoyed every minute of it. He looked up at the trees and kept a sharp lookout for animals, but there seemed to be no animals about, although there were birds high up in the trees.

Suddenly Mr. Badger stopped.

"Hark!" he said.

"What does that mean?" asked Mr. Lobster.

"It means listen especially hard," answered Mr. Badger.

They all stood still, listening. There was not a sound except leaves stirring overhead.

"What is the matter now?" asked Mr. Bear finally.

"I heard a sound. Someone is following us. It was a stealthy rustle."

"Like danger?" asked Mr. Bear.

"Exactly," said Mr. Badger.

So they all listened and looked all around again, but there was not a sound and not a creature to be seen but the three explorers themselves.

They continued their exploration. Mr. Lobster marveled at the trees, some of them with green moss on their trunks and some with black bark and some with snow-white bark. He was so busy looking around and touching things with his feelers to satisfy his curiosity that he soon forgot all about the stealthy rustle.

Then Mr. Badger cried out again.

"Hark!"

And they all listened and looked, but there was not a sound and not a creature.

"Very strange," said Mr. Badger. "There is something going on here that we know nothing about."

"I thought you knew everything," said Mr. Bear. "You always talk as if you did." Then he laughed. It was the first joke he had ever had on Mr. Badger.

Mr. Badger pretended he didn't hear that remark of Mr. Bear's.

"This is serious," he said. "I think it is the beginning of a new experience, probably an adventure or a narrow escape. We must keep together."

They went on slowly, but now both Mr. Lobster and Mr. Bear also listened carefully, and both of them heard the rustling behind them. Several times they all stopped and listened. Once Mr. Badger rushed off into the woods to look, but he saw not a single creature.

"This is very bad," he said when he returned. "Someone is following us, and he is invisible."

"Like the wind," said Mr. Lobster.

"Yes," agreed Mr. Badger.

Mr. Lobster trembled a little in the joints of his shell, but he assured himself that he was not afraid.

"I think I am getting dry," he hastened to say. "Perhaps I had better go in the water for a little while."

Mr. Bear shivered. Then he said: "It is cool in these woods. Let us go out in the sun again."

So they all went out on the beach for a time and continued their travels. Mr. Lobster spent several minutes in the water, and he wondered if it would be polite for him to walk around the island under water, where there were no stealthy rustles. He decided not to suggest it to Mr. Bear and Mr. Badger, and so he returned to the shore.

After they had walked for a long time on the beach Mr. Badger started to walk toward the woods.

"An explorer goes everywhere," he said.

There was nothing for Mr. Lobster and Mr. Bear to do but follow. They knew that friends always stick together, no matter what happens or what danger may threaten; but they much preferred walking somewhere else.

All day they walked, and all day someone followed them through the woods. Mr. Lobster became more and more eager to return to his new home under the water. Mr. Bear was very nervous. His back hairs were standing up straight, and he growled in a low tone as he went along. Mr. Badger walked in an especially dignified manner with his legs stiff and his eyes gleaming, which were sure signs that he was angry and ready to fight if necessary.

At last, when it seemed as though the island would go on forever, Mr. Bear saw his boat.

"We are back," he said with a great sigh of relief, and his back hairs went down again.

But just then there was the stealthy rustle right behind him, and his hairs immediately stuck right up straight again. He let out a fearful growl and jumped. But there was no one to be seen.

It was dusk now, and the woods were dark. The three friends stepped out on the beach.

"Well," said Mr. Bear, trying hard to speak calmly, "now that we have explored this island we can go home." He looked longingly at his boat.

"No," said Mr. Badger, "we can't do that. An explorer always stays a long time away from home. You know, staying away from home is the most important part of exploring, and we can't break the rules."

"Are you sure that is a rule?" asked Mr. Bear.

"Oh, yes," answered Mr. Badger confidently. "Also, I have observed no creatures on this island, which is important."

"There are birds here," said Mr. Lobster.

"Birds don't count," answered Mr. Badger. "They live only in trees. They cannot claim the ground. No, we are the only creatures I have seen on the island. Therefore we must do a most important thing."

"Do tell us!" exclaimed Mr. Lobster.

"We must claim this island for our own. An explorer always claims the places he goes, if no one else is there."

"But we don't want this island," protested Mr. Bear. "We want our own homes. At least, I do, and I wish I were home now. Besides, this island is worthless."

"We don't know that for sure, for we have only been around it," said Mr. Badger. "And even if it is worthless, it doesn't matter. An explorer claims places no matter how worthless they are. That is another rule."

Mr. Bear groaned.

Mr. Lobster was instantly curious to know how the island would be claimed.

Mr. Badger went right on talking. "Since there is no one else here—"

"There is a stealthy rustle," interrupted Mr. Bear.

"Invisible things do not count," said Mr. Badger, "and please do not interrupt again. This is one of the most important ceremonies of exploring." Then he paused, looked all around, and said in a very loud voice: "Since there is no one else here, I now claim this island to be the private property of Mr. Lobster, Mr. Bear, and Mr. Badger!"

"I don't want it," said Mr. Bear.

"Hush!" said Mr. Lobster.

"And because of his wisdom and bravery in helping us get here," went on Mr. Badger in the same loud voice, "I name this island Mr. Lobster's Island."

There was just a single instant of silence after that solemn announcement. Then there came the most amazing cry from the woods.

"Treason!" cried a voice. "Treason!"

Mr. Lobster's pride at having an island named for him was instantly shattered.

Mr. Bear shivered.

Mr. Badger, not being afraid of anything, made a jump and ran straight for the woods where the voice came from.

Soon he returned, shaking his head. "I didn't see a soul," he said.

"That means trouble," said Mr. Bear.

"Pardon me," said Mr. Lobster, "but will you tell me what treason is? I am sure there is nothing by that name at the bottom of the ocean."

"Treason is really bad business—like stealing and such," admitted Mr. Badger. "Or, if you are the absolute boss, anything you don't like you call treason. If you have an enemy, then you call anything he does treason. It is very serious usually."

Mr. Lobster and Mr. Bear shivered and trembled.

"Do you suppose we are the enemies of that creature who cried out?" asked Mr. Lobster.

"Yes, I suppose so," said Mr. Badger.

"And is he our enemy?"

"Yes."

"A fine situation, indeed!" exclaimed Mr. Bear. "Now how about going home?"

"Never!" declared Mr. Badger. "That would be retreating, and a hero never retreats. We shall now spend the night here. You and I will guard the boat, Mr. Bear. Mr. Lobster can go into the water. Tomorrow something will have to be done."

With these words he started for the boat, and Mr. Bear, wishing he were a lobster for the night, had nothing to do but follow him.

Mr. Lobster went into the water and hurried away to his new home. "Life is indeed strange," he thought. "I am the kindest person in the world, and I wouldn't harm a soul. And here I have an enemy, and I have not even seen him. I am afraid tomorrow may be a very bad day for me, for I have no idea how to deal with enemies."

And a little while later he said to himself, "Life is like exploring: one never knows what he will see or what will happen; and one must always have wisdom and courage. And if one's life is successful he will discover new and wonderful things—just as explorers do. In spite of tomorrow and other troubles, I love exploring and I love life."

There Is
Serious Trouble

WHEN MR. LOBSTER woke up in the morning the first thing he did was to catch a large breakfast. He had an idea that it was going to be a busy day, perhaps a very hard day, and he knew that he would feel stronger in an emergency if he had had a good breakfast. "For," he told himself, "even wise persons sometime have emergencies, but no wise person starts the day without breakfast when he is at home, and I am temporarily at home. A good breakfast is the best beginning to almost any problem, and I think that today is going to be a problem."

He felt rather full under his shell when he started for

shore, with the result that he crawled slowly and contentedly, admiring the seaweed and shells along the way,
and stopping to chat with a large crab who said that he
was visiting in those parts.

Mr. Badger and Mr. Bear were waiting by the boat. Mr.
Badger was looking very brisk and determined. His eyes
were especially bright. Mr. Bear did not look eager at all.

"I shall stay on my boat," said Mr. Bear. "This boat is
my property, and no one can accuse me of treason while
I am on my own property. I don't like this treason business, and I say we sail for home."

"I say that we have a meeting to decide what to do,"
said Mr. Badger.

"No, thank you," said Mr. Bear. "Our meetings all end
the same way: you have an idea, and we have to do
what you say. I don't understand it, but that's the way it
always is."

"Some persons are natural leaders," said Mr. Badger
modestly. "And I'll bet that if I have an idea Mr. Lobster
won't be satisfied until he knows what it is."

Mr. Lobster knew very well that Mr. Badger would
have an idea, for Mr. Badger was full of ideas. And Mr.
Lobster was curious already, for even a good big breakfast does not change curiosity in the slightest.

"If you have an idea," he said, "I do want to know it.
I have had a very pleasant night, but now that I am ashore
again I realize that I have an enemy and I am not contented. I wonder what I shall do."

"An enemy must be conquered," said Mr. Badger firmly.

"I would rather change my enemy into a friend," said Mr. Lobster. "Couldn't we do that?"

Mr. Badger scratched his head and thought for some time. Then he said, "I never thought of that before, but I believe it is a very wise suggestion. Mr. Lobster, you still amaze me with your wisdom."

"I love peace and contentment," said Mr. Lobster, "as you already know; and I don't see how we can have peace and contentment and an enemy at the same time."

"Very true," agreed Mr. Badger. "And now the very first thing to do is to find our enemy so that we can change him. I say that we immediately search this island and find him."

"There you go!" exclaimed Mr. Bear. "That's your idea, and a dangerous one, too! It just means looking for serious trouble, as if we did not have enough already. Don't you know that enemies always fight? That is what an enemy is for."

"I beg your pardon," said Mr. Lobster, "but if we do not fight, then certainly the enemy cannot fight all by himself, and so nothing unpleasant will happen."

"Mr. Lobster is right," said Mr. Badger. "He is always right."

Mr. Bear sighed and growled softly. He saw that no one wanted to go home with him. It gave him a rather lonely feeling to think that his friends never seemed to follow his ideas, and he wished desperately that he could do some brave thing or have some great idea that would make Mr. Badger and Mr. Lobster think he was courageous and clever. He wanted so much to be important, and he did not feel important at all.

Mr. Lobster was not exactly afraid, but the joints in his shell were a little shaky when he thought of actually seeing an enemy face to face. It would be a new experience, and not the kind he wished for. The question was: Would it be a pleasant experience in the end? However, thinking over Mr. Badger's idea of searching the island, he *was* sure of one thing: he was terribly curious. He said to himself, "I have done strange things before to satisfy my curiosity, and I know that I shall do this. For I wonder what my enemy looks like. And I wonder why he shouted 'Treason.' And I wonder what he will do when we find him."

Then Mr. Badger interrupted his wondering.

"Well, Mr. Lobster," Mr. Badger was saying confidently, "I suppose you vote to search the island."

"Yes, I do," answered Mr. Lobster, realizing that it was a most important decision.

"That settles it," said Mr. Badger. "You and I are going anyway. If Mr. Bear insists on staying here, he may."

"Oh, no, I'm coming," said Mr. Bear. "I am practically resigned to my fate. I felt it in my bones it would turn out this way."

Mr. Badger led the way until they were in the woods. Then the three friends spread out and walked along slowly, three abreast, and looking around at every step. Every little while Mr. Badger would say "Hush!," and they would stop and listen. But they saw nothing, and no one heard the stealthy rustle behind them. The island seemed deserted and still.

When they had walked to the middle of the woods, where it was stillest and shadiest and the leaves were thickest, Mr. Bear called out loudly:

"Is there anybody here who claims this island?"

There was no answer.

So they started back toward the beach. Everyone was somewhat nervous by now, not knowing how soon the voice would cry out, or the rustling be heard behind them.

"Maybe he is really invisible," remarked Mr. Badger.

Mr. Bear shivered at the thought.

They kept on walking for hours, until once more they could look far ahead and see the ocean through the trees.

"Who owns this island?" called out Mr. Badger.

There was not a sound in reply.

"If no one owns this island we claim it again," shouted Mr. Badger.

"Treason!" The cry came from right behind Mr. Bear, and he jumped straight up in the air and growled at the same time.

"The enemy!" cried Mr. Badger. "We have found him!" And he ran to the very place the cry had come from.

There were only low bushes not thick enough to hide any creature, and yet when Mr. Badger got there not a creature was in sight. They all looked around, but the place seemed absolutely empty.

Mr. Badger cocked his head and looked up among the branches of the trees. There was no one up there.

"I don't like this," muttered Mr. Bear.

Mr. Lobster crawled over to investigate. He was nearer the ground than the others, and he saw things that they overlooked. When he walked on the beach he noticed all the colors and patterns in the sand; and in the woods he noticed the veins in the leaves, and the blades of grass, and all the small things that larger creatures would never notice at all. And now, as he crawled about under the bushes near where Mr. Bear and Mr. Badger were, he saw something that they had missed.

"Look!" he exclaimed.

There was a large hole in the ground.

"That must be where he lives," said Mr. Badger. "Let us speak to him."

"Do you think we need to?" asked Mr. Bear.

"Yes," answered Mr. Badger. "Now that we are here, we must settle this matter. Let us all get ready."

The three friends moved away a respectful distance from the hole and all stood waiting. It was an exciting moment. Mr. Bear's back hair was up. Mr. Lobster was so excited and curious that he couldn't keep his joints quiet, and his shell trembled in every possible place.

"Whoever you are, please come out!" called Mr. Badger in his loudest voice.

"We are not fighting!" called Mr. Bear hastily.

There was a pause. Everyone held his breath.

And then, without a sound, came a head and two

gleaming eyes, and then a tremendous snake up from the blackness of the hole—a snake feet and feet long. The creature coiled himself and lifted up his head and ran his tongue in and out, so that he was fearful and wicked to see. Then he hissed.

At that awful sound Mr. Bear, who had been sitting up, fell over backwards in a heap; but he very hurriedly scrambled to his feet and exclaimed:

"We are not fighting, please!"

The snake simply looked at them, his head swaying back and forth in the most evil manner. Then he hissed again.

Mr. Lobster was fascinated. He found himself moving his long feelers back and forth in exact time with the swaying of the snake's head.

Mr. Badger's hair was standing up straight now, and his eyes had a glint in them, a glint of red. But he didn't move.

"So," he said calmly. "A snake."

"How dare you!" exclaimed the creature. "How dare you insult me in my own home! It's treason! Can't you see that I am no snake, but a serpent? Who ever saw a snake my size?" And he hissed in a most disgusted and outraged manner, and his head kept swaying back and forth.

"I beg your pardon," said Mr. Badger. "It was a slip of the tongue. I am not afraid of anything, for I happen to be a badger, but I did not mean to insult you. Of course you are a serpent, and the finest specimen I have ever seen."

The snake stopped swaying for a moment.

"Fine words, indeed!" he said. "But I am too wise to pay any attention to flattery."

"We are explorers," said Mr. Badger in a polite way. "I am Mr. Badger. There is Mr. Bear and there is Mr. Lobster."

"I have seen you all before," said the snake unpleasantly. "In fact, I have seen too much of you."

"Pardon me, but were you the stealthy rustle?" asked Mr. Lobster.

"I was."

"And did you cry 'treason' last night?"

"I did! How dare you claim this island when it is mine? If that isn't treason, I'd like to know what is!" The snake was angry now, and his tongue darted in and out, and he hissed fiercely.

The three friends were silent.

Mr. Lobster sighed, and after a moment of thought said, "I suppose I have lost my island then."

"Lost!" exclaimed the snake. "How can you lose something you never had? This is my island. It has always been my island, and it always will be!"

"Oh, I beg your pardon," said Mr. Lobster.

There seemed to be nothing for the three friends to do. Everything they said was wrong. The snake, who was really tremendous and very long, was swaying back and forth in a most threatening manner, his shiny eyes watching them carefully, and the wickedest expression on his face. It looked as though the three friends had found the most dangerous enemy possible.

IT LOOKED AS THOUGH THE THREE FRIENDS HAD FOUND
THE MOST DANGEROUS ENEMY POSSIBLE.

Mr. Lobster's head was now swaying back and forth just like the snake's, he didn't know why, and he had a queer feeling under his shell, and his mind was filled with wonder. He was sure that he was getting dry, and he wanted to hurry back to the ocean, but he couldn't take his eyes off the snake's shiny eyes.

Mr. Bear began to moan softly to himself in an unhappy sort of way that showed that he felt unusually miserable.

Mr. Badger, whose eyes were still alert and gleaming, and whose hair was still standing up straight, was thinking as hard as he could but saying nothing.

It was a most awkward and unpleasant moment.

"Well," demanded the snake, "are you going to leave my property?"

"We were going home," muttered Mr. Bear. "I said long ago we ought to go home."

"I feel a little dry," Mr. Lobster managed to murmur.

Then Mr. Badger spoke.

"Of course," he said, "we are all sorry that we claimed your island, but you must understand that explorers always claim whatever they find, and we are explorers. We did not know that you were here. We are going to return to our boat now and decide what to do, and we shall call on you tomorrow."

"Decide!" screamed the snake. "You will decide! You will leave my island this minute! You will all leave this very day!" And he hissed so that Mr. Bear and Mr. Lobster both expected something terrible to happen at once.

"We shall decide," said Mr. Badger in his calmest tone, just as though the snake had said nothing. "I must also tell you that we are all heroes, and heroes are never afraid." Mr. Badger looked the snake straight in the eye. "We shall see you tomorrow," he concluded.

The snake hissed terribly.

Mr. Badger started to walk away very slowly, with his legs very stiff.

Somehow Mr. Badger's courageous words and his action made it possible for Mr. Lobster to take his eyes from the snake, and he too started to crawl toward the ocean.

Mr. Bear came along grumbling and muttering.

"I knew it," he was saying. "Mr. Badger can always get us into serious trouble. Claiming the island is what did it. I knew we didn't want it anyway. Now I guess I was right for once, and it is high time we took my boat and went home."

"We shall see," said Mr. Badger.

There was something strange about Mr. Badger's tone, something like anger, which was not like good-natured Mr. Badger at all.

"You don't mean that you are really going back to see that serpent again, do you?" asked Mr. Bear.

"No one can threaten me," said Mr. Badger. "It is true that we cannot claim this island, since it is the serpent's, but as we only claimed it by mistake and explained it all politely the serpent should have been courteous. Also, since he does not need all the room on the island, he should have invited us to visit. Instead he told us to get off—and, what's more, he hissed. That was the same as a threat, and threats make me angry."

"Are you angry now?" asked Mr. Lobster.

"Yes, I am," answered Mr. Badger.

"What are you going to do?" Mr. Lobster felt a little doubtful about returning to see the serpent. "Can you change him from an enemy to a friend?"

"We shall see," answered Mr. Badger.

"You make me as nervous as the serpent did," said Mr. Bear. "All you say is 'We shall see.' I know what we shall see, and it's more trouble."

"I am going to think things over now," said Mr. Badger, paying no attention at all to Mr. Bear's complaint. "Please excuse me for a while." He started to walk away.

Mr. Lobster said good-by to Mr. Bear and Mr. Badger and crawled into the ocean. He was glad to be under water again, and glad to hurry away to his new home, for he wanted to think over things, too. Especially he wanted to think over the serpent's head swaying back and forth, and why he had swayed also just because the serpent had swayed. That had been a strange business.

"Serpents are very strange," he kept saying to himself. "Very strange." And, saying that over and over as he lay in his home, he fell asleep without thinking a single new thought.

An Enemy
Is Changed

IN THE morning Mr. Lobster found Mr. Bear and Mr. Badger on the beach. Mr. Bear was walking back and forth in a state of agitation, talking to himself and growling softly.

"Mr. Badger refuses to go home," he said to Mr. Lobster.

And Mr. Badger was walking by himself in deep silence, thinking so hard that he didn't even notice Mr. Lobster's arrival.

Mr. Lobster realized that this was indeed a serious morning. The three friends had to go and see the serpent and make friends with him, or else sail away home and leave the island forever.

So Mr. Lobster began to crawl back and forth by himself and think as hard as he could, just like Mr. Badger.

For a long time the three of them went back and forth on the beach, and there was not a sound except Mr. Bear's soft growling and the songs of birds from the woods and the whisper of small waves on the sand. It was such a beautiful day that it seemed a pity to spend it all in thinking.

About noon, when the sun was high overhead, and Mr. Bear was nearly exhausted and Mr. Lobster was feeling rather dry, Mr. Badger suddenly stopped walking.

"We must have a meeting now," he announced.

"Thank goodness!" exclaimed Mr. Bear. "At last I can have a rest."

"I must get wet," said Mr. Lobster, and he hurried gratefully for the ocean.

When he returned, they gathered near Mr. Bear's boat, at which poor Mr. Bear looked longingly, hoping that the meeting would decide that they would sail home, although he knew that any meeting with Mr. Badger could never turn out so pleasantly.

"Now," said Mr. Badger, "this is important. It is a council of war or a council of peace."

"Pardon me, but what is a council?" asked Mr. Lobster. "I have never seen one."

"A council," explained Mr. Badger readily, "is a meeting where all the people present are very important and only big things are discussed. It is very different from an ordinary meeting."

"I see," said Mr. Lobster. "I suppose all of us *are* important."

"And that serpent is so big, he is enormous," said Mr. Bear sadly.

"Exactly," said Mr. Badger. He looked all around before speaking again, as though he were making sure that no one but Mr. Lobster and Mr. Bear could hear him. Then he said in a low tone, "And a council is always secret. That is a rule. So we must be careful!"

He had already succeeded in making Mr. Bear nervous and Mr. Lobster curious, and they were both as silent as could be.

"I have thought this matter over," he went on, still speaking so that no one else but his two friends could hear. "I hate to admit it, but this is the serpent's island because he got here first. But that does not excuse him for being inhospitable to wanderers—and discourteous as well. And I cannot forget that he threatened me—me, a badger! If this is a council of war we must decide to drive the serpent away and take the island for ourselves." He paused to see what the others would say.

Mr. Bear spoke up at once.

"Fighting is uncomfortable," he said.

"It seems to me," said Mr. Lobster, "that driving the serpent away from his own island would be even more discourteous than he was. And I am sure that a hero is never discourteous. So how can we do that?"

Mr. Badger heaved a long sigh.

"I might have known that you would think of that, Mr. Lobster," he said. "You are altogether too wise. And I was sort of hankering for a good fight."

"Fights are very seldom good," replied Mr. Lobster. "And even if someone else does wrong, that is no excuse for our doing wrong."

"True," agreed Mr. Badger. "Of course you are perfectly right, but the truth is sometimes disappointing. Well, I guess we shall have a council of peace. Would you like to hear my idea?"

"Are you sure it is a peaceful one?" asked Mr. Bear.

"Yes, it is this: I have learned from experience that anyone who is really fierce and strong and heroic never has to threaten; so you can be sure that anyone who does boast and threaten is really an inferior creature. So I believe that the serpent is really not a serpent at all, but only a snake; and I believe we can make a bargain with him."

Mr. Lobster, although he trembled in every joint at the thought of seeing the serpent's head swaying back and forth, and looking into those strange eyes again, was instantly eager to see what Mr. Badger would do.

"I will go with you," he said, "if you want me to."

"Fine," said Mr. Badger. "Then we are decided. Are you ready to go, Mr. Bear?"

"I am never ready to rush into danger or unpleasantness," answered Mr. Bear, "but I know that I have to go, whether I am ready or not. It has always been so when you and Mr. Lobster decided anything. So let us get started and get it over with as soon as possible."

They started at once, Mr. Bear going last and looking over his shoulder at his boat as long as he could see it. When they were deep in the woods he paused once or twice, as though contemplating a retreat, but it was impossible to retreat with such a leader as Mr. Badger. So he went on, and before long they were all at the entrance of the serpent's home.

Mr. Bear looked around and picked a place behind a thorn bush. He hoped that serpents did not like thorns.

Mr. Lobster was nearer the hole in the ground. He was wondering what he could look at if the serpent's head began swaying back and forth and he began swaying himself.

Mr. Badger stood directly in front of the serpent's home. "Now this may be serious," he said to his two friends, "and you must be ready to help me if there is trouble and I need assistance."

"Please remember that we had a council of peace," begged Mr. Bear from behind the thorn bush.

Mr. Lobster curled his tail tightly.

"We are here to discuss matters," proclaimed Mr. Badger in a loud and firm tone. "Will you please come out?"

There was a moment of silence. Then the serpent appeared, sliding very slowly, his head held up in a dignified and fearless manner. When every inch of him was in sight he coiled himself neatly, gave his tail a flick to put it in perfect position, raised his head as high as possible, and spoke.

"I endeavor to be reasonable," he said, his eyes gleaming, "and so I have come. But a serpent never goes back on his word. You have committed treason, and I won't have you on my island."

It was not exactly a friendly beginning, and Mr. Bear was ready to leave at once without any further words.

But Mr. Badger was not ready to give up.

"It occurred to us," said he, "that perhaps you did not understand fully that we are wanderers and explorers, and that anything we did that you did not like was only a mistake."

"Only a mistake, indeed!" the snake said fiercely. "There is no excuse for mistakes! Only stupid persons make mistakes!"

"Then you have not changed your mind?" asked Mr. Badger, still speaking courteously.

"A serpent never changes his mind!"

There was a most uncomfortable silence—in fact, a disagreeable silence. The meeting seemed to have come to an end before it had really begun.

Mr. Bear, who was peering through his thorn bush, leaned forward to see what Mr. Badger would say or do next. Mr. Badger's eyes now had red in them, a dangerous sign with all badgers, and he wanted to fight the serpent. But there was something uncanny and shivery about that strange creature. No matter how angry and brave Mr. Badger felt, when he looked at those glittering eyes and that swaying head he couldn't quite get started fighting, no matter how much he wished to. It was an entirely new experience for Mr. Badger.

Mr. Lobster looked the other way when the serpent's head began swaying back and forth. He wanted to look again and again, but he didn't. He looked at a leaf instead. And he was curious. He thought: "If the serpent never makes a mistake and never changes his mind, then he must be perfect. What a wonderful thing to be! And I wonder if he is poisonous."

And, wanting to satisfy his curiosity, he forgot that the situation was a very serious one and spoke to the serpent.

"Pardon me for asking," he said in his polite way, "but are you poisonous?"

At that very moment, and before the serpent could answer, Mr. Bear leaned forward so far that he lost his balance. Quickly he put his foot out and stepped down very hard. He stepped on a thorn. And he let out the loudest, the fiercest, the worst growl he had ever made. The woods rang with it.

Like a black flash the serpent uncoiled himself, put his proud head down, and darted down the hole. He was gone, and the three friends were alone again.

"Bravely done!" exclaimed Mr. Badger. "Mr. Bear, you are a wonder to think of growling."

Mr. Bear had not meant to growl at all, of course, but now he felt quite pleased with himself.

"That fixed him!" he said.

MR. BEAR LET OUT THE LOUDEST, THE FIERCEST,
THE WORST GROWL HE HAD EVER MADE.

There was a moment of silence while the three friends wondered what to do next. Then Mr. Lobster realized something important.

"It seems to me that I have a good thought," he said. "If the serpent is really poisonous, would he run away from Mr. Bear's growl?"

"Why, no! Of course not!" exclaimed Mr. Badger. "Mr. Lobster, you have solved everything! It is your wisdom again, and I say brains always win. For certainly the serpent is not poisonous at all. And so he is not a serpent at all either!"

And Mr. Badger walked right over to the hole in the ground.

"Come back here at once," he called, and he spoke in no uncertain tone.

At first there was no sight or sound of the strange creature, but then he appeared. He came very slowly, and he coiled himself without taking any pride or pleasure in it.

"Are you poisonous?" demanded Mr. Badger.

The creature hung his head in shame, and was silent.

"Answer me," said Mr. Badger.

"No," came the answer in a low voice. "I am not poisonous at all."

"Then you are not a serpent," declared Mr. Badger in his sternest manner.

"No, I am just an ordinary snake." The poor creature's head was down to the ground.

"And you deceived us." Mr. Badger's voice was sharp. He had been fooled himself the day before and almost fooled this time by the snake, and people who have been fooled are angry when they find out.

"Yes—and now you have made my life miserable by discovering the truth," said the unhappy snake. "All my life I have wanted to be poisonous and terrible, and all I really am is utterly harmless. It is my great shame. You have no idea how sad it is to look dangerous and be utterly harmless."

Mr. Lobster already felt a good deal of sympathy for the snake just because he looked so unhappy, for Mr. Lobster's heart was so soft that he never could bear to see other creatures unhappy or suffering. But he couldn't understand why the serpent wanted to be poisonous.

"Would you mind telling me why you want to be poisonous and terrible?" he asked.

"Well," said the snake, "you see, this is my island, and I wanted to be the ruler of it and have a great deal of authority. I love authority. And how can I have authority unless I am poisonous and terrible? I have always dreamed of being known far and wide as the sinister serpent—and now my dream will never come true."

"What is 'sinister'?" whispered Mr. Lobster to Mr. Badger.

"'Sinister' is the wickedest there is," answered Mr. Badger promptly.

Mr. Lobster addressed himself to the snake. "I don't know a great deal about authority," he said, "because I have never had any. And I should think that it would be a nuisance. But, anyway, I should say that the best way to be a ruler would be to be friendly and helpful and wise. If I were you, I would consider being poisonous very unimportant."

"And I want to say at this point," put in Mr. Badger quickly, "that Mr. Lobster is one of the wisest creatures in the world, and that everything he says is true."

Mr. Bear muttered unpleasantly:

"And that snake told a lie. He said he was a serpent— and I believed him."

The snake looked more ashamed than before, if that were possible. He was completely crushed.

"I will think it all over," he said humbly.

He began to uncoil very slowly and without any enthusiasm, like a piece of old rope.

"Oh, pardon me," said Mr. Lobster, "but before you go, as you are not a serpent but only a snake, can you change your mind and let us stay on your island?"

The snake brightened up.

"Do you mean that I still have authority, even if I am not poisonous or terrible?" he asked.

"Of course," answered Mr. Lobster. "One can have authority and be the kindest creature in the world. This is still your island, and we are asking your permission to stay here. We are all friendly creatures, you see."

"Well," said the snake, and he paused a moment while the three friends waited breathlessly, and his head came just a little further off the ground. "Well, I will let you stay. Perhaps, when I feel better I shall come and see you."

"Thank you," said Mr. Lobster courteously. "That is most kind of you."

And the snake slowly disappeared down the hole then, not waiting for any more words with the three explorers who had so changed him.

Mr. Badger and Mr. Bear and Mr. Lobster went happily through the woods. Mr. Badger was especially happy, as he had the greatest love and respect for Mr. Lobster and he was always glad when Mr. Lobster's great wisdom solved a problem.

"Mr. Lobster saved the day," he said. "He is more than ever a great hero."

"That's all right," said Mr. Bear. "Mr. Lobster is always a hero, and he asked the snake the question. But who scared the snake down the hole, I would like to know?" He gave a low growl.

"You did," said Mr. Lobster promptly. "And I believe that the person who really saved the day was you. I believe you were the most important, Mr. Bear."

Those words were sweet to Mr. Bear. At last he was important. At last he had saved a day. He walked proudly through the woods, happier than he had been for a long time.

"You know," he said, "I believe I am going to like this island. It is a most pleasant place, and I shouldn't be surprised if I found honey on it yet."

When they had reached the boat Mr. Lobster went into the water for a light lunch, and he began to think things over, as was his custom after every important event.

"I trust this has been a valuable lesson for the snake," he said to himself. "And I hope that now he will be happy. But there is one thing I am curious about: being cross and being unhappy often go together. I wonder whether the snake was unhappy because he was cross, or cross because he was unhappy."

And, thinking it over for some time, he decided that it would have to remain a mystery, because it would be discourteous to ask the snake for an answer. So he crawled happily along, looking for lunch and not worrying about anything.

The very next day the snake came to the beach and spoke to the three friends. "I have decided to be friendly and see what it is like," he said. "And I have thought of something. If you would like to borrow my island for a while, I will lend it to you, and while you are here you may do as you wish."

"Thank you very much," said Mr. Lobster.

"We do appreciate it," said Mr. Badger. "You see, an explorer simply has to discover something that he can claim, and it is most discouraging to sail as far as we did and discover an island and then find out that someone else has discovered it first. Now you won't mind if we just claim this island while we are here, will you?"

"Not at all," said the snake.

"And does that include the woods and any honey in the trees there?" asked Mr. Bear.

"Oh, yes, you may as well claim everything."

So Mr. Bear and Mr. Lobster and the snake were quiet

and attentive while Mr. Badger made a solemn proclamation and once more claimed the island and named it Mr. Lobster's Island. This made the three friends very happy, and the snake seemed pleased.

When Mr. Badger had finished, the snake started for the woods.

"I must be going," he said, "as I very much prefer the woods to the beach. Sand is not pleasant to glide over, but leaves are very soothing to the stomach, and certain kinds of moss are delightful. So I spend most of my time in the woods, but I shall be glad to see you when you come my way. Before I go, I wonder if you would do me a favor?"

"We shall be glad to," said Mr. Lobster.

"Well," said the snake, "you may think it strange, but I am still a little sensitive about not being poisonous. I am afraid it will be a long time before I can be really happy over being an utterly harmless snake. So would you mind not mentioning the fact to anyone?"

"I am sure we shall keep your secret," said Mr. Lobster. "And I hope you realize that probably you are the largest and most handsome snake in the world, and the only one who owns an island. Islands are a great luxury, and owning one is a great distinction."

The snake lifted his head at those kind words, and some of his old pride returned. He went gliding into the woods a much happier snake than he had been before; and he left behind him three brave explorers who were also happy.

The Pleasures
of Exploring

NOW THAT matters were arranged to the satisfaction
of all, the three friends could once more forget all unpleasant things, and it was decided that they would remain on the island until they had explored every inch
of it.

Mr. Lobster wanted to travel completely around the
island under water, so that he might know all about the
bottom of the ocean in that neighborhood. He hoped
that there would be many caves and many forests of seaweed. And he felt that there must be a good many kinds
of small fish.

Mr. Bear had dreamed so long of finding honey that he said he would explore the woods inch by inch in hopes of finding a honey tree where the bees had a home. "Now I can enjoy these woods," he said. "You don't mind a stealthy rustle if you know that a friend makes it." He still felt more important than he had ever felt at home; so he was happy to stay on the island as long as Mr. Badger and Mr. Lobster wanted to.

As for Mr. Badger, he felt that he had had a great victory, and he intended to enjoy the beach. "I shall explore every bit of it carefully," he declared. "I almost feel as if I owned it myself. But I want to take it easy for a while; so, if Mr. Lobster will just bring me some clams, I shall do some fishing. Fishing is practically loafing, and I love loafing."

So that was the way things were settled.

Mr. Lobster searched the ocean and brought Mr. Badger a good supply of clams, which he put in shallow water near shore, where Mr. Badger could reach them. And Mr. Badger made himself a burrow at the edge of the woods and lined it with dry leaves so that he could live underground and sleep in the kind of place he liked best. He said to Mr. Lobster, "Of course, anyone with any sense at all knows that if you must live on earth the only place for solid comfort and no one to bother you is underground."

Mr. Bear went to work to search the woods. "I shall have a home in a cave," he said. "All powerful creatures live in houses or caves. But I shall see if I can find where the bees have hidden honey before I decide where to live. If I find honey, I shall live near there. A home near honey is perfect."

He went off into the woods, not worrying about the snake at all, he said, but growling every now and then as he went along, just to make sure that everyone knew who was coming. He considered that in the dark woods where he was a stranger a little noise like a growl once in a while was a great comfort.

Mr. Lobster took to the sea, although he planned to come ashore and crawl on the beach and in the woods once in a while so that he could keep in practice living out of water. Also, he was still very curious about birds and trees and such land things, and he liked to watch birds flying, which was a wonderful thing he was most curious about. So he couldn't think of spending all his time under water, although he knew, in spite of what Mr. Badger and Mr. Bear had said, that under water was really the best place of all. "I suppose," he said to himself, "that each person thinks his own home is the best; just think of all the best places there must be in the world! It is a very comforting thought."

Before the three friends separated they agreed to meet from time to time, just as they used to before they started exploring. In the meantime Mr. Bear's boat was left alone and deserted, floating quietly with its bow resting on the beach and very little in it except the water jug, which was still empty, and the coil of rope.

All through the summer and the first days of September

with its cool nights and fresh breezes, the weather was perfect for exploring. Day after day the island lay in the bright sun, and the ocean was marvelously blue. The three friends were having a wonderful time.

After a week of hunting, Mr. Bear found an enormous store of honey in a hollow stump where he could reach it with scarcely any effort at all. When he made this discovery he rushed to tell Mr. Lobster and Mr. Badger.

"Exploring is truly wonderful!" he exclaimed. "This is the greatest find of my life! Probably I shan't see you for a few days because I shall be too full to travel." And he rushed away to the woods again.

"Well," said Mr. Badger to Mr. Lobster, "I believe I shall have a feast myself. The fish here have an unusually fine flavor—much better than any others I ever ate. I hope you don't mind."

"Oh, not at all," said Mr. Lobster.

Then, being left entirely alone and without any plans to meet his friends until their feasting was over, he continued his travels alone.

The next day he came out on the beach some distance from the boat. For a time he watched the birds flying, and he watched the moving of the tree tops, bent by the mysterious and invisible wind, that wanderer of the sky who never rests and yet is never tired. And the rustling of all the leaves fascinated him. "How interesting it is," he thought. "Some of the wind is pushing the clouds across the sky, which must take a great deal of strength, and some of it is just playing with these leaves. It is strong, and it is gentle. You can't ever see the wind, but you can see where it is."

And then, while he was watching the trees, he noticed that a slender tree just beyond the edge of the woods seemed to have different leaves from those on the trees near it. There were patches of bright blue amongst the green leaves. "I must ask Mr. Badger about that," Mr. Lobster said to himself.

Next he saw a bird alight in a tree, and he thought, "I wish I could fly through the air just once to see what it is like."

For a time he considered taking a short crawl in the woods, but then he decided to continue along the beach.

He had not gone very far when he came to a huge black boulder with a line around it which showed where the tide came, and seaweed was hanging down below the line. He crawled around it and looked up the beach and was surprised to see another creature traveling in the same direction that he was. Mr. Lobster looked very carefully. He felt sure that the other creature was the talkative turtle, but as they were both going the same way, and he could see only a huge shell and a short tail, he was not sure enough to call out.

So he began to hurry, crawling as fast as he could to catch up with the shell. As the turtle was moving too, Mr. Lobster had to move his eight legs faster than he had ever moved them before. Soon he was gaining on the turtle. He hurried more. When he reached a spot just behind the short tail, he called out, "Wait a minute!"

and fairly rushed past so that he could see the creature face to face.

It *was* the talkative turtle. Mr. Lobster recognized him at once. But the turtle, seeing Mr. Lobster rush past him, gave a single gasp of horror and then pulled in his head completely out of sight.

Mr. Lobster was amazed. It seemed a most discourteous greeting.

"I beg your pardon," he said politely, "but aren't you the turtle who gave me a ride last fall? I am Mr. Lobster."

"Impossible! Go away!" The turtle's voice came from way inside his shell. "You are no such thing! I am seeing things."

"But I *am* Mr. Lobster. I couldn't be anybody else," said Mr. Lobster.

"Lobsters don't walk about on dry land. Oh, I am seeing things! I am seeing things! I am going crazy!" moaned the turtle.

"Oh, no!" exclaimed Mr. Lobster. "Don't be afraid. You may remember that you told me that you explored islands when you wanted to get away from everyone. Well, I go on land also, and I have been exploring this island. I am now an explorer, too, you see."

The turtle cautiously put out his head and opened his eyes. He looked very carefully at Mr. Lobster.

"I guess it's the truth after all," he said finally. "Will wonders never cease? I thought it was your ghost, or that I had lost my mind. You know how it is. Sometimes when you think you've gotten away from every one and everything, you come across the very worst thing possible. You really gave me quite a turn. And exploring! The idea! Well, here I am, two hundred and twenty years old and still learning new things. This will certainly be a lesson to me: never think you know it all!"

Mr. Lobster was almost out of breath just from listening, for the turtle was now talking as fast as though he had not been frightened at all.

"I hope you are well," he said.

"Oh, fine, fine. Nothing so healthy as a turtle, you know. Best luck on earth to be a turtle, I've always said!"

"And I trust that you had a nice winter," Mr. Lobster said.

"Oh, yes. Yes, indeed. Nothing like southern waters, you know, for comfort and ease; and there are many more islands in the south then there are here. Islands all over the place. Ocean's full of them. Of course, the place is overrun with sharks and swordfish and tuna, but I don't mind them."

The southern waters did not sound very attractive to Mr. Lobster. He considered sharks and monstrous fishes unpleasant creatures. He decided to change the subject.

"I should like to have you meet my friends, Mr. Badger and Mr. Bear," he said.

"Oh, no, please don't insist," protested the turtle. "I'm on my vacation, and I prefer to wait a few days before I meet anybody. There's so much going on in the ocean, you know, and I've only just this minute come ashore to get away from it all. After a time, after a time. After all, what's the good in hurrying? So many people want to do everything today. Ridiculous, I say. Ridiculous! Do it to-morrow. Do it a week from tomorrow. Or in two or three years."

"Perhaps you would like to have me go away," Mr. Lobster suggested.

"Not unless you want to. Don't feel that way. Old friends are like old places you've known a long time. No trouble at all. No trouble at all. Besides, I believe I'd like your company. You're a good listener, and I do like a good, intelligent listener. Gives me someone to talk to, and I'm a natural talker, you know. And there's no one I know around here except a serpent, and I steer clear of serpents. Can't hurt me, of course, but I don't feel just right in my stomach when they're around. You come along with me."

So Mr. Lobster and the turtle spent three days walking together while Mr. Bear and Mr. Badger feasted. Although Mr. Lobster got a little tired of listening all the time and only putting in a small word every now and then, he found the turtle most interesting. And he learned so much from the stories of the turtle's travels that he considered the three days profitably spent.

"In a way," he said to himself when he was thinking things over, "just listening is very restful and it is one of the easiest ways of being polite. Also, if you listen to the right person you learn a great deal, and the turtle seems to be the right person."

The fourth day the turtle said that he was going back into the ocean for a day or two. "I shall be glad to meet your friends when I come ashore again, if I am not too tired," he remarked. "You may meet some of my distant relatives if you continue your travels here. There's a small pond in the woods, and several turtles live there. Only mud turtles, and very inferior and disagreeable, always biting; but they are relatives and I have to admit it. Well, good-by for a while."

He ambled slowly away to the water, and Mr. Lobster went in search of Mr. Badger and Mr. Bear. He met them both walking along the beach, looking for him.

"I hope you have both feasted well," he said, after he had told them about meeting the talkative turtle again.

"Oh, yes," said Mr. Badger. "That is one thing I always do perfectly. It is such a pleasure to rest one's brains and use only the stomach for a time, and you know how I love pleasure."

"Me too," said Mr. Bear. "And I've had such a good time I forgot to growl for three days."

"Well, it's time for action now," said Mr. Badger cheerfully. "We must all do something. We must have some excitement."

"Can't we just have pleasure for a little while longer?" asked Mr. Bear.

"Excitement is the best pleasure of all," answered Mr. Badger.

"I don't feel sure about that," muttered Mr. Bear, "but we'll see."

"I know one thing I should like to do," said Mr. Lobster. "There is a small tree I discovered which has blue

amongst the leaves, and I am curious about it. I want Mr.
Badger to explain it to me."

"Then we shall go there at once," said Mr. Badger,
who was always eager to explain.

They started along the beach, but they had gone only
a short distance in the direction of Mr. Lobster's tree
when there came a voice from the woods.

"Where are the explorers? Where are the explorers?"

"It is the snake!" exclaimed Mr. Bear. "I hope it doesn't
mean trouble."

"Perhaps he wants his island back," suggested Mr.
Lobster.

"Where are the explorers?" came the cry of the snake
again. "I need help!"

"Here we are!" called Mr. Badger. "We are coming!"

The three of them hurried toward the sound of the
voice, and the snake kept calling as though he were in
great distress.

They found the snake in such an unhappy condition
that it was no wonder he had called out so. For there was
a large knot tightly tied in his tail.

"I have been to the pond," he explained. "There is
some beautiful mud there, and once in a while I go to
glide back and forth on it. It soothes my nerves. And today I coiled up in the sun to take a nap after I had finished gliding, and I dreamed that I was poisonous and
fierce, and that I was attacked by a lion. I fought and I
fought. I coiled tighter and tighter around the lion. It was

a terrible battle. And then, all of a sudden, I woke up and there was this horrible knot in my tail. It is a disgrace. I could never face anybody in such a condition. What shall I do?"

"Does it hurt?" asked Mr. Lobster.

"It hurts my feelings," said the snake.

"And that is the worst kind of hurt," said Mr. Lobster wisely; "so we must see what we can do about it. Mr. Badger is very clever, and I am sure that we can untie you if he takes charge."

Mr. Badger was only too glad to take charge, and he made an examination of the knot. It was a very tight knot indeed, and enough to make any self-respecting snake feel unhappy; but for an old sailor like Mr. Badger it seemed comparatively simple.

"You take hold of the beginning of the snake's tail," said Mr. Badger to Mr. Lobster.

"How can he?" put in Mr. Bear, who was very much interested in the matter. "The snake's tail doesn't begin anywhere, because he is all tail. All it has is an end."

"Hush!" said Mr. Badger. "Anything that has an end has to have a beginning."

"I'm not so sure," persisted Mr. Bear. "Things that have a beginning don't always have an end. Look at the earth and the ocean and such things. They never end, but they must have had beginnings."

"Well, I have both," said the snake to decide the matter. "I will show you."

And he showed Mr. Lobster where to take hold.

Mr. Lobster took a firm hold. He held on so tightly that when Mr. Badger began to untie the knot the snake hissed. This startled Mr. Lobster so that he let go.

"Please hold on," begged the snake. "I didn't mean to hiss, but I couldn't help it."

Mr. Lobster took hold again. Mr. Badger pulled harder and harder at the knot. Mr. Lobster held on even tighter.

The snake hissed again, which was really quite embarrassing for him, for it sounded so impolite and he didn't want to appear impolite at all. But this time Mr. Lobster held on just the same, and after a few minutes of hard work Mr. Badger got the knot untied and the snake was perfect again.

"I can't thank you enough," said the grateful snake. "I see that you are really true friends, and I only wish that I could give you something. But I own nothing but my island, and I hope you won't take that for keeps."

"Friends do not expect any return for help," said Mr. Lobster. "We are glad that we could help you. And now we must be going."

The snake went off happily, and the three friends returned to the beach to search for the tree Mr. Lobster was curious about.

"It all goes to show how superior bears are," said Mr. Bear. "You never see a bear getting into trouble with his tail. We know better than to have such long ones."

They went steadily on, but it was nearly night before they came to Mr. Lobster's tree. Since it was too dark for

MR. BADGER GOT THE KNOT UNTIED AND THE SNAKE WAS
PERFECT AGAIN.

Mr. Badger to see the top of the tree, they decided to wait until morning. Mr. Bear and Mr. Badger settled down in the woods for the night, and Mr. Lobster crawled into the ocean.

Mr. Lobster Flies
Through the Air

WHEN MR. LOBSTER came ashore the next morning it was rather late, for he had been hungry after his long crawl the day before, and he had spent a long time catching breakfast. And it was such an unusually large breakfast that he crawled very slowly afterwards.

Mr. Badger and Mr. Bear were already on the beach, and Mr. Badger had been examining the trees.

"Good morning," he said to Mr. Lobster. "Is that the tree you were curious about?"

Mr. Lobster looked up.

"Yes," he said. "Isn't that a strange color for leaves?"

"Those are not leaves," explained Mr. Badger. "Those are grapes. That is why they are blue. There is a grape-vine growing up the tree."

"Grapes," said Mr. Lobster. "Well, well. I wish I could see them closer."

"They're sour grapes," said Mr. Badger firmly. "Not worth bothering about."

"Can you tell that they are sour without even tasting them?" asked Mr. Lobster, who was amazed at Mr. Badger's knowledge.

"Oh, yes. You see, grapes that you can't reach are always sour."

Mr. Lobster did not understand that at all, but for the time being he decided to ask no more about it. Instead he crawled around the tree several times, studying the whole situation and thinking about the grapes and about the tops of trees. What Mr. Badger had said did not wholly satisfy his curiosity, for he had been curious about the tops of trees for a long time, and now he felt that he must learn about them.

"Mr. Badger," he said, finally, "do you ever climb trees?"

"I should say not," answered Mr. Badger. "The ground is the place for me. I wouldn't think of going into a tree without wings. It wouldn't be sensible."

"How about you, Mr. Bear?" asked Mr. Lobster. "Do bears climb trees?"

"Oh, yes," answered Mr. Bear with some pride. "You mustn't pay any attention to Mr. Badger. Everyone knows that it is fun to climb trees, and the only ones who never climb them are those who don't know how." Mr. Bear chuckled at his own remark. He was still feeling important, and the honey had made him exceedingly good-natured. Also, it pleased him to tease Mr. Badger.

"Would you mind climbing that tree and getting some grapes for me, then?" asked Mr. Lobster.

Mr. Bear went over to the tree and stood on his hind legs and looked up to the very top. It was a slender tree, and it looked very bendy.

"I'm sorry," he said. "This tree isn't big enough for me. If I climbed it, I am afraid it would break and I would come crashing down. Large bears never climb small trees—and I am a very large bear."

Mr. Lobster was disappointed. And he was more curious than ever. It seemed as though he must find out about the grapes himself. So he kept crawling around the tree. He even wondered if he could climb it, although he knew that lobsters never did such things; but when he tried to reach up the tree he saw that he could not even reach the first branch.

He started to crawl away, and it was then, just as it seemed as if he would have to give up the whole idea, that he saw something hanging down from the top of the tree. He had not noticed it before because he had been crawling near the trunk of the tree. He crawled over to the thing now, and he saw that it looked like a small rope and that it hung from the top of the tree to the ground.

"What is this?" he asked.

Mr. Badger and Mr. Bear came over to look.

"It is one of the grapevines," said Mr. Badger.

"I wonder if it is strong."

Mr. Bear reached up and took hold of the vine and pulled. As he did so, the top of the tree bent down.

"Look!" exclaimed Mr. Lobster. "It bends the tree down! If you could pull that down farther and farther, Mr. Bear, you could bring it right down to the ground and I could see the grapes and the top of the tree."

Mr. Bear began to pull slowly on the vine. The tree bent over and over, like a long bow.

Mr. Lobster was delighted. At last he was going to see the top of a tree. And at the thought of satisfying his curiosity he became so excited that he trembled in every joint of his shell.

Nearer and nearer came the tree top, and he could see the bunches of shining blue grapes.

"It pulls hard now," said Mr. Bear, grunting. "Something seems to be pulling it back."

"Oh, please pull it all the way to the ground," begged Mr. Lobster. "It is almost here."

"I'll help," said Mr. Badger, and he took hold of the vine, too.

Mr. Badger and Mr. Bear were both grunting now, and both pulling as hard as they could. The top of the tree came down until the leaves were touching the ground.

"Hurry up!" panted Mr. Badger. "We can't hold it down very long!"

Mr. Lobster crawled in among the leaves. What a satisfaction it was to be right in the top of a tree! It was almost as good as being a bird!

He reached up a big claw to get a bunch of grapes, but he couldn't quite touch the bunch he wanted. So he grabbed a small branch and pulled himself up into the tree top so that he was not touching the ground at all.

Just then something happened, no one knew how or why. Mr. Bear felt the vine slipping out of his grasp, and he pulled down with all his strength. Mr. Badger pulled, too.

Snap! The vine broke!

Mr. Badger and Mr. Bear shouted at the same time.

"Look out!"

It was too late. Mr. Lobster didn't have time to get back on the ground. All that he could do was hold on to a branch. And the tree straightened up, and the top of it with the grapes and Mr. Lobster went flying through the air with a rush and a swish that took his breath away in a terrifying manner. Mr. Badger and Mr. Bear were left in horrified silence. The tree was standing straight as an arrow, and Mr. Lobster was perched in the very top of it, in the midst of the grapes and leaves.

For a minute or two no one could say a word.

Finally Mr. Badger spoke in a very small voice.

"Are you there, Mr. Lobster?" he asked.

"Yes, I'm here," answered Mr. Lobster, also in a very small voice.

He looked down through the leaves at the ground, and

MR. LOBSTER WENT FLYING THROUGH THE AIR
WITH A RUSH AND A SWISH.

it looked so far away that he shivered. He said to himself, "If I ever fall from here I shall break all to pieces," and he hung on for dear life with both big claws.

"You will have to pull me down now," he called to his two friends below.

"We can't," said Mr. Bear miserably. "The vine is gone. There isn't anything to pull by."

Mr. Bear had spoken the terrible truth. There was no way to pull the tree down, and yet Mr. Lobster was at the top of it, and no lobster could ever live in the top of a tree for very long. The very worst had happened.

"This is terrible!" exclaimed Mr. Lobster. "I shall get dry up here, and then I'll be gone."

"At least you won't starve," said Mr. Badger, trying to be cheerful. "You can eat grapes."

"I don't feel hungry," said Mr. Lobster unhappily.

"It is a disaster," moaned Mr. Bear. "I should have known things were going too smoothly. Whenever things go too smoothly there is some serious trouble that follows, and this is the worst trouble we have ever had. Before, Mr. Lobster was always with us to help us, but this time he is in the top of a tree. A terrible disaster—a terrible disaster!"

"Perhaps I shouldn't have pulled," said Mr. Badger.

"I know I shouldn't have pulled. I am too powerful," said Mr. Bear.

"No, it was my own fault," insisted Mr. Lobster, like a true friend and hero. "It was all caused by my own curiosity. You must blame no one but me."

But Mr. Lobster's words did not make things any better. They all knew that once a bad thing has happened it does no good to talk about the blame, for the only thing that does any good is to set matters right.

"We must think," said Mr. Badger. "We must all think hard until we have an idea."

Mr. Bear and Mr. Badger sat down under the tree to think. Mr. Badger was always silent when he was thinking, and now he did not make a sound. Mr. Bear was thinking, too, but he was never silent when he was unhappy, and he was most unhappy now. So he growled and moaned softly all the time. It was a dismal scene.

Up in the tree Mr. Lobster held on tightly.

"This is worse than when I was lost in the woods," he said to himself. "And all my own fault. Sometimes being wise is no help at all. I am afraid curiosity is stronger than wisdom or I shouldn't be here. If I could only get back into the ocean I should be especially happy, for I have flown through the air like a bird, and I have been in the top of a tree and looked around. But now I am only miserable. There are times when one's finest accomplishments give no satisfaction at all."

He looked down on the island and the ocean sadly. There was the ocean so near, and yet he could not possibly enter it. He had never before looked at the blue water and felt sad, but now the sight of the sea, which he knew was cool and salt, made him so unhappy that he decided to look the other way and see nothing but woods.

While the three friends were thinking desperately, the

day was passing. Fortunately Mr. Lobster was somewhat shaded by leaves, and the afternoon was dark and cloudy, so he did not suffer yet from dryness. But in the back of his mind he knew that he *would* get dry sooner or later.

"Have you thought of anything yet?" he called down finally. "It won't be long before I'll be getting dry."

"I can think of nothing but beavers," said Mr. Bear. "If there were only a beaver here he could gnaw the tree down."

"And I can think of nothing but wings," said Mr. Badger. "If only I had wings I could fly up and save you."

"Thank you both," said Mr. Lobster, "but there are no beavers here, and we have no wings."

"True," said Mr. Badger.

No one seemed to be having very comforting thoughts.

"It might be a good idea to ask the snake's advice," said Mr. Bear. "Perhaps he knows someone who could help us. I will go and get him."

"And that reminds me of the talkative turtle," said Mr. Lobster. "He may be coming out of the ocean again by now. Do go and see if you can find him anywhere on the beach. He has been everywhere, and he must know a great deal."

"Hang on until we return," called Mr. Badger, and he started down the beach.

Mr. Bear plunged into the woods, going in such a hurry that Mr. Lobster could hear him crashing through the bushes and making a great racket. He hoped that Mr. Bear would not frighten the snake.

Now Mr. Lobster was left all alone, without even the sympathy of his friends to console him, which made his position even worse than before. "Next to being just plain unhappy," he said to himself, "the worst thing is being unhappy and alone at the same time."

And he was alone for a long while, for it was nearly dark before Mr. Bear and Mr. Badger returned.

Mr. Bear and the snake came first.

"This is most unfortunate," said the snake. "I have not forgotten what you did for me, and I will help you if I can, but I don't know a thing to do at present."

Then Mr. Badger and the turtle arrived.

The turtle looked up into the tree.

"Well, it's true," he said. "It just doesn't seem possible, but it is. And I say there are limits. First you are walking on a beach, Mr. Lobster, and give me the shock of my life, and now you are up in a tree. Most ridiculous thing I ever heard of. Absurd, I say! Absurd! A lobster in a tree. We must do something about it!"

"I am very sorry to cause all this trouble," said Mr. Lobster humbly.

"Never mind that," said the turtle briskly. "Too late to be sorry now. Doesn't do a bit of good. Not a bit of good."

Everyone was silent.

Poor Mr. Lobster wondered about the turtle's words. "It doesn't seem to me too late to be sorry," he thought. "If I had been sorry before this happened it would have been too early; but surely when I am right in the middle of terrible trouble it is just the time to be sorry."

The turtle and the snake had evidently met before, for they seemed to know each other.

"I don't suppose you climb trees, do you?" the turtle asked the snake now.

"Oh, no," replied the snake.

"Well, then, we shall have to get a bird," said the turtle calmly, "and all the birds have gone to bed for the night. Can you hold on there all night, Mr. Lobster?"

"Yes, I think I can if I don't get entirely dry," said Mr. Lobster. He did not speak with enthusiasm. The thought of being all night in the tree made him shudder.

"Don't worry about that," said the turtle quickly. "It is going to rain tonight. That's the reason I am ashore. I love to hear the rain on my shell. It is excellent for my nerves, and I am very nervous today. First I come ashore to get away from everything and meet you on dry land, and now I have come ashore again and met nothing but trouble. But never mind me. I shall help you no matter what it does to my nerves. In the morning we shall see; and now, if you don't mind, I shall say 'Good night.'"

With those words he pulled in his head and was ready for the night and the rain.

The snake said that he would return in the morning, and glided off into the woods.

Mr. Badger and Mr. Bear and Mr. Lobster said their good nights in small unhappy voices, and Mr. Bear and Mr. Badger went to their own shelters.

Mr. Lobster was alone again.

"Everyone is comfortable but me," he thought sadly.

Soon the wind began to blow gently, and the tree moved back and forth. Mr. Lobster hung on tightly and hoped for the best, but he felt sure now that nothing could happen but the worst. As the wind blew harder and the tree swayed more and more, he began to feel dizzy. The rustling of the leaves and the thrashing of branches in the storm made a hideous noise. And then it began to rain.

The rain, even though it was not salt water, of course—and Mr. Lobster liked only salt water—kept him cool and wet all night while he swung back and forth and back and forth in the tree top. Such a night it was—a terrifying night! And it seemed to go on forever!

But the morning finally came, and the sun came out bright and warm.

"Now," thought Mr. Lobster, "if something doesn't happen pretty soon I shall certainly get completely dry."

The turtle put his head out, remarked to himself that it had been a beautiful night and that his nerves were now soothed, and looked about him. The snake came gliding from the woods. Mr. Badger and Mr. Bear came hurrying down the beach together.

"Are you all right?" called Mr. Badger anxiously.

"No, I am afraid I am not all right," Mr. Lobster had to answer. "But I am still alive."

"Remember that you are a hero," said Mr. Badger. "A hero never gives up."

"We must get a bird," said the turtle. "Does anyone here know a bird?"

At first no one seemed to know any birds. Then Mr. Lobster remembered.

"We know a sea gull," he said.

"Oh, yes!" exclaimed Mr. Badger. "There was a sea gull who stole our picnic one time, and we treated him very kindly. Maybe he would help us."

"Where does he live?" asked the turtle.

"By a certain river that flows into the ocean near a big cliff," said Mr. Badger. "It is a most beautiful place."

"I know where that is," said the turtle. "It is quite a distance, but I have had such a soothing and restful night that I feel able to travel at tremendous speed this morning. We turtles look slow, you know, but you ought to see us under water! I will get the sea gull. Hold on, Mr. Lobster! Just hold on!"

Before anyone could think of anything else to say, the turtle had crawled into the water and was gone. There was nothing to do now but wait.

The snake and Mr. Badger and Mr. Bear remained under the tree. Every little while one of them would try to give Mr. Lobster courage by calling out: "Hold on. It won't be very much longer now."

Poor Mr. Lobster held on, but his big claws were now so tired that they ached. And, as the long morning passed, he got drier and drier. By noon his tail felt so dry that he feared he would never be able to curl it tightly again. And when a lobster cannot curl his tail he is in a very bad way.

"I am getting very dry," he finally said to his friends. "I fear that the turtle will be too late."

"No, no! Don't say that!" protested Mr. Badger.

And then Mr. Bear, who was looking out to sea, cried out:

"Look!"

It was the sea gull. He came flying straight to the island and landed on the beach.

"You are saved!" cried Mr. Badger.

"Here I am," said the gull. "I remember Mr. Lobster's kindness to me. What can I do?"

"Get Mr. Lobster out of the tree!" exclaimed Mr. Badger excitedly. "Hurry!"

The sea gull flew up to Mr. Lobster. Everyone waited breathlessly to see him pick up Mr. Lobster and bring him to earth. But, instead of helping Mr. Lobster, the gull flew down to the beach again.

"I am sorry," he said, "but Mr. Lobster has grown so big that I could never lift him."

"Then I am not saved," said Mr. Lobster miserably. "Nothing can save me."

At this moment the turtle came crawling out of the ocean.

"Whew!" he said. "I guess that is a record! Never say a turtle can't hurry. Is everything all right now?"

"Everything is all wrong," moaned Mr. Bear. "It always is. Mr. Lobster is too heavy for the sea gull."

"What's that? What's that? Too heavy?" The turtle was amazed.

"If you only had a rope," said the sea gull. "I've seen people on ships do all kinds of things with ropes."

Mr. Lobster had about lost all hope, and he was so dry and tired now that he could hardly speak. But when he heard the sea gull mention a rope he immediately remembered the wonderful long rope he had brought on the exploration.

"My rope," he called down in a weak voice. "It is in Mr. Bear's boat."

"I'll get it!" cried Mr. Badger, and he dashed up the beach.

In two minutes he was back, dragging the rope behind him. The sea gull, without wasting an instant, took one end of the rope in his claws and flew up into the tree. There he pulled the rope over a strong branch. Then he gave the end to Mr. Lobster.

"Here," he said. "Do just as I say: take this end in one claw and hold on for dear life. Keep the other claw on the tree. When I tell you to let go of the tree, take hold of the rope with both claws. Then we can let you down to the ground."

Mr. Lobster followed the sea gull's directions, and the sea gull flew down to the beach.

"You are the strongest," he said to Mr. Bear. "So you take hold of the rope here, and when I tell you to, just let the rope out slowly."

Mr. Bear took hold of the rope firmly.

"Now let go!" called the sea gull to Mr. Lobster.

Mr. Lobster was terrified, but he let go of the tree. Now he was holding fast to the rope with both claws.

"Let him down," said the sea gull to Mr. Bear.

Mr. Bear began to let out the rope very slowly and carefully. Everyone was anxiously waiting to see what would happen. Not a word was spoken.

The sea gull's plan worked! Down came Mr. Lobster at the end of the rope, dangling like a huge fish. It was a strange sight.

"Marvelous!" exclaimed the turtle. "Marvelous! Never thought I would live to see a sight like this!"

Slowly Mr. Lobster came down and down, getting nearer and nearer to the ground.

And then he stopped! And there he hung in mid-air, still many feet above the ground.

"Go on," ordered the sea gull.

"Yes, go on!" cried Mr. Badger.

"I can't," said Mr. Bear. "I've come to the end of the rope. There's no more to let out."

Everyone groaned.

"I can't hold on much longer," gasped Mr. Lobster. "And if I let go now I shall be broken."

It was the most desolate moment of all.

"I am afraid you will have to pull him up to the top of the tree again," said the sea gull. "We shall have to get a longer rope."

"It's no use. Never mind," said Mr. Lobster weakly. "I won't last that long. I might as well let go now. Farewell—"

"Wait a minute! Don't let go!" cried the snake, who had been silent all the while. "I will be a rope! Quick, Mr. Bear, just pull the end down so that I can take it in my mouth, and then you can take hold of my tail!"

Mr. Bear pulled the rope down, and the snake took the end in his mouth. Then Mr. Bear took hold of the snake, just as if the snake were a rope also. Once more Mr. Lobster began to come down.

"Hurry," he said in a whisper. "Hurry if you can."

It was most uncomfortable for the snake, for he was being stretched out straight, and Mr. Lobster was heavy. But he said not a word of protest, and he did not hiss.

Down, down . . . Mr. Lobster touched the ground.

"Saved!" cried Mr. Badger. "Saved!"

"Let go!" exclaimed the sea gull.

Mr. Lobster let go. At last he was back on earth.

"Thank you! Thank you!" he managed to say weakly. "Every one of you helped to save me. Now I must go into the ocean."

He crawled slowly to the water, his tail, which was very dry, dragging limply behind him. But he was happy once more, for he knew that he was saved and that soon he would be himself again.

And all the others were happy, too, for it was true that every single one of them had had an important part in rescuing Mr. Lobster, and nothing makes people so happy as to rescue someone.

Mr. Bear Has
a Great Shock

By THE next morning Mr. Lobster was completely recovered from his harrowing experience, although he
knew that he would never forget it as long as he lived.

"I am through with trees and flying through the air,"
he told Mr. Badger and Mr. Bear. "In the future I shall
leave them both to the birds."

Mr. Badger and Mr. Bear agreed that was a wise decision.

"But it *was* exciting," said Mr. Badger. "Think what a
great thing it will be to remember! It was the narrowest

escape of all, and it took more people to get you out of trouble than any other escape. That is a record."

The snake came to the beach to see if everything was all right. He was still somewhat lame from being stretched, he said, but he was happy.

"It is the first time I have ever helped anybody out of trouble," he explained, "and it has given me a most pleasant feeling. I am sure that it was a valuable experience, and that I am a better snake now."

Those words made Mr. Lobster feel that he had not suffered in vain.

The sea gull had flown away home, but the turtle came out of the ocean to see Mr. Lobster once more.

"I'm on my way," he said. "Glad to see you looking so fit this morning, Mr. Lobster. Very glad. Never like to see anyone in trouble. Makes me nervous. All your own fault, of course. You shouldn't go into the tops of trees."

"I shan't do it again," said Mr. Lobster.

"Well, well, never mind," the turtle went on in his usual rapid manner. "Never too old to learn a lesson, I say. But I must be going. Must be on my way. I hope you don't mind my saying so, but it has all been rather confusing for me, you know, after coming here to get away from everything. Think I'll look for another island and have a good rest."

Mr. Lobster thanked the turtle again for saving his life, and he thanked the snake. The turtle returned to the ocean, and the snake disappeared into the woods. So the three friends were there on the beach, and Mr. Lobster expressed his gratitude again to Mr. Badger and Mr. Bear.

"Don't mention it," said Mr. Badger. "We're just friends and heroes together. And explorers, of course, although I think that it is about time to think of sailing for home."

"I suppose it is," agreed Mr. Lobster. And he thought of his real home with longing. He realized that he had been gone a long time.

"I hope we haven't got to hurry," said Mr. Bear.

"Why, I thought you were ready to leave long ago," said Mr. Badger.

"Well, I haven't eaten all the honey yet."

Mr. Badger chuckled.

"We couldn't wait for anything so unimportant as honey," he said in order to tease Mr. Bear.

Mr. Bear gave a small growl, the first one in many days.

"Honey is very important," he said gruffly.

"But we had better wait a few days until the wind changes," Mr. Badger went on, pretending that he was paying no attention to Mr. Bear, "and of course we can all do whatever we please while we are waiting."

Thus it came about that Mr. Bear went into the woods to eat the rest of his honey. Mr. Lobster and Mr. Badger had other things to do. In the first place, Mr. Badger had not forgotten that they had sailed on their exploration without any bait for fishing. So it was decided that Mr. Lobster should gather some more clams, which could be kept in shallow water until the day of departure.

This kept Mr. Lobster busy for two days, and it kept him happy as well, for he caught several good dinners and lunches while he was hunting clams. Also, he was getting excited over the thought of returning home.

On the third day, in the afternoon, Mr. Badger took the water jug.

"There is a spring in the woods right near the beach just a short distance from the boat," he said. "I discovered it some time ago. I shall fill this with water and put it in the boat."

Mr. Badger had no more than gone when Mr. Bear came out of the woods. He looked very full and completely satisfied.

"You know," he said to Mr. Lobster, "this has been quite an exploration, but I am ready to go home now. Not much use staying anywhere after the honey is gone."

"I think we are sailing tomorrow," said Mr. Lobster.

Before Mr. Bear could say anything in reply, they both heard a great shouting from up the beach. It was Mr. Badger, who was calling as loud as he could.

"Mr. Lobster! Mr. Bear! Come here! A great discovery!"

They both hurried toward Mr. Badger, wondering what was going to happen now. When they reached the spot where Mr. Badger was waiting he led them to a part of the beach right next the edge of the woods.

"It is tremendous!" he exclaimed as he led the way, "perfectly tremendous! Dozens and dozens of them!"

"Dozens of what?" asked Mr. Bear.

"Eggs!" said Mr. Badger.

"I never saw an egg," said Mr. Lobster.

"Eggs are round things that new birds come out of," explained Mr. Badger breathlessly. "The owl told me about them. Look!"

Mr. Lobster and Mr. Bear looked. There in a hollow scooped in the sand were small round eggs. As Mr. Badger had said, there were dozens and dozens of them.

Mr. Bear sniffed.

"I am not interested in eggs," he said. "I never eat them."

"I am interested in them if birds come out of them," said Mr. Lobster, "but I don't see how there is room for wings inside of those eggs."

"Probably they grow their wings after they come out of the eggs," said Mr. Badger. "I don't know about that."

"Well, it makes no difference to me," Mr. Bear remarked. "I am not interested in eggs, and we are going home tomorrow."

"I am afraid we can't go home tomorrow," said Mr. Badger seriously, "on account of these eggs."

"I don't understand," said Mr. Lobster. "Please explain."

"Eggs have to be kept warm or the birds in them never come out," explained Mr. Badger. "The owl told me. It is terribly important. And I think there must have been an accident, and the bird who was sitting on these eggs is lost. So we must keep them warm and save the little new birds."

Mr. Bear gave a low growl.

"You mean that we can't leave because of these miserable eggs?" he demanded.

"Yes," replied Mr. Badger. "It was a bird who saved Mr. Lobster's life, and so we must save all the birds in the eggs. Heroes can never forget their obligations."

"I suppose you are right," agreed Mr. Lobster, "but what shall we do?"

Mr. Badger thought seriously for a few minutes, looking at the eggs all the while.

"I have an idea," he said finally. "It is this. Of course, Mr. Lobster is too cold to sit on them. He could never keep them warm even if he is a hero. And I am too small to cover so many eggs. I should be resting right on top of them and break them all."

"I know what's coming," said Mr. Bear at this point. "Please don't say another word."

"Mr. Bear must sit on the eggs," said Mr. Badger very firmly, not paying the slightest attention to Mr. Bear. "He is so big that he can cover this hole and all the eggs without breaking them."

"Never!" cried Mr. Bear in a rage. "It would be ridiculous for a bear to sit on eggs."

"This is not ridiculous. It is our duty, and duty is never ridiculous," said Mr. Badger. "Don't you agree, Mr. Lobster?"

"I am afraid you are right," said Mr. Lobster, "although it is rather hard on Mr. Bear."

Mr. Bear growled then, and it was no small growl either.

"Just my luck!" he said. "Just when everything is going beautifully, and I have had plenty of honey, and we are ready to go home—this happens! Life is full of nothing but sorrow for me."

"Think of all the poor little birds," said Mr. Badger.

"I hate birds!"

"Never mind," said Mr. Lobster. "I am sure you will be happy when it is all over, for it will certainly be a good deed, and you are bound to be happy when you do good deeds."

Mr. Bear only growled in reply.

He was miserable, and he felt ridiculous indeed. He was sure that it was silly for a bear to sit on eggs. And yet he knew that he was helpless. Whenever Mr. Lobster and Mr. Badger agreed on anything, it had to be done.

So, with a great deal of grumbling and growling, and the strangest look on his face, Mr. Bear lay down on the sand so that he covered the place where the eggs lay.

"You can pretend you are a bird," said Mr. Badger.

"Go away!" growled Mr. Bear. "If I have to sit here after I get hungry, you will have to bring me my food, and now you can leave me alone."

Mr. Lobster and Mr. Badger thought it best to leave Mr. Bear alone as he suggested.

"He is really very cross," observed Mr. Lobster when they had gone some distance.

Mr. Badger began to laugh, and he laughed until the tears came to his eyes.

"It is the funniest thing I have ever seen in my life," he

WITH A GREAT DEAL OF GRUMBLING AND GROWLING,
MR. BEAR LAY DOWN ON THE SAND.

said. "That enormous creature sitting on those eggs and growling all the time. I can hardly keep a straight face when I am near him."

"I suppose it is necessary?" said Mr. Lobster.

"Absolutely," said Mr. Badger. "That is the best part of it—to have something necessary and funny at the same time. It is so unusual."

The next morning, when they returned with a fish for Mr. Bear, they could hear poor Mr. Bear growling and muttering to himself as soon as they drew near.

"How long do I have to stay here?" he asked.

"Oh, you never can tell," said Mr. Badger. "Sometimes it takes weeks."

"Then that settles it," said Mr. Bear. "If you think I am going to wait here weeks before going home—and just for dozens of little birds—you are mistaken. I am leaving right now."

"Probably the bird did most of the sitting, and it may take only a few days," said Mr. Lobster, trying to be encouraging.

Mr. Bear snorted, but he did not move.

"You must remember that you are a hero," said Mr. Badger. "You will be very important."

For the first time since he had started sitting on the eggs Mr. Bear had a gleam of happiness. Being important was a new thought, and it made his task a bit easier. He settled back in some comfort now.

But his task was not finished by any means. Day after day passed, and the endless sitting became a great trial to

Mr. Bear. Often he was cross at Mr. Badger, who had caused the whole thing by discovering the eggs, and who, Mr. Bear suspected, was really enjoying the situation.

And each day they all became more and more excited about the eggs and what would come out of them. It was hard to wait.

Mr. Lobster, in the kindness of his heart, was sorry for Mr. Bear, and he did everything in his power to give Mr. Bear comfort and joy. So he spoke encouragingly to Mr. Bear about the birds.

"I am sure they will be beautiful," he said.

"I don't know. I'm not very lucky," remarked Mr. Bear in a gloomy tone. He was feeling depressed because he wanted to go home and it seemed as if the birds would never come out of their eggs.

"Perhaps they will be sea gulls," said Mr. Lobster.

"They may only be sparrows."

"They might be eagles."

Then Mr. Bear brightened up.

"I never thought of that," he said. "Do you think that is really possible? Eagles! Think of it—the most important birds there are!"

After that Mr. Bear was much happier, and everyone was in even greater suspense. This whole business was one of the strangest things the three friends had ever encountered, and they began to feel that some great event was going to happen.

Fortunately, the weather was fair and warm, so Mr. Bear did not suffer from being out all the time, day and night. And he began to get some pleasure from ordering Mr. Badger to bring more and more fish. In fact, he did his best to keep Mr. Badger working, even ordering meals when he was not very hungry.

But it was the thought of the glorious eagles that gave Mr. Bear the greatest comfort.

"I am positive they will be eagles," he said to Mr. Lobster one day.

Mr. Lobster wasn't so sure about the eagles. However, he was now so curious about what was going to come out of the eggs that he could hardly sleep nights. The very thought of it made him tremble with excitement, and he came ashore earlier and earlier in the morning and stayed there all day waiting. Mr. Badger was kept busy catching fish, but he also hovered around Mr. Bear and the eggs as much as possible.

The three friends were all more excited than ever before, and it was plain that something would have to happen pretty soon or they wouldn't be able to eat or sleep or do anything but wait for the coming of the birds.

One afternoon, just as Mr. Badger was hurrying to Mr. Bear with his supper, the great moment came.

Something stirred in the nest under Mr. Bear, and he felt it plainly.

"There is something happening!" he called out.

"Hurry!" called Mr. Lobster to Mr. Badger.

"The eagles are coming!" exclaimed Mr. Bear.

Mr. Badger dropped his fish and came on the run.

Mr. Bear tried to look extremely important.

"I have done it," he declared proudly.

"What? Tell me at once!" cried Mr. Badger, who was now very much excited but could see nothing.

"I have hatched the eagles," answered Mr. Bear.

"Do wait a few minutes more," advised Mr. Badger. "We must save them all."

"You mean I must save them all," said Mr. Bear. "I think I get the credit for this! And please remember that these eagles are mine!"

He waited for a few minutes. It was so exciting that Mr. Lobster had to hold his breath to keep still. Then, very slowly, and in the most dignified and impressive manner, Mr. Bear rose from the nest and carefully stepped to one side before turning to see what had come out of the eggs.

Before Mr. Badger or Mr. Lobster could see a thing, Mr. Bear made a hideous sound of pure horror. Then he growled in frightful rage.

Mr. Badger and Mr. Lobster looked.

Out of the nest came scrambling forty-three little black turtles!

"Turtles!" exclaimed Mr. Badger.

"Oh!" gasped Mr. Lobster. "The turtle said that he had distant relatives living in a pond on this island. He said they were just mud turtles."

It was a dreadful moment, a crushing moment for all of them. But for Mr. Bear it was the most horrible disappointment of his life.

He turned and started to walk away, his head hanging

down. The forty-three little mud turtles followed him. Frightful sounds were still coming from deep down in Mr. Bear's throat.

Mr. Badger was trying to keep from laughing.

Mr. Lobster was stunned.

"Mud turtles!" Mr. Bear was saying. "My whole life is ruined. I am the unluckiest person on earth. All great sorrows fall upon me. I am disgraced forever. All on account of Mr. Badger. No one will ever believe that I am a hero after this."

He was slowly walking down the beach. The forty-three turtles were still following him. Mr. Lobster and Mr. Badger started after Mr. Bear and the turtles. It was a strange procession, indeed.

"I give you my word of honor," said Mr. Badger, "that I never knew turtles came from eggs."

"Do not speak to me," growled Mr. Bear, not even looking around. "Never speak to me. I am going away by myself—probably forever!"

"Oh, don't go!" exclaimed Mr. Lobster.

"That is life," Mr. Bear went on, just muttering miserably to himself. "You think you are going to hatch eagles, and you hatch mud turtles instead."

With those sad words he looked around at his two friends. When he did so, he saw the forty-three mud turtles following him. At that shameful sight he let out a most fearful growl of rage, gave a great jump, and started running as fast as he could. He dashed across the beach and into the woods and disappeared.

More Troubles—But
a Happy Ending

FOR THREE days Mr. Lobster and Mr. Badger waited for
Mr. Bear to return. There was not a single sign of him.

"I am afraid we have had another unfortunate experience," said Mr. Lobster.

"It looks that way," said Mr. Badger. "My idea certainly
turned out very badly. It is a great pity."

"Do you know what happened to the mud turtles?"

"Yes," said Mr. Badger, "they have all gone into the
woods, either to look for Mr. Bear or to find the pond
where mud turtles live."

"If they could only have been eagles," sighed Mr. Lobster.

"Well, I wondered about that, I confess," said Mr. Badger, "although I did not say anything."

"You did?"

"Yes. To tell the truth, you know I just cannot resist starting a little trouble once in a while. The owl told me that birds usually have only five or six eggs in their nests, or at most a dozen. So I was a little suspicious when I found the eggs, there were so many of them; but I thought it would be fun to make Mr. Bear sit on them. And I never dreamed of turtles!"

"Mr. Badger, sometimes you amaze me," said Mr. Lobster.

"Yes," said Mr. Badger, "I suppose I do. Sometimes I amaze myself."

The next day Mr. Lobster and Mr. Badger decided to get the boat ready for the voyage home and then go and search for Mr. Bear. Everything was made clean and neat. The rope and fish lines and water jug were all put aboard. The supply of clams was left in the water where they could be gotten easily. Mr. Badger waded into the water and washed the boat, and he worked so hard that Mr. Lobster suspected there was something on his mind.

"You are working very hard," he observed.

"Well," said Mr. Badger, "perhaps Mr. Bear will feel happier and less angry with me when he returns if he finds his boat in good order and ready to sail for home."

"We must start searching for Mr. Bear this afternoon," said Mr. Lobster. "We must get the snake to help."

But in the middle of the afternoon, just when the work on the boat was finished, the sky began to darken. Mr. Lobster and Mr. Badger had been working so hard that they had not noticed the weather at all. Now they looked up into the sky and saw that there was going to be a bad storm.

"We are going to have a tempest," said Mr. Badger. "I guess I had better go to my burrow. The only place to be in a tempest is underground."

"I prefer the ocean, of course," said Mr. Lobster. "I shall return when the storm is over."

The storm raged all that night. There was thunder and lightning, and a gale of wind that whipped the trees and roused the ocean to fury. Great waves pounded on the beach, making a thunderous and mighty sound, and shaking the earth so that Mr. Badger in his burrow thought the whole island was going to be pounded to pieces. And Mr. Lobster, whose temporary home was in shallow water, knew from the sand in the water and the stirring all about him that there was a great tumult going on. It was the kind of storm that makes you think the whole world is in confusion.

Early in the morning the wind died down. By the time the blackness of night was fading and it was time for the sun to come up, the dark clouds went far out to sea and disappeared. The sky grew brighter. But the waves were still big and crashed hard upon the beach.

It was difficult for Mr. Lobster to get ashore because of the waves, but he succeeded after being rolled over and over several times, and he hurried up the beach to find Mr. Badger.

Mr. Badger was just coming out of his burrow.

"What a night!" he exclaimed. "We must look after the boat."

They hurried to the little cove where the boat was kept.

The boat was gone!

"We are done for now," said Mr. Badger.

They both sat looking at the place where the boat had been. Neither of them could think of anything more to say. The disaster was too great.

And while they were sitting there miserable and speechless there was a sound of hurrying from the woods and Mr. Bear came running toward them.

"No more of this for me!" he was saying. "One more storm like that and there will be no island left. It will sink just like the other one I was on. I am going back to my home on solid land!"

Then he paused for breath and looked around.

"Where is my boat?" he demanded.

"Gone," said Mr. Badger.

"Where is it gone? I want my boat!"

"It must be floating on the sea," said Mr. Lobster. "The storm did it."

Then all three friends were speechless. Mr. Bear seemed to have forgotten about the mud turtles. At last he gave a growl of complete sadness.

"Whatever happens next is always worse than what happened before—if it happens to me," he said. "We are lost."

"We are still on the island," said Mr. Badger.

"To be on an island forever is the same as being lost," said Mr. Bear.

"Maybe the boat will float back," remarked Mr. Lobster, trying to think of something cheerful.

"We can never go home," said Mr. Bear, paying no heed. "All I know is that we can never go home. That is what comes of exploring." And he looked hard at Mr. Badger.

"I guess you're right," said Mr. Badger, "unless we swim home."

Everyone knew that Mr. Lobster was the only one who cared to be in the water.

It seemed a most unhappy end to the summer. No one wanted to talk about it. No one said a word about the turtles or the adventures they had had. For the time being everything was sad, and everything joyful in the past was forgotten.

"I suppose we shall have to borrow the island from the snake for quite a long time," observed Mr. Lobster.

"No, I shall do something about this," said Mr. Bear in a firm voice. "I have been disgraced by mud turtles, and now my boat has been taken away. I can stand no more. I shall do something!"

"What?"

"I don't know yet, but I shall do something, I tell you."

After that it was evident that Mr. Bear had a secret. For that very afternoon he said to Mr. Lobster and Mr. Badger:

"I shall have special business on the other side of the island, and if you don't mind I should like to be by myself."

There was nothing for the three explorers to do but stay on the island and make the best of things. Mr. Lobster tried to pretend that his temporary home was as delightful as his real home; but he knew that it was not so. And Mr. Badger tried to be bright and cheerful and made a good many jokes; but no one seemed to laugh at them.

Every day Mr. Bear would disappear for hours. When he returned he was always sticky and wet and covered with sand. But he would not say a word about where he had been or what he had been doing.

Mr. Lobster grew more and more curious day by day, but he was far too polite to inquire about a secret.

Every morning and every afternoon when Mr. Bear returned from his secret business the three friends walked along the beach, searching the shore to see if Mr. Bear's boat had drifted in, and looking out over the ocean to see if it was anywhere in sight out there.

It was a most discouraging procedure as the days went by and there was no sight of the boat. Mr. Badger said that they would have to make a raft, but when they looked on the beach for wood there was nothing large enough to make a raft that would hold Mr. Bear.

It was early one morning, before Mr. Bear had left to

go off on his secret, that the last great event of the summer happened.

Mr. Badger was gazing out over the ocean. "Look!" he exclaimed. "Look out there!"

Everyone looked.

There was Mr. Bear's boat, floating some distance from shore. Every one of them recognized it at once.

"My boat!" cried Mr. Bear.

"Quick, Mr. Lobster!" said Mr. Badger. "You can pull a boat. You must swim out and pull it ashore."

"I am sorry," said Mr. Lobster, "but you will remember that you left the short rope on the seat of the boat, and there is no anchor rope because we had to cut it off. So I am afraid there is nothing I could pull the boat by, even if I swam out there."

It was true. Mr. Lobster could not get the boat after all, and he was the only one who was at home in the water.

"I will get my boat!" declared Mr. Bear in a loud voice. "It is my boat, and I shall do something about it!"

And then, before amazed Mr. Lobster and Mr. Badger could say a word, Mr. Bear walked down to the water and went right out into the ocean. In another instant he was swimming straight for the boat.

"It's marvelous!" exclaimed Mr. Badger.

They both watched, scarcely believing their eyes. It was impossible that Mr. Bear, who hated water, could be swimming in the ocean. And yet he was! And he swam without a pause straight to the boat and then climbed up over the side and got into it. In a moment or two Mr.

MR. BEAR WALKED DOWN TO THE WATER AND
WENT RIGHT OUT INTO THE OCEAN.

Lobster and Mr. Badger saw the white sail being hoisted. The boat started sailing along with Mr. Bear at the helm.

Mr. Bear brought the boat to shore like an old sailor and ran it gently up on the beach.

"There!" he said.

"I thought you hated water and couldn't swim!" cried Mr. Badger.

"I do hate water," said Mr. Bear, "but I felt that I had to do something to redeem myself after the hideous affair with the mud turtles and the loss of my boat. Every afternoon I have been on the other side of the island learning how to swim."

"That was your secret!" exclaimed Mr. Lobster.

"Yes, I decided not to talk any more about my accomplishments beforehand," said Mr. Bear.

Mr. Badger drew himself up very stiffly.

"Mr. Bear," he said, "I am proud of you. I am proud to know such a creature as you. You are a true hero!"

"And I am proud of you, too," said Mr. Lobster. "You are the most important hero of all, for if it had not been for you we might have stayed here forever!"

It was the greatest moment of Mr. Bear's life. He had never before been so happy.

"Now we can sail," he said.

Mr. Badger ran and collected the clams that had been saved for the occasion. Then they all got in the boat. Mr. Badger took the sheet and tiller. Mr. Bear gave a push away from the beach.

There was a twinkle in Mr. Badger's eyes.

"And where shall we go?" he asked.

"Home!" cried Mr. Bear.

"Home!" cried Mr. Lobster.

"Home!" cried Mr. Badger himself.

And they were all perfectly happy.

RICHARD WARREN HATCH (1898–1959) grew up in Pennsylvania but lived for most of his adult life in Marshfield, Massachusetts, in a house that had been continuously occupied by his family since the middle of the seventeenth century. After graduating from the University of Pennsylvania in 1918, he joined the US Naval Reserve Flying Corps and later served during World War II. It was while stationed on an aircraft carrier that he came up with the idea of writing about the adventures of a very old lobster. From 1925 to 1941 Hatch taught English at Deerfield Academy, eventually becoming head of the English Department, and during the 1950s he lectured at the Center for International Studies at MIT. In addition to his books for children, he also wrote novels for adults set in coastal Massachusetts towns.

MARION FREEMAN WAKEMAN (1891–1953) was born in Montclair, New Jersey, and attended Smith College before joining the Art Students League. She was a member of the National Association of Women Artists and exhibited her work at the National Academy of Design, the Montclair Art Museum, and Smith College.

TITLES IN SERIES

31901063755377